CALLIE
ENDICOTT

—

That Summer at the Shore

HARLEQUIN® SUPER ROMANCE®

Recycling programs
for this product may
not exist in your area.

ISBN-13: 978-0-373-60824-9

THAT SUMMER AT THE SHORE

Printed in U.S.A.

ABOUT THE AUTHOR

As a kid, Callie Endicott had her nose stuck in a novel so much it frequently got her into trouble. She majored in English in college to support her addiction to stories, but it wasn't enough. Out of desperation she turned to writing, and now when she isn't walking on a beach or taking a mountain forest trail, she usually has her nose stuck to a computer screen. That is, when she isn't feeding her cat, scooping the litter box...and listening to Myna purr. The guy in her life doesn't appreciate the distractions, but that's another story....

Callie enjoys hearing from her readers. You can reach her at Harlequin Enterprises Ltd., 225 Duncan Mill Road, Don Mills, Ontario, Canada M3B 3K9.

For Mom and Dad.

PROLOGUE

ZACK DENNING BREATHED in the tangy scent of seaside vegetation as the bulldozer bit deep into the soil. For seventeen years he had worked for this moment.

Mar Vista. My own resort.

He'd saved, invested, made the right contacts, learned along the way, calculated for everything imaginable…and now he was finally breaking ground.

"It's a big day," said Phillip Atchison, his architect, during a lull in the noise from the heavy machinery.

"Yes." Zack nodded, holding his triumph at bay. This was just the beginning, with the greatest risks and challenges still ahead. Nevertheless, he could see it all in his head, the way he'd been seeing it since he was a kid and everyone thought it was a pipe dream.

Phillip understood his ideas and had been excited by the opportunity to design classic architecture that recalled an era of gracious stability. Equally important, they'd incorporated luxury amenities, state-of-the-art electronics and a killer resource center. A guest could run an international company from Mar Vista…or forget the outside world existed.

Leaving the bulldozer, they walked toward the trailer, which would serve as Zack's home and office while the construction phase progressed. Later he would have an apartment over the administrative offices.

"It's too bad your family couldn't be here for the groundbreaking," Phillip commented.

"My folks were going to come, but something… came up."

Zack's mood chilled. He didn't want to explain his brother's damaged body and the months of surgeries and therapy yet to come. Brad had gone through hell since being hit by a roadside bomb in Iraq. Their parents were in Bethesda, Maryland, where he was being treated at National Naval Medical Center. The doctors kept saying they had to be patient, but it wasn't easy.

"Maybe they can come for the grand opening. And you've taken lots of photos that you can send them," Phillip said, dropping his arms. "They're on the internet, aren't they? Or do they resist using computers and email like my folks?"

It took a second for Zack's brain to refocus. "No, they love email," he answered, patting his digital camera. He'd already sent dozens of pictures to his parents and brother, hoping it would raise their spirits. His jaw hardened. The resort had to be a success—the family needed *something* to go well.

They climbed onto the landing in front of the trailer and studied the terrain leading down to the Pacific Ocean. Weather reports indicated relatively dry conditions for the next several months—ideal for contouring the acreage for the golf course and completing the major structures. They were disturbing as few of the natural features as they could, which helped their timeline. Mar Vista would nestle into the land as though it were always meant to be there.

The golf-course design also employed existing features, while still creating eighteen holes that each had its own unique challenge. Zack didn't care much for playing golf himself, but he'd paid close attention to what the enthusiasts of the game had to say about a good course.

"It would be nice if there wasn't a public road on the north end," Phillip said.

Zack kicked a clod of dirt from his shoe. "True, but I've examined similar issues at other resorts. It doesn't seem to be a problem if the atmosphere is right, and the situation here is better than most because the road only leads to the public beach."

"What about the section *north* of the road? I noticed the old for-sale-by-owner sign is still there. That strip of land is too narrow for the main resort, but the view is spectacular and your guests would love exclusive access to the water."

Zack suppressed a laugh. Phillip "noticed" that for-sale sign whenever he came to Warrington. "Actually, my real-estate agent is contacting the owner with an offer."

"Wonderful."

Zack saw the wheels turning in his architect's eyes. "Don't get busy with blueprints," he warned. "Even if the seller accepts, I can't afford to develop for at least two years." If it wasn't for a recent investment in his portfolio panning out better than expected, he wouldn't have been able to consider buying the property in the first place.

"What if the owner decides not to sell and builds something that clashes with Mar Vista?" asked Phillip.

Zack grimaced. "My landscape architect and I have a contingency plan. We're leaving green space with trees where we can plant one of those tall evergreen hedges as a buffer if necessary. It isn't a great solution, but it would help."

Phillip whistled. "That's expensive, particularly if you put in mature bushes."

"Less expensive than losing the right atmosphere."

"Can't argue with that. Well, best of luck. I'll be back regularly to meet with the contractor and monitor the progress."

They shook hands, and Zack watched the architect drive away. The roar of the bulldozer drowned out the roar and crash of the ocean, but it was sweet music. In due time Mar Vista would be open for business. He already had stacks of prospective reservations from people who knew him through his years of management at other resorts.

His cell phone rang and he checked the caller ID. It was his real-estate agent.

"Yes?"

"Hi, Zack, it's Janet Trent," she said. "I met with George Jenkins, and he's willing to sell. I floated the lower figure by him so we'd have leeway for bargaining, but he accepted without countering."

"That's terrific," Zack exclaimed.

"George wants the deal to close fast. As I told you, he's a nutty old coot. Not stupid, though. I tried to convince him to list the property with me several years ago, only he didn't want to pay the commissions. Now to speed things up he said he won't ask for a reduction of the agent's commission for representing the buyer. So, are you sure you want to go ahead?"

Zack rubbed the back of his neck. Spending the majority of his financial reserve was a huge risk. "Will he sell to someone else if I don't?"

"There's no telling. The resort is going to raise property values. George hasn't been well and obviously wants to sell, so he could decide to cash in with another developer."

Zack winced. A motel or subdivision might be tolerable, but what if it was worse? Images of a cheap trailer park filled his imagination, complete with neon signs and rusty, single-wide trailers crowded too close together. It wasn't impossible, and something like that could destroy the five-star rating he hoped to earn. He couldn't risk it happening, even if buying the land left him with little financial cushion.

"Let's do it," he told Janet. "Get the documents to me as soon as possible. It's interesting that he didn't quibble over the lower offer."

"Yes. As we discussed, I started at fifty thousand under your top number. I expected to dicker with him for a while, but he just wrote out the parcel numbers and signed the papers."

An extra fifty thousand in his pocket wasn't much when it came to a project as big as Mar Vista, but every bit helped.

Zack ended the conversation and switched off the phone with a satisfied smile.

Nothing stood in his way now.

CHAPTER ONE

ZACK CROSSED THE golf course in a loping stride. Now that the resort was open for business, he was too busy for the lengthy runs he liked, so he fit in exercise whenever he could.

The rising sun shot gold rays across the landscape. It was a favorable time of day to take promotional pictures, and he made a mental note to mention it to the photographer. A webcam on the website might also be worthwhile—a long-view camera that showcased the elegant sweep to the Pacific Ocean.

"Hey, boss," Rick Lopez, the senior groundskeeper, said as Zack got to the seventeenth hole and surveyed the yellow blotches of dying turf, glaring against the surrounding green.

"Have you figured out the issue?"

"Too much fertilizer and it burned the grass. We'll lay fresh sod immediately. We're lucky this happened toward the end of the course or the early players would catch us working."

Zack scanned the nearby scenery. "Are you positive this is the only site?"

"Yep. All clear."

"Find the idiot responsible and send me a memo."

Rick bent and pulled at the grass, examining a few blades. "Two of my guys were out here Monday night. The equipment could have malfunctioned. It's hard to see in the dark and the burns aren't critical. In most cases I'd let the grass come back on its own. But I'll follow up."

Zack nodded and sprinted to his SUV. He knew there wouldn't be an *idiot report.* Rick hired his own crew and was loyal to them. He also came as a package—his wife, Trudy, was a top-notch office manager. Zack had lured the duo from a prestigious golf course on the East Coast. It wasn't easy persuading Rick to make the move, but a hike in salary and the chance to build his reputation at a new California resort had finally won him over. As for Trudy, she was happy as long as she could work in the same location as her husband.

Sliding behind the wheel of his Mercedes SUV, Zack seized the radio microphone.

"Base," he snapped.

"Good morning, boss," Trudy answered.

"Has anyone teed off yet?"

"Several went a quarter of an hour ago."

Zack tensed, despite the situation being under control. "Rick says he'll resod before they get that far."

"I can delay them with my Lady Godiva impression," she offered.

"We don't have a horse available," Zack told her, trying to choke down his annoyance. Trudy's light-hearted approach usually made him smile; lately it was wearing on his nerves. Didn't anyone else understand how critical it was that the resort run perfectly? It wasn't just *his* money on the line—his parents had invested their retirement savings in Mar Vista.

"I'll take the riding mower. My alabaster skin will look fabulous in the rising sun."

For a moment Zack wondered what people would think if they overheard this conversation. "Uh… your husband might object."

"Yeah, he's a real killjoy. He insists on full safety gear when you roll that shiny machinery out for a spin. I keep telling him that he shouldn't fuss—I've driven everything from an 18-wheeler to a baby carriage."

Baby carriage…?

Jeez.

Were babies on her mind? The Lopezes didn't have any kids and had never mentioned starting a family in the years he'd been acquainted with them.

Zack's stomach churned as he recalled a box of saltines lying on Trudy's desk. She'd been sick a couple of days the past week…improving by noon. He pinched the bridge of his nose. It was best not to dwell on potential complications—it only drove him crazier.

"Did the early birds go together, or are they in separate groups?" he asked.

"They're together, and they decided to walk instead of using your fancy golf carts. That gives us longer to fix things. Anyhow, Rick says it's mostly cosmetic and doesn't affect play."

"Appearances matter. We're aiming at a five-star rating," Zack retorted.

The microphone amplified Trudy's breath as she sighed. "That's why Rick is taking care of it at the crack of dawn."

"Okay. What's the status on the linen?"

There was a brief pause. "No need to worry about that, either. I'll make certain the delivery guy stays while each piece is checked and double-checked. The head of housekeeping is also on the warpath, and you know how she gets."

"Tell me when the delivery arrives. I want to be there."

"Sure, boss," Trudy said after another pause.

Zack started the ignition and turned onto the road, pleased with how well the new SUV handled. He didn't require such an expensive vehicle for his daily inspections, but a Mercedes signaled luxury and success to the clientele. Attention to detail was his trademark.

As a high school senior he'd deliberately begun working through each position in the leisure industry. Initially he'd gotten a job as a bellboy, then one in laundry, followed by housekeeping, groundskeeper's assistant, a turn at the reception desk and various other jobs, including a summer as activity director on a cruise ship. It had helped pay expenses as he earned his MBA and complemented his education with practical experience. Many managers or owners took the fast track to the executive's suite, spending a token stint in the different departments, but he'd wanted to learn the business at every level.

Yawning, Zack sucked down a gulp of coffee. Morning wasn't his favorite part of the day. He liked sleeping in, preferably next to an attractive female companion. That hadn't happened in a long time; too much was riding on the project to let anything distract him.

With his digital camera, he clicked photos at various sites around the resort. They were for his personal records; professional tripod jockeys were handling his advertising needs. But he routinely compared his snapshots to the project blueprints and his original vision. So far so good.

All at once he slammed on the brakes and stared. *What is that?*

Dumbfounded, he gaped at a row of colorful sandwich boards toward the end of the public road.

Local Produce—Opening May 19
Some Organic!
First Come, First Served
Strawberries
Raspberries

Loganberries
Leaf Lettuce
Greens
And More....

An arrow pointed down the small unpaved track on the undeveloped portion of his acreage. Sitting smack-dab in the middle of one of the finest ocean views on the California coastline was a bright blue trailer adorned with more signs, each wilder than the last.

His foot hit the accelerator.

JAMIE CONROE HELD the trailer awning with her right hand, pushed the brace with her other hand and nudged the pole with her toe. She'd been struggling to get it up for ages. Why her grandfather had invented such an ungainly system she'd never know. When she'd tested it in the barn last October, she had promised herself to devise a better plan. Now she was getting ready to open the fruit-and-vegetable stand, and thanks to her procrastination, she was performing an acrobatic act.

In the back of her mind she registered the sound of tires on gravel. It was probably a farmer. Whoever it was, they'd have to wait. If she could just get that darned brace in the spot it needed to be...

A harsh voice broke her concentration.

"What the devil are you doing?"

She jumped, the canopy slipped and the pole whacked her left temple.

"Ouch!" she yelped as the heavy canvas dropped and shoved her against the trailer's painted aluminum siding. Slouching, she considered remaining in temporary defeat, but it wasn't very comfortable. The corner of a box was digging into her hip, while the awning's fabric was sandy and had a musty odor after three years in storage.

Jamie wriggled her head free and glared at the man. "Could you have found a *slightly* more awkward moment to shout at me? Perhaps when I was blindfolded and walking a tightrope?"

To give him credit, he lifted a handful of canvas, poles and ropes so she could hop out of the mess.

"You didn't answer my question," he said.

"Which question was that?"

He gestured incredulously. "I should think it's obvious. What are you doing here?"

Jamie gazed dolefully at the tangled lines and poles. *Rats.* She'd have to begin all over again. "I thought you were being rhetorical. This isn't rocket science. It's a sun canopy."

"No. I mean the whole thing. This…this trailer and those signs."

Massaging the knot forming on her forehead, Jamie studied the stranger. She knew him from newspaper articles—Zack Denning. The *Warrington Gazette* regularly printed editorials on the "genius" entrepreneur who'd built the luxury resort next door. His picture was hard to miss, though she hadn't paid much attention to the world since arriving in Warrington this past September.

She'd spent the winter in seclusion, making the excuse that she was busy with her silver jewelry casting, but mostly she was sorting out her new life. Now that she'd emerged from solitary, she was focused on reopening the seasonal produce stand. Local growers were delighted; Granddad's business had been a profitable outlet for them.

"Well?" Denning demanded.

She had no idea what the trouble was, but would enjoy giving him a verbal runaround for his belligerence.

"It's a fruit-and-vegetable stand. Farmers bring their harvest. We sell it. Selling is when you exchange one product for another commodity, usually money," she explained as if he were a child in need of instruction.

"You can't put anything here," he said, barely containing a growl.

"Sorry. Free trade is an old tradition, commonly called 'commerce,' or occasionally 'capitalism.' Look it up. Communists don't approve, but Americans are fond of the practice."

"I've no objections to what you do, as long as it's not on ground belonging to me."

"Poor fellow," she commiserated. "I always heard men were supposed to be spatially adapted—you know, with the roaming ability for tracking game.

Maybe you missed getting that gene. My section is the acre including the beach that's immediately north of the public road. You own the rest, except the state beach and the tract with my house on it." She traced a simplistic map in the dirt to illustrate.

"No. The water forms my property line, making it a private beach for the acreage between the main road and the salt flats. I realize you have a house lying north of my section with access two miles east, off the main road. But you aren't entitled to cross my land to get there, and it definitely doesn't mean you can drag that horrible trailer onto my resort. This site may not be developed, but it's still Mar Vista."

She raised her chin. Zack Denning didn't need to sneer as if Granddad's 1950s travel trailer broke the law. Admittedly, the brilliant aqua was startling. An enterprising junk man with a load of overstocked paint had peddled it to her grandfather over a decade ago. The neighbors had joshed Granddad until they got used to calling the trailer that "Little Blue Fruit Stand."

"As I explained, this particular acre isn't yours, Mr. Denning. It's mine, and the attorney gave me the documents to prove it. Granddad may have been color-blind and a little odd from living alone, but he was sharp as a tack and didn't sign a scrap of paper unless he was sure of the facts."

"I own this land," Denning said. "Understand? It's mine. You can't fast-talk your way around it."

Jamie waved a finger at him. "Repetition does nothing for you legally."

"We'll see about that."

He stomped to his Mercedes, groping for something in his pockets. After a moment he slapped his thigh in apparent frustration, as if he couldn't find what he was looking for. Then he reached into the SUV, pulled out a radio or walkie-talkie and spoke into it. From the little she could hear, it sounded as if he was talking to someone named Trudy.

Interesting. The newspaper had endorsed him, and they were normally conservative when it came to newcomers. Presumably they'd never had the pleasure of seeing him acting like a jerk. Of course, anyone could have a bad day; her ex-husband specialized in them, especially the arrogant-asshole kind of day.

Granted, Zack Denning *was* good-looking with his dark brown hair and eyes. If he ever smiled, he'd devastate feminine hearts right and left.

She shrugged. It made no difference that he was a hunk. Life had gotten simpler since she decided to forgo romance. No more hassles about dating. No more hopes dashed. And best of all, no more worries about how to dress. She wore whatever she fancied without wondering if a guy would find her appealing. It was incredibly freeing. Her friends marveled at her willingness to do without sex, but it had been so lousy in her marriage, it didn't seem much of a loss.

Right now her only concern was getting the awning in place. She knew it could be done. Granddad had managed it, even when his arthritis acted up. Adjusting the poles and ropes, Jamie tugged the canvas, pushing, poking and nudging until the stupid structure fell into the correct position. A sea breeze rippled the edges and she hurriedly tied the lines to their stakes.

Pleased, she inspected her accomplishment. This used to be her grandfather's favorite season; he loved the company of his customers after a winter in isolation. He'd passed his summers sitting in a worn wooden chair, talking to tourists and townspeople, filling dozens of journals with their stories…some of them scandalous. They made a fascinating social history of the area.

As a kid she'd spent Augusts in Warrington. While Granddad chatted with customers, she played in the sand or devoured library books. And when he let her, she sold produce. But now that the Little Blue Fruit Stand was hers, she didn't know if she wanted to work there daily, or hire someone to run it for half the week.

Humming, she began scrubbing the trailer floor with a bleach solution. The small interior space was for personal use and she wanted it clean.

"I need you to deal with this, Deputy." She heard a voice through the open door.

It was Zack Denning.

He must have summoned the authorities to enforce his opinion. *Fine*. The overbearing jerk would learn what immovable meant after dancing that tango with *her*. She scrambled to her feet and stepped out to see a blond man in a khaki uniform standing next to the darker and leaner Zack Denning.

"Is something wrong?" she asked.

"Uh—yes." The officer shifted nervously. "Trespassing is against the law. You have to...um...leave if you don't want to be arrested."

"Hmm," she said. "That's a serious threat, and I won't resist if you take me in. However, false arrest is also serious, particularly since you haven't questioned my side of the story. Sadly, it could be a career-ender if the people of Warrington hear you helped a rich outsider bully a resident who's legally on her own property."

The young man swallowed, his Adam's apple bobbing with ridiculous speed.

"Not that I want that to happen to you, Officer," Jamie assured him. "But even if folks appreciate the income Mr. Denning brings to the community, they won't like him using the sheriff's office to throw his weight around."

She turned and assessed Zack Denning.

"You know, Mr. Denning," she said, "you ought to be law-abiding and neighborly in these rural parts. For example, I could have charged *you* with trespassing and disturbing my peace, but I chose to let bygones be bygones."

A second official vehicle drove in and parked near the trailer. "Good God," the driver exclaimed as he slid from the front seat. "It's Jamie Conroe—or didn't you get married?"

"Married, divorced and back to Conroe," she said. "So you're finally on the right side of the law, Curt. How did you get elected sheriff after painting Badger's Suck, Warrington Wolverine's Rule on the city water tower following your senior homecoming game?"

Curt chuckled. "Easy—I convinced everyone that reformed troublemakers spot trouble quicker than anyone else." He hauled her into a hug. "This is great. You're here and the Little Blue Fruit Stand is opening again. Mom will be thrilled. She's big on organic lately. When did you come back to Warrington?"

"Last September."

"No kidding? What happened to getting in touch with old friends?"

"I needed to regroup...after losing Granddad."

Sympathy crossed Curt's face. "It must have been rough with the two of you being so close. All the same, it's terrific to see you. What's going on here?"

Jamie tried not to laugh as she glanced at Zack Denning. The deputy was edging away from the entrepreneur as if he had symptoms of the plague. Nevertheless, the "genius" seemed up for the challenge.

"Sheriff," he said, "I'm Zack Denning, owner of the Mar Vista Resort."

"Should we all genuflect when you say that?" Jamie mocked.

He scowled as Curt choked and vigorously rubbed his hand over his mouth before responding. "Curt Saldano, Mr. Denning. I must have missed meeting you at the monthly chamber-of-commerce gatherings. I'm usually asked to attend, along with the Warrington Police chief."

"Did he go to any of those meetings?" Jamie asked in an aside to Curt, and he gave her a single, negative shake of the head.

Hasn't joined, he mouthed.

"This woman is intruding on private property," Denning said, scowling at Jamie. "You don't have to arrest her as long as she removes those signs and gets that contraption out of here. *Immediately.* I run a high-end resort and this eyesore is unacceptable."

Curt pondered it silently and then lifted an eyebrow at Jamie. "What have you got to say, kiddo?"

"This is Granddad's place." She folded her arms over her stomach. "And has been for sixty years. He gave it to me in his will."

"And that wily fox would have nailed it tight with titanium," Curt affirmed with a grin.

Zack Denning's features smoothed into the bland mask Jamie had endured at too many official lunches with her ex-husband. Tim loved to spar with people and knew exactly how to conceal his emotions…and the truth. The thought had barely formed before she mentally spanked herself. It wasn't fair to compare anyone to Tim, and it didn't encourage her resolve to leave the past behind.

"Sheriff," said Denning, "I recognize what's happened. Ms. Conroe trespassed in ignorance. I presume her grandfather was George Jenkins. Apparently, she isn't aware that he sold this property to me a year and a half ago."

"'Fraid not," Jamie countered. "He sold some other pieces. Trust me, he would *never* sell this parcel."

"Fortunately, I have the deed in my safe," Denning said coolly. "I'll give you four hours to move your belongings. That's all."

"Wow. Your staff must tremble when you look at them with that calm, intimidating stare." Jamie stretched lazily. "Luckily, I don't work for you and I'm on my own turf, so I'm not quaking in my boots. And by the way, you're not the only one with a deed."

"You're trespassing," he said furiously. "You have to—"

"We can't initiate action without proof of who holds the title, Mr. Denning," Curt interjected. "At present it's a civil disagreement over boundary lines. Not a criminal matter."

Denning's eyes narrowed. "I see. Ms. Conroe, my lawyer will be contacting you." He climbed into his gleaming-black SUV and sent gravel flying as he made a sharp U-turn.

Curt frowned. "Yikes, Jamie. That's one angry man. Ring me if he causes trouble."

"I'll be fine," she asserted, her jaw stiffening. Curt had once acted as a big-brother defender during her childhood trips to California. But she'd acquired a few life lessons since then—you had to stand up to bullies, if only for your own self-respect.

ZACK WENT DIRECTLY toward the office instead of finishing his morning rounds, keeping his speed low to avoid drawing attention. Mar Vista was doing even better than he had hoped and he wouldn't let anything blow it. Jamie Conroe was a blip on his problem radar. He'd teach that smart-mouthed brunette the definitions of *land purchase* and *title*. The sheriff might be swayed by a pretty face, but the state police could be brought in if necessary.

"Boss, have you got your ears on?" Trudy asked over the radio, and Zack grabbed the microphone.

"Here, Trudy."

"You okay? Did you take care of the intruder? I hope they didn't have a weapon."

"No weapon," he answered, "but her trailer might be lethal."

"Excuse me?"

"Never mind." Zack checked his watch. "Call my lawyer. I want a video conference when I get back."

"She might not be in this early, or she could be with another client."

"Try. Warn her that she may need to fly here today or tomorrow."

Trudy whistled. "What's in the frying pan this time?"

"A property-line dispute. It's got to be dealt with ASAP."

"Gotcha."

Putting the microphone on its hook, Zack saw a familiar couple ready to tee off. The Langianos waved. He drew to a stop and forced a pleasant smile.

"Roger, Suzy, how are you doing?" he asked.

"Mmm, wonderful," the woman said. "But I've been eating so much that I told Roger we had to walk it off rather than take a golf cart. Restaurants like your Sunfish Grotto ought to be against the law."

"I'm glad you're enjoying it," Zack replied; years of practice as a manager had taught him to show amiable hospitality to his guests, and nothing else. When people were on vacation they expected a world where difficulties just disappeared.

"We appreciate your chef's candor about his ingredients," Roger added. "With Suzy's allergies, it makes things easier."

"I'll share your comments with the kitchen. Chef Gordon has a daughter with food sensitivities, so he understands."

The investment in a top chef was paying off. None of the other chefs Zack had interviewed were willing to provide a list of ingredients for their special recipes. These days a lot of folks were concerned about their food. It fit the modern trend toward health awareness, so Zack had kept searching for someone who shared his vision. *Oh, Lord.*

Yesterday Gordon had mentioned that a produce stand was opening nearby. He wasn't happy with their current supplier and hoped for a new source. It had to be Jamie Conroe's trailer, and Zack could imagine how appalled his patrons might be if they discovered their fruits and vegetables were coming from that hideous place. Maybe he was overreacting, but you couldn't predict what would alienate clients.

The Langianos continued to the course and Zack drove to the administrative parking lot. He got out, moving casually until he was beyond the view of guests. The management area was more austere than the rest of the facility; the luxurious ambience was saved for their clientele.

"Trudy," he barked, "did you reach Kim?"

"Yep. She's waiting for you."

Zack tapped his fingers as Trudy put the call through to his office. The computer screen opened to Kim Wheeler. She was one of the most beautiful women he'd ever met, though at the moment he was interested only in her keen legal mind.

"There's a woman, Jamie Conroe, squatting above the beach with a decrepit trailer. And the color it's painted is downright offensive," he said without preamble. "She's planning to sell fruits and vegetables there and is claiming she inherited the land from her grandfather. Something has to be done. *Now*. Mar Vista golfers, and anyone going to the beach, might see it. Other guests going horseback riding and—"

"Good morning to you as well, Zack," Kim interrupted. He reluctantly nodded a greeting. Kim rarely let him get away with anything. In college they'd lived together for several months until she had told him they weren't suited for each other. Although they were no longer lovers, they'd stayed friends, and when she had gone into corporate law, he'd put her on retainer as his attorney.

"Sorry," he apologized, "but this is important. This woman claims to own the first acre adjacent to the state beach on the northwest section. It's where the public road ends at the water and a dirt road takes off at a right angle in the middle."

Kim pulled up something on a second computer. "I see it on the map, a rectangular chunk along the waterfront. That's some of the real estate you rushed to buy without checking with me, isn't it?"

Ouch.

She'd ragged him unmercifully for failing to consult her on the transaction. There just hadn't been enough time—old George Jenkins had insisted on closing the sale as fast as possible. Zack had also been distracted by his brother's hospitalization and the construction commencing on the resort, but he wouldn't make excuses.

"Yes," he said shortly. "It's one of the last parcels I bought."

"I doubt we can resolve this today. Chances are we'll need an official survey to settle the matter."

"Can you get a court order to get her out in the meanwhile? I guarantee she'll ignore any no-trespassing signs I post, and they wouldn't look good to my guests anyhow. Oh, and get this—the county sheriff is a pal of Ms. Conroe's. I probably can't expect support from him or his deputies."

Kim shook her head. "I don't think a judge can issue an injunction unless there's substantive evidence that it's not her property."

"Damn."

"I'll keep you updated on our progress. Just don't purchase any more real estate without talking to me first."

The screen went blank before Zack could devise a suitable retort. He sank back in his chair and gazed into space. Jamie Conroe's fruit stand might not be so bad if it was charming or offbeat instead of just tacky. He could hide the more obvious signs of her presence with a tall hedge, but planting fully grown shrubbery was a costly remedy for a temporary condition.

And it shouldn't be necessary. That was the galling part.

To think he'd congratulated himself on securing

that particular piece of land, protecting his resort from this sort of thing.

Now?

He'd simply have to take care of it. Ms. Conroe would soon be investigating a different site for that shabby little trailer.

CHAPTER TWO

JAMIE OPENED BLEARY eyes, awakened by the persistent noise from her BlackBerry cell phone.

No one, repeat, *no one* had the right to call before eight in the morning, particularly when she'd spent most of the night doing her silver casting. Not that anyone else knew she was short on sleep. She focused on the caller ID to see if it was her exhusband. Tim had begun phoning her last winter, though she'd changed her cell number twice to avoid him. It was jarring to know his voice was a single button away, so she'd stopped listening to messages and never answered unless she recognized the caller.

She switched the BlackBerry off without answering and dropped a pillow on top of the landline extension. Rolling onto her side, she fell asleep.

A heavy pounding on the front door woke her an hour later. Didn't *anybody* respect a woman's right to sleep in? Apparently not, since the pounding continued. She dragged herself out of bed and donned a clean bathrobe.

Swell. It was Zack Denning and a blonde woman in a business suit.

"Coming," she yelled over the racket, waiting until it stopped before turning the knob.

The woman was finely coiffed and sculpted, a sharp contrast to Jamie's faded pink terry wrap and messy morning hair. It probably accounted for why Denning was staring at her. Tough. She was done with trying to impress men with clothing and makeup.

She smiled sweetly. "Can I help you? The vegetable stand isn't operating yet, but I can put you on a reservation list for strawberries. How many flats can you use?"

Denning's lips thinned and she could have sworn she saw a vein throbbing in his forehead.

"Ms. Conroe?" the woman queried.

"That's me, aside from the part I left in my bedroom."

"Please excuse us for waking you, but I've been calling for several days. I also tried your mobile number after my assistant got it from your business license. You never answered so I left a message, but maybe you weren't able to get back to me."

"If that's a nice way of asking whether I bother answering the telephone, the reply is usually no, unless I know who's on the other end. Basically, that means no blocked numbers. And I don't listen to messages."

The woman blinked. "Oh. I was working from home and should have considered that."

Jamie tightened the belt on her robe. "Not everyone has my bias about it—and you still haven't explained who you are."

"I'm Kim Wheeler, Zack Denning's lawyer."

"You mean a macho tycoon actually hired a woman as his attorney? But I bet he was the one hammering dents into my door. Those manicured hands of yours never did anything so rude." To Jamie's satisfaction, Denning's jaw clenched.

"Ms. Conroe," he said, "you've delayed resolving this too long already and name-calling is hardly appropriate under the circumstances."

"I didn't call you a name, but I'd like to know when you think it's appropriate to throw one around."

"That's…"

The lawyer's elbow hit him in the ribs, cutting his words short. Interesting. It was a safe wager that Kim Wheeler and Zack Denning knew each other quite well.… They were the classic image of a power couple.

"Please ignore him, Ms. Conroe," the woman said. "Mr. Denning is impatient concerning this matter since his resort is nearby. I agreed to bring him if he…"

"Kept his trap shut?" Jamie cheerfully completed the sentence.

"I told him to let me handle things."

"Good luck."

The corner of the attorney's mouth twitched.

"May we come in and discuss the problem regarding your property lines?"

"It isn't my problem. It's his. Or do you think my grandfather's will could have been probated for a piece of property he didn't own? This is a waste of effort."

"Can we try?"

Jamie scrunched her bare toes and shivered. "You'll have to wait a few minutes. I don't argue real estate while wearing a bathrobe."

"Wait?" Denning exploded. "So that you can duck out the rear while we're standing here?"

The woman's elbow slammed his ribs again and Jamie laughed. "I like you, Ms. Wheeler. And because of that, I'll invite you—and only you—into my living room. After I get dressed we can talk without testosterone getting in the way."

Denning started to say something, and Kim shook a furious finger in front of his nose. "Zip it," she ordered.

Laughing some more, Jamie gathered her bathrobe close and unhooked the screen door, then secured it again once the lawyer was in the foyer. "There's a porch swing you can use," she offered to the glowering man outside. "Fair warning, though, the cushions may be coated with cat fur. I'll give Ms. Wheeler a ride when she's ready if you want to head back to your resort."

Or I'm ready to kick her out, Jamie added silently. No, most likely that wouldn't be necessary.

She guessed that Kim Wheeler, Attorney-at-Law, would be on her best behavior.

Jamie shut the door and motioned toward the main room. "Go on in."

"Is the furniture furry there, too?" Kim inquired with a friendly tilt of her head.

"It isn't as bad. I regularly vacuum the house, but admitted defeat on the porch. Marlin's fur is overwhelming in the middle of his spring shed."

"Holy Toledo." Kim gazed at the massive black cat lying in a patch of sunlight on the hardwood floor. Marlin stretched, lazily flexing his claws. "Is he a special breed?"

Jamie gave Marlin an affectionate stroke with the arch of her foot. "Officially, he's a house cat. Unofficially, I heard that a panther ran away from a wildlife park and spread his genes before being caught, except that might be a tall tale. I'm not sure if there are bobcats in this region. Supposedly they can interbreed with domestic felines, so that's another possibility."

"Maybe he's a mutant."

"Could be."

Leaving Kim to get acquainted with Granddad's aging companion, Jamie shuffled to the bedroom and stared in the mirror, wondering what she could wear. Should she retrieve the remaining clothing from her previous life, a time when her ex-husband had expected her to wear outfits as fine as Kim Wheeler's? She'd sold the majority through a consignment shop, but she had some left in a box at the back of the closet. The right apparel made an undeniable impact—look how she felt with Ms. Wheeler sitting on her couch, garbed in a high-priced suit.

Pulling out the box, Jamie suppressed a wave of nausea. The green evening gown on top was strapless and too taste-specific for the consignment shop. She'd worn it once, the night they went to the company Christmas dinner, the year prior to the divorce. Tim had admired how chic and sexy she appeared until they got to the banquet hall and he saw the CEO's wife dressed in a similar color. She couldn't have known what the woman would wear, but he'd told her if she'd had a speck of sense she would have chosen black, same as the other wives. His cold fury had made her shrivel inside.

Suddenly Jamie crammed everything into the carton and booted it across the floor. She refused to be intimidated. An expensive suit collected cat fur the same as her jeans, but jeans didn't need dry-cleaning.

Zack leaned against the solid porch pillar after seeing the volume of cat fur on the cushions.

He'd supposed Jamie Conroe would be living in a ramshackle beach shack, not a large and well-maintained home from the early-twentieth-century Arts and Crafts era. It was an architectural style he liked, though he'd emulated an earlier period for Mar Vista. And it wasn't just the Conroe house that was so striking. The north side had an incredible view across the tidal flats to the ocean, and the front boasted a restful forest scene.

A signal came over the SUV's radio and Zack hurried to his vehicle.

"Boss, are your ears on?"

He lifted the microphone. "I'm here."

"Your mother didn't know whether you'd replaced your cell phone yet. She wanted to remind you that Brad is arriving. His flight lands at 11:20."

Crap. The resort had an airstrip for private planes and chartered flights, but Brad was coming into a commercial airport, eighty miles from Warrington. Zack ground his teeth in frustration. How had he forgotten? *He* was the one who'd suggested Brad come to California after the doctors and therapists advised a change of scenery might be beneficial.

Zack checked his watch. "Thanks, Trudy. I'm leaving immediately. Can you send a car to the Conroe place for Ms. Wheeler?"

"I'll call the garage."

He signed off and dialed Kim on his cell phone.

"She's getting dressed," Kim said crisply. "And I'm making friends with a mutant cat. Practice patience for once."

"Mutant? Forget it. I have to go. Brad is flying in, and I'm picking him up."

"Great! Do you have a vacancy at the resort? I'd love a chance to visit with Brad."

"We'll take care of you, Kim. Listen, don't let

that Conroe woman try to wiggle out of the situation. Be firm."

"I'm curious, Zack. When did you receive your law degree? I missed the graduation ceremony." The light humor in Kim's tone didn't conceal the underlying warning. *Don't interfere.* She seemed to think he'd done enough damage.

"Okay, okay," he grumbled. "It's just that she has a habit of talking in circles."

"Sounds smart. She should be a lawyer."

"I'm counting on you being smarter."

"That's what you're paying me for. And wait till you get the bill for this trip—I'm adding twenty percent for the extra trouble you've caused. Tell Brad hello and that I'm looking forward to seeing him." The phone disconnected.

Zack started the SUV. It was galling. He'd been required to cool his heels on a porch as if he were a delivery boy. Now he had to go before anything was settled.

He hit the accelerator until he was going the speed limit…and a little above.

KIM WHEELER RUBBED the cat's big ears and listened to the purr rumbling from his chest.

"Marlin, huh?" she said.

"Marrooow."

"Fur flying or not, you are magnificent," Kim whispered.

She cocked her head, her thoughts drifting. So,

Brad Denning was visiting his brother. The last time she'd seen Brad, he was en route to Iraq—the perfect spit-and-polish marine. He could have walked off a military recruiting poster. She'd met him at the airport during a five-hour layover. They'd discussed his upcoming tour of duty over dinner and she'd hidden her concern for his safety.

"Don't forget I'm trained for this," he'd told her—apparently, he'd seen her concern after all.

She'd hugged him and watched as he disappeared down the concourse. Brad had been in her life almost as long as Zack, and the idea of something happening to him was unbearable.

That was, what…three years ago?

And something *had* happened, but now he was home and slowly recovering.

Kim glanced around the room. It glowed with sunlight, satiny wood floors and cream-colored paint. Lovely paintings hung on the walls, and beautiful pottery and glassware sat in strategic spots.

A thud echoed in the house. Kim didn't worry that another exit was being used for a secret departure—Zack wasn't rational when it came to Jamie Conroe *or* Mar Vista. Kim understood his reasons, but he wasn't helping. It would be simpler to investigate the matter without him. Inheritance was a potentially emotional subject, though Jamie had been calm when she'd made that excellent point about her grandfather's will going through probate.

Acting as Zack's attorney was challenging. Before she'd agreed to represent him, they'd had an in-depth discussion, which involved assurances that their past relationship wouldn't be an issue. It had worked so far, and he probably followed her advice slightly more often than he would for someone he didn't know as well.

Marlin shoved his nose into her palm.

"By the way," she announced to the feline, "I'm a lawyer. Any objections to that?"

The cat shut his eyes sleepily and purred. A very un-lawyerly giggle escaped her throat. She'd met at least two people who'd taught their dogs to growl when they even *heard* the words *lawyer* or *attorney.*

JAMIE FOUND KIM WHEELER seated on the large, comfortable sofa. Marlin, never a slouch in demanding attention, was draped over her lap, purring like a diesel motor.

"You must be covered with fur," Jamie said. "I'll put him out back."

"Don't be silly. I think cats are great."

"I doubt the hothead on the porch feels the same."

Kim snickered. "That's *his* problem. But it doesn't matter anymore because he's driving to the airport. His brother is arriving from Maryland."

"And the jerk would have had a fit if you'd gone along." Jamie sat on the arm of the couch and swung her legs. She was glad she'd kept Zack Denning and his bad vibes out of her home—it made maintaining peace and tranquillity easier.

"He wants to clear things up as soon as possible," Kim said diplomatically.

"Yes, I figured that out when he asked the deputy sheriff to throw me off my own property."

Kim frowned. "I apologize about that."

"I'm not holding it against him. Don't have to—it's my land."

"You seem quite certain."

Jamie swallowed a yawn. She would have preferred having this debate after a decent night's sleep. "I have a deed *and* it's in my grandfather's will—the one he revised when he sold his other parcels. The real estate he left me is the section with the house and barn, plus the acre on the beach."

Kim removed a folder from her briefcase. "Over eighteen months ago, Zack purchased several tracts north of the road. He understood they included everything to the water's edge. You're welcome to see the sales agreement."

"There's no need. Granddad wanted to leave my brother some cash, so he sold some of the land he owned, but not my two sections. He was a romantic—that's why he gave them to me." Jamie smiled. She'd loved her grandfather's idealistic streak. "My brother doesn't have a sentimental bone in his body, which is strange. That trait commonly passes through the males in our family."

"So you're the sentimental sibling?"

"I don't cry at sad movies, but I'll keep the land, and David wouldn't."

"May I see the deed?"

Jamie went into her office and opened the document file Granddad's lawyer had given her. She flipped through the contents and found both deeds. She made duplicates on her scanner-printer and took them to the living room.

Kim Wheeler studied the deed to the waterfront property. "I have to compare this to Zack's paperwork," she said finally. "And we may require an official survey."

Jamie shrugged. "Fine, but I'm not budging, and the Little Blue Fruit Stand is opening on Wednesday to get the business going smoothly by the Memorial Day holiday. Granddad's records indicate it's a busy weekend."

Kim tucked the copies into her briefcase. "If you don't mind me asking, why run your business on *that* land? It's on a dirt road, at the dead end of a public access. There must be more profitable locations."

"It makes a profit, which I can use, but the stand isn't solely about selling produce. Granddad could have gone closer to the highway, but he *didn't* because he wanted to spend his days by the beach. His customers liked going there, too. It can happen that way in small towns. And he got tourist traffic, too."

"I see."

Jamie yawned again. "Sorry. I was awake till four."

"Couldn't sleep?"

"I was working—got caught up in a new design and didn't notice how late it was. I make jewelry and market it in local tourist and gift shops."

"You'll have to show me your jewelry sometime," Kim said politely. "But I should go now and let you go back to bed."

"Don't you need a ride?" Jamie asked.

"If I know Zack, he's likely arranged for a car to collect me."

"And forgot to tell you, right?"

"He's concentrating on other things."

Jamie tried not to sound bitter as she said, "Sure, there's *always* an excuse for people acting badly."

ZACK DROVE INTO the airport and parked. He raced inside the terminal and read the arrivals and departures boards—he wasn't late after all; Brad's flight had just landed.

At the security checkpoint, Zack watched the passengers greeting friends and family, or searching for the baggage-claim area. It took a minute to recognize the thin form limping in his direction. Somehow his mental picture of Brad as a healthy, muscular marine hadn't changed, even though he'd visited his brother in the hospital. Brad still had the military haircut and neat appearance, yet the man beneath the clothing seemed shadowed and broken.

Hell, he *had* been broken.

But he was getting better; the therapists said so.

He'd simply hit a plateau and would benefit from a fresh environment.

"Good to see you, bro." As they clasped hands Zack tried not to reveal anything except a hearty welcome.

"I know. I look like crap." Brad grinned wryly, obviously seeing through Zack's effort. "I wish you hadn't needed to drive so far to get me, but the doctor recommended I travel on a larger plane."

"I was happy to come. Got your luggage checked?"

"A small duffel."

"Not *that* small, I hope," said Zack, and then realized he sounded overly jovial. His father had warned him to act natural—only, what was natural? Certainly not having your brother nearly blown apart by a roadside bomb. "Aren't you staying for a while?"

Brad's face was hard to read. "I don't require much and I can buy more. There must be stores in town."

"And a shop at the resort."

"Thanks, but I'll stick to something less grandiose. I'm sure the shop caters to your high-toned guests, not ordinary jarheads."

"Hey, those high-toned guests pay the bills," Zack reminded him jokingly. "But it *is* mostly golf gear and leisure stuff, so it may not suit you. Feel free to borrow from my closet if you can't find what you want."

They stopped for the duffel bag. Zack carried it easily and slowed his steps to Brad's pace.

Brad whistled when he saw the Mercedes. "Pricey vehicle."

"We have to provide an atmosphere of luxury. It's part of the aura that keeps visitors returning. They come to be pampered."

"You're the expert."

Settling into the passenger seat, Brad eyed him. "You seem okay. But what's going on? Mom hasn't gotten any emails from you for a week and she says that's odd."

"It's nothing to worry about," Zack said calmly, and realized he should send a note so it didn't appear as if anything was wrong; his folks didn't need to lose any more sleep. "A woman is squatting on my land next door. She has a deplorable trailer and thinks she's going to use it to sell fruits and vegetables. Kim is here, attending to the situation."

"What about the police?"

"Ms. Conroe claims she owns the property, and the sheriff insists it's a civil matter. She has this way of verbally twisting things. Kim actually seems to *enjoy* her," he ended in disgust.

"What's she like?" Brad asked.

"Long brunette hair, stubborn chin…smart mouth."

"Hmm. She's made quite an impression on you. I'll have to meet her."

"It won't be on *my* beachfront land if you do."

Brad chuckled, at the same time sending him an odd look. Zack wasn't sure how to react, so he remained silent as his brother tilted his seat back and went to sleep.

Quite an impression.

True. Jamie Conroe had done that, dragging her ugly trailer to the site and putting up those signs. He'd remembered that she was pretty, but still had thought of her as a rugged farmer type in overalls. This morning the sun had gleamed on shining, sleep-rumpled hair, and her worn pink bathrobe had sagged, revealing soft skin that sloped into very sweet curves. Not that he'd seen much. Nor was he interested.

Ten minutes passed and Brad stirred restlessly. "Sorry for flaking out."

"Go ahead. Sleep."

"I'm a master of cat naps. We had to grab them whenever we could in Iraq and be alert at an instant's notice."

"Do you want to talk about it?"

Brad shifted and massaged his left leg. "I appreciate the offer. Mom and Dad try, but I can see it bugs the hell out of them."

"What about post-traumatic stress. Is that a problem?" Zack probed. The frank question was a risk, yet he and Brad had always been honest with each other, and Dad had said to be himself.

"Some. I've spoken with the counselors, and they think I'm handling it."

"I'm here if you want to talk about anything."

"I know," Brad agreed. "Right now I'd rather focus on something different. Tell me more about this woman who's got you so bothered. Is she attractive?"

Jamie Conroe wasn't on Zack's list of favorite topics, but he couldn't refuse after offering his brother his choice of subjects.

"If I'm being honest, she's very...attractive," he said, picturing the woman he'd seen earlier. "Mid to late twenties. A delicate complexion, particularly for someone who works outside. And she's got gorgeous blue eyes." It was strange that he recalled so many details.

"You mentioned she had a smart mouth. What kinds of things does she say?"

As Zack reluctantly described some of the conversations he'd had with his neighbor, Brad smiled, finally laughing so hard that he started coughing.

"My God, bro." Brad caught his breath in his damaged chest. "This woman really has your number."

"I guess she knows what buttons to push. Maybe she's a con artist."

"Kim will deal with it. How's she doing, anyway?"

"She's high profile now, really in demand."

"But how is she personally?"

"Terrific," Zack said. "Stunning as ever. And you know Kim—she's unflappable. The perfect attorney."

Brad scratched his ankle. "Is she spending the night?"

"Trudy assigned her a guest room. I'd invite her to stay with us, but she draws a distinct professional line. I'm her client. She's my lawyer."

"That's Kim's style."

"She's looking forward to seeing you."

Brad didn't respond. He stared at the passing scenery and Zack wondered what he was thinking. Did it upset him to be with people who'd known him before he was injured? Zack almost asked, then saw Brad was asleep again.

As the SUV approached the resort's entrance, Brad roused himself.

"Are we here?"

"This is it," Zack said, hearing the pride that crept into his voice. He slowed to prolong the moment; none of the family had visited until today.

He'd spent a hefty sum on the stone entry to establish a defined border between the outside world and the place he'd created. The words *Mar Vista* were fastened to the stone arch in bold bronze letters. The coastal air was already putting a subtle patina on the metal.

"Mar Vista?" Brad questioned.

"It means 'Sea View,'" he explained. "We're in

California, so it seemed fitting to have a Spanish name—something catchy and easy to remember."

"I thought your name would go on the thing."

"The corporation is Denning Enterprises, but a resort should have a gracious title."

The road curved through a grove of evergreen trees and then opened to the buildings nestled on the gentle slope. Care had been taken during construction to preserve as many of the trees as possible, and the buildings were reminiscent of the great lodges built in the Edwardian era. To the north occupants had a view of the coastline; to the west was the golf course and the brilliant blue ocean.

"Lord, Zack," Brad said, staring at the vista. "You've done a damn fine job."

"I'm glad you like it. Every penny I have is riding on this, and money from the folks, too. I'm going to make it a success."

"That's what you'd say when we were kids and the teacher declared something couldn't be done."

"And I never failed to pull it off." Zack parked in his private space and gestured. "My apartment is above the offices. You can rest or do whatever you want. There's a garden with reclining chaises, or a pool if that appeals— Oh, and a hot tub and sauna. In the meantime, I should go to—"

"Work?" Brad finished.

"I can free up some hours later this afternoon."

"Don't change your routine. I'm sick of people tiptoeing around me and making special arrangements. Mom and Dad haven't had a normal life since I came home."

Yeah, Brad would hate that. Zack was the bull-headed son, determined to win no matter what, while his brother was the easygoing one. Few things had surprised Zack more than when Brad entered the Marine Corps. Yet he'd done well, rising in the ranks and becoming highly respected by the soldiers under his command.

He showed Brad the apartment, urged him to order from room service or one of the Mar Vista restaurants and trotted downstairs.

It was time to locate Kim and find out how soon Jamie Conroe and the Little Blue Fruit Stand would be gone.

CHAPTER THREE

THE SURVEYORS ARRIVED with their gear the following Thursday morning. Jamie had a steady stream of customers the first hour, and soon the surveyors drifted over. They bought three baskets of strawberries and ate them on the spot.

During a quiet pause in business, Jamie settled in her Adirondack chair and took in the familiar scents and sounds. Her grandfather's heavy wood chair had dated to the 1950s. Instead of dragging it from the house, she'd found two made from recycled plastic. It would be too weird to use his, anyhow. Even as a kid she'd never sat in his chair—it belonged to Granddad and nobody else.

The day was unusually warm. This part of the coast didn't get much hot weather; it was moderate most of the year.

Mmm.

Jamie yawned.

Ocean waves crashed on the shore and the sea shimmered brilliant blue with streaks of greenish-aqua. It was no wonder that Granddad had loved this place; it was peaceful and wholesome. The sunshine was blissfully soothing, and she could always sketch a pendant or bracelet design if inspiration came to her.

Crunching gravel nudged her eyelids open. The approaching vehicle was a black van with Mar Vista in gold lettering on the door and Denning Enterprises in smaller print below. The logo was striking—a lone cypress and soaring seabird.

Jamie stretched, ready to rev up her brain for another verbal bout, but neither of the men who climbed from the van was Zack Denning. The driver seemed genial and innocuous, and his passenger was thin and pale, with a narrow scar above his left eye. He walked with a limp and hugged his arm to his rib cage as if it hurt. She recognized the cautious posture too well.

"Hello," the driver called. "I'm Gordon Chen. Your sign says you carry certified organic fruits and vegetables."

"Yup. More and more people are eating pesticide-free."

"That's great. I'm looking for someone to supply the restaurants at Mar Vista. Dealing directly with growers is time-consuming, so I was hoping we could come to an agreement that would benefit both of us."

Jamie shifted in her chair, clinging to her tranquillity. "Let me guess. You'll be able to buy all of my produce, so there won't be any reason for me to keep the stand going."

Gordon frowned. "I'm not sure what you mean. I don't want you to quit your business. Quite the contrary."

"In that case, you'd better get oxygen for your boss. He'll be gasping for air when he hears the news."

The second man laughed and Jamie was struck by the difference it made in his appearance.

"Morning," he said. "My name is Brad Denning. I hitched a ride to come and meet you."

She extended her left hand to shake so he wouldn't have to move his injured side.

"I'm missing something here, but it isn't important. Are you interested?" Gordon asked. "I'm choosy about what goes into my kitchen and want someone equally careful to coordinate my produce." He must be the chef, which accounted for his air of confidence.

"I'm interested," she assured him. "And I can work with the organic farmers to get you a wider variety than what I stock. The biggest problem is that I don't have a large enough truck, and there's no point in getting one for a single customer."

Gordon shrugged. He seemed unusually easygoing for a high-priced chef. "I can send a guy to get my orders. It's still an improvement over having a dozen sources delivering throughout the day."

"The other problem is that for now the stand is only open for the summer and I may not want to do it year-round," Jamie explained. "At present I'm a one-person operation."

"Let's have a trial period and see where we go from there," Gordon suggested.

They discussed the arrangements, and he took her email address so he could send his orders electronically. As they were leaving, Brad Denning gave Jamie a friendly smile. He was nothing like his obnoxious brother.

"It was good meeting you, Jamie."

"Likewise," she said, yet she couldn't help sniggering once she was alone.

She was now a Mar Vista supplier.

How much oxygen was Zack Denning going to need?

BRAD WINCED AS the van bounced entering the public road. His fist went instinctively to his aching thigh, but he dragged it away. They'd told him the pain would ease; his shattered bones would strengthen and wasted muscle rebuild. In the meanwhile he was treating it as survival training…one step, one minute at a time.

"Nice lady," Gordon commented. "What was that stuff about her closing?"

Brad hesitated. He didn't think Zack would relish the staff gossiping about his disagreement with Jamie Conroe. His brother had changed; in some ways he was nearly a stranger.

"I'm sure it's nothing," Brad said as Gordon

parked close to the kitchen. "Ms. Conroe seems to have a unique sense of humor."

"Yes. It should be entertaining getting to know her." Gordon hung the keys on the central message board and returned to his kitchen. He was a nice guy and hadn't minded Brad dropping by one afternoon to scrounge a snack. Gordon had prepared the sandwich himself—a masterpiece of roast beef, cheese, sautéed mushrooms and spicy peppers piled on fresh-made sourdough bread. Brad had eaten it with Gordon clucking over him like a brood hen.

Since then the chef had pressed a number of dishes on him that he claimed were experiments, but were obviously intended to tease the appetite of a recuperating patient.

Clearly, if Gordon hadn't become a chef, he would have been a mother.

Brad set out to walk the perimeter of the resort, willing his body to cooperate. At the hospital they'd dictated the amount of exercise he should get, but he'd outmaneuvered them by covertly visiting the rehab center in the middle of the night and using the equipment on his own.

Lord.

It was tough accepting that his old life might be over...a life in which he'd served his country. People didn't always understand. It wasn't the battles or adrenaline he missed; it was doing something for folks he'd never even met.

"Hi there," Rick Lopez called as Brad passed his

open office window. "I saw you on the course. Are you taking up golf?"

"There's no chance in hell. Knocking a ball around a manicured lawn isn't my style."

Rick chuckled. "I beg your pardon.... Manicuring those greens is hard labor. But you're right—it isn't for everyone. Between you and me, I don't believe our fearless boss loves the sport, either. Zack is so grim practicing his swing. I swear he only plays so he can converse with the guests and join with a group in unavoidable circumstances."

Naturally.

Everything Zack did nowadays was to support his dream. The resort was a marvel, but it wasn't an atmosphere where Brad felt comfortable.

Nonetheless, Mar Vista and its ritzy counterparts were Zack's world.

And Kim Wheeler's.

Kim.... Brad rubbed his jaw. He'd enjoyed seeing her, however briefly. She was more polished and beautiful than ever, wearing discreet evidence of her professional achievements. He imagined those diamond studs on her ears would cost three or four months of a soldier's pay.

On Tuesday after the Memorial Day weekend, Zack read the surveyor's report in disbelief. It plainly indicated that the real estate he'd purchased *didn't* include the section where Jamie Conroe had her fruit stand. He owned the beach north of it, not the entire waterfront.

"Hey, Zack. Snap out of it," Kim commanded over the video-teleconference connection.

"How did this happen?"

"There were a number of parcels involved, Zack. You were preoccupied with construction and made the deal in a hurry."

"In other words, I should have had your office check it."

Her lips curved in humor. "Actually, few buyers have a lawyer review a real-estate transaction until closing, although large companies usually bring in an attorney from the beginning. I didn't check your other purchases and they were successful."

That was six years ago, when the land had cost less and he'd bought it on speculation. Had success with his first batch of acquisitions led him to a hasty decision with the second?

"What are my options?" Zack asked.

"You might have a chance in court if you think the seller was deliberately misleading."

"I don't know if Jenkins did anything wrong, and I doubt we could prove dishonest intent if he did. It would be a nasty fight. People liked the old guy, odd as he was."

Kim nodded. "And they'll be protective of his granddaughter. You're a smart businessman, Zack. Negative relations with the local community is extremely costly in the long run. My suggestion is to work it out with Ms. Conroe. She isn't a bad sort."

Zack pictured Jamie's stubborn face. "*She* doesn't like *me*."

"And whose fault is that?"

"Don't rub it in. I'll have the real-estate agent contact her with an offer."

Kim tapped her pencil on the desk thoughtfully, and a corner of his mind appreciated the technology for doing video teleconferences. It wasn't face-to-face communication, but closer to it than the phone. This way he could read her body language and get a feel for what she was thinking.

"I have a suspicion Ms. Conroe won't sell," Kim said. "There's a sentimental attachment. Other solutions are possible, though. For example, she makes jewelry. How about featuring her pieces in the gift shop? In return, she may relocate the stand."

He stared at the computer monitor, appalled. "For Pete's sake, I can't put cheap bits of beadwork on sale here. We carry top-end items like art glass and original sculptures."

"Look for an accommodation." Kim sounded exasperated. "Talk to her. She might compromise if she realizes the potential impact on your operations."

Zack glanced at the map on which the property lines had been clearly drawn. "You've got higher hopes for her goodwill than I do."

"If nothing else, you have your contingency plan

to build around her and border it with a tall hedge or stone wall. Your guests would still have a private beach since you aren't required to provide access between her two sections. She has to use the public road the same as everyone."

Zack groaned. He'd gotten used to the idea of having all that lovely, undeveloped land to himself. It was so much less complicated.

"Make nice," Kim ordered. "You do it with difficult patrons. Swallow your pride and pretend she's a VIP client staying in your King Louis suite."

"I don't have a King Louis suite. What's your schedule over the next couple days? Unless you ticked her off, I'm sure she'll listen to you more than me."

"We got along fine." Kim scanned her iPhone, and then shook her head. "I can't get away for a while. Anyhow, *you* should be the one to take care of this. Like it or not, she's your neighbor and you've got to mend fences. Begin with an apology for trying to get her arrested. It wasn't your finest moment."

He groaned again.

"I have to go, Zack. I've got a meeting with the mayor in twenty minutes."

"The mayor? Show-off."

She laughed as he disconnected.

Zack was convinced Kim was getting malicious amusement from the situation. He grasped his coffee and sucked down half the cup, wishing it had a dash of whiskey. Aside from his emergency fund, he'd sunk every penny into Mar Vista, along with the assets his parents had insisted on investing. If the resort didn't turn a profit and his loan defaulted, could he at least salvage their money?

Hell. There was no reason to assume the worst; he'd deal with it. And in the meantime, he would ensure everything continued to run properly.

He hit the intercom button on his desk. "Trudy?"

"Yes, boss."

"Do you have those purchase orders and invoices ready for me to review?"

"I forwarded them to your computer."

"Thanks."

He clicked on the files, making notes and adding his approval as needed. Trudy had rejected a requisition for room deodorizers and sent a memo to housekeeping that guest rooms were to be so clean that fragrance wasn't necessary. *Excellent.* Trudy knew his position on the issue. Apparently, the housekeeping supervisor was pleased with the replacement linens. The prior lot must have been defective, though they'd come from a leading company for luxury hotel linens.

Zack started on the invoices, only to grit his teeth when he saw the third one. *Of course.* Jamie Conroe must have chortled when she topped her paperwork with Little Blue Fruit Stand Enterprises.

Resigned, Zack added his authorization for payment. Maybe the Mar Vista restaurants would furnish enough income that she'd abandon her trailer. It had to be easier to manage supplies for one customer than to spend a full day vending vegetables to dozens of different people.

The lunch hour passed before he was finished. He got out his keys and squared his shoulders. No more procrastinating; he had to tackle his chief headache.

On the way, he drank the cup of stale coffee sitting in the SUV. Caffeine might help him cope with the woman.

The blue trailer wasn't quite as vivid as his memory had made it, or else the shock value had diminished.

Jamie was half reclining in a green chair, legs extended in long, languid lines. She seemed to be asleep. Her dark hair fluttered in the breeze and her creamy complexion was highlighted by the eyelashes resting on her cheeks. Today she wore jeans and a T-shirt that revealed the curves he'd glimpsed at her house.

No cosmetics.

No jewelry or accessories.

No special attempt to look attractive or appealing.

Yet something in the scene tugged at Zack's gut. It didn't make sense. Jamie was the opposite of the women who inhabited his world. True, he'd been living like a monk, too buried in work for socializing, but still....

"Are you going to buy strawberries, or keep examining me for weak points?" she said suddenly, startling him.

"I thought you were asleep."

"The sound of tires on gravel is a decent alarm system." Jamie raised her eyebrows. "If you're here to complain some more, go ahead and give it your best shot."

"I...I want to apologize. I shouldn't have called the sheriff. And you were correct—this is your land. The surveyors' report came this morning."

"Wow. That must have hurt." She rose from the low-slung chair in a graceful twist.

Zack grimaced. She couldn't know how much it hurt, or how hard it was to follow Kim's advice to be nice. "As I said, I'm very sorry. I was under the impression your grandfather sold me everything, including this beachfront acre."

Her blue eyes grew stormy. "Are you saying he cheated you?"

"I'm only..." Zack stopped. It was galling; even if George Jenkins had cheated, it meant *he* was the chump. Zack couldn't afford that kind of reputation in corporate circles. "No, not at all, but I *would* like to acquire this section. Name a price."

"It isn't for sale."

"Are you planning to build?" he asked.

"Heavens, no. Granddad would haunt me."

That was reassuring. All he had to worry about was a summer fruit stand—except summer was his busiest season. In the next few months the resort was solidly booked with reservations from high-profile guests, as well as old friends and clientele who knew him as a manager in other locations. Most were coming because of their acquaintance with him, and they'd *keep* coming if Mar Vista met or exceeded their expectations. And while it was possible that Jamie's hideous trailer wouldn't sabotage the resort, it wouldn't be good for it, either.

"I'll pay you a fair amount," he said. "Extremely fair."

"It isn't a question of price." Her gaze was clear and seemed free of guile. Yet it made no sense that she didn't care how much she could get. A woman who eked out a living peddling fruits and vegetables had to be short on money.

"If you aren't going to develop the site, why not take the cash?"

"To be sure no one *else* builds on it. It isn't you personally. No one gets this land. It's Conroe soil and it stays in the family."

The scent of strawberries wafted into Zack's consciousness. His stomach grumbled, a reminder that he'd skipped both breakfast and lunch. Jamie grinned at the noise and held a bowl of fruit in his direction. "Have some. My treat."

"I'm fine."

"It's a free sample of what your restaurant is serving for dessert tonight," she said. "You do know that we're in business together, don't you?"

"I saw the invoice."

Her lips twitched. "Did you fire your chef for crossing enemy lines?"

"No. Gordon is in charge of his kitchen. I'm lucky to have him."

Jamie jiggled her bowl to tempt him, and the glistening red berries made his mouth water. It was also a reminder that if he'd eaten something instead of gulping numerous cups of coffee, he might be doing a better job of handling this situation.

"So, top chefs do rule their territory," she mused.

"That's one way of putting it." Zack thought of Gordon's contract. It gave him broader authority than anyone else employed at Mar Vista, even Rick Lopez. The competition was fierce for a chef with Gordon Chen's standing. Zack probably couldn't have gotten him if he and his wife hadn't wanted to raise their children in a rural setting like Warrington, California.

"Poor Mr. Denning. There's a fiefdom in his kingdom that he can't command." Jamie ate a berry with unabashed pleasure, then licked a bead of ruby juice from her finger.

Zack hung on to his resolve and concentrated.

"Come on," she urged. "Declare defeat and eat a few."

"I don't need anything." His voice came out stiffer than he'd intended. "I want to discuss…"

His words were interrupted by the crunch of truck wheels on gravel. The pickup parked and the passengers ambled across to look at the spinach. Another car pulled in behind them.

"Excuse me," Jamie said. "You comprehend the importance of customers, don't you? People who buy what you *want* to sell. Catch my drift?"

Yeah, he got it. She refused to part with her land. But surely there was something he could offer... perhaps pay for renovations to make her produce stand more acceptable, though moving her was his top choice. His guests would still see the signs as they approached the resort, but he could have new ones painted that were rustic and charming, rather than garish.

"Loganberries?" queried one of the newcomers as she lifted a basket and sniffed. "I've never heard of them."

"They're yummy," Jamie told her. "Kind of a cross between a raspberry and a boysenberry. Delicious in jam, pies, whatever."

"We're staying at the state park," the woman said, wrinkling her nose. "No camper. Roughing it, or I'd bake a pie."

Jamie smiled, a wide, unaffected smile that transformed her ordinarily pretty face into something truly striking. "That reminds me of the summer my mom made jam using a camp stove. She swore she'd never do it again. Tell you what— if you have a covered pot, you can make berries and dumplings."

"Really?" the woman said, plainly intrigued. "We have sugar and I brought biscuit mix for pancakes."

"That's all you need. Cook it the same as you'd cook chicken and dumplings, only sweetened, and drop the dough into the simmering berries."

"Yum. I'm going to try that." She selected three pints, and told her husband they should come again before their vacation was over.

Zack had planned to wait for Jamie's customers to leave so they could finish their discussion, but he couldn't be sure of getting her full attention with the constant disruptions. It was amazing that people drove this far from town and the main highway to buy fruits and vegetables. The view was a plus, of course, and her produce was first-rate.

"Thank you for speaking with me, Ms. Conroe," he murmured. "I'll contact you when it's more convenient."

"Whatever."

Just then a young woman squealed and hugged her. "Jamie Conroe. I heard you were here."

"Kristie, you look *fantastic*. How are you?"

"Great. You know what? I married Greg Norton, the way I predicted. He finally noticed me the last year of college. And I made him pay for taking so long.... He chased me for weeks before I'd go out with him. I loved it."

The two women chatted as Zack strode to his car. He definitely had to find a strategic location for their next encounter—on his turf, rather than hers. He'd learned long ago that the person who controlled the environment had the advantage in a negotiation.

JAMIE DREW A breath of relief after Zack's departure. The customers were arriving fast and furious—it was strange how they came in waves.

Although Granddad's stand had always been popular, the volume of shoppers had amazed her until she'd realized the locals knew about the land dispute. Some were showing their support; others were curious. On top of that, she got plenty of tourist traffic. It was a bonus week. She sold out every afternoon except for bits and pieces.

It *was* a demanding schedule. She had to meet growers before five in the morning, assemble the load for Gordon and count boxes as they were packed into the Denning Enterprises truck at five-thirty. Despite his pickiness, Gordon wasn't difficult to deal with, and jabbing Zack Denning was a perk. She just wasn't sure the extra profit was worth it.

Zack's apology had come as a surprise, and Jamie suspected his lawyer was responsible. Not that he'd genuinely sounded sorry; it was more like he thought Granddad had swindled him. If there was one thing she knew for certain, her grandfather had played fair. She had no idea how the mix-up had occurred, but she wouldn't let anyone malign one of the best men she'd ever known.

Swallowing, Jamie tried to recapture the peace she'd felt earlier. Why let Zack Denning spoil things?

Yet deep down, Jamie knew part of her trouble stemmed from guilt—she hadn't been here when Granddad was putting his affairs in order. She should have come, but her marital problems had kept her away. She'd been trying to hold things together, and was embarrassed to be with her family and admit what was happening. It was Tim's attempts to keep her from visiting Granddad during his final illness that had tipped the scale. She'd stood up to him and walked out.

Perhaps it was okay that she couldn't easily relax after a confrontation—she didn't want to forget how to defend herself.

Footsteps broke the quiet and she saw Brad Denning.

"Gordon tells me the strawberries are tasty," he called. His limp was more pronounced than the day they'd met, and the creases on his forehead were deeply drawn…from pain, she guessed. He must have pushed himself to get this far.

She grabbed the dish of fruit samples and offered it to him. "I hope you aren't as pigheaded as your brother. He wouldn't even eat a small one, though his stomach was growling louder than an angry grizzly bear."

Brad chose a juicy berry and popped it in his mouth. "I can be pigheaded, but not over food. I don't know any jarheads dumb enough to turn down a tasty meal."

"Jarheads?" Jamie asked.

Pride flared in his eyes. "It's a nickname for a marine."

"Oh, I remember now. Have a seat."

Sinking into the other chair, he sighed. "This is the farthest I've gone in a long time. But it's great to get outside for exercise instead of on a therapist's treadmill. I…uh, I've had to do some rehab recently."

"I'll give you a lift back if you don't mind waiting. It's on my route to the bank."

"My ego says no. My common sense says thanks."

Jamie had the feeling that Brad would prefer accepting a ride from her, rather than his brother.

"This is the perfect spot to take a break. Have more berries."

Brad took the bowl and ate several strawberries, then gestured at her empty displays. "Don't you keep stock for late customers?"

"Nope, unless I have a reservation for something. That's why I'm still here. An old friend of Granddad's is coming for the four flats I've got stored in the trailer. Otherwise, as I put on my sign, first come, first served. I order the amount I think I can sell and usually get to close early."

"You sound experienced."

"As a kid I spent every August with Granddad,

so my policies and attitudes come from him. He also had thorough records on the daily turnover."

"That must make it easier."

He seemed drowsy and his left hand scratched his shoulder before settling onto his lap.

Jamie's sensation of peace returned. She liked Brad Denning. It was bizarre that he was the brother of such an arrogant jerk, but siblings *could* be very different. Her own brother didn't look like her, and they certainly didn't have much in common.

As Brad slept, her brain chewed on designs for her next jewelry project. She'd taken a silver-casting class in college for fun. Tim used to be snide regarding her efforts, so it was an ironic triumph that selling the expensive clothes he'd insisted she wear during their marriage provided the money she'd needed for tools and supplies. Hopefully, marketing her jewelry would be a real supplement to her fruit-stand earnings.

Jamie stiffened, despite the comforting warmth of the sun. Tim had been nauseatingly smug in court, claiming she wouldn't be able to live without him. Fat chance, just like the split lip he'd given her when she told him she was leaving for good. She restrained a giggle as she recalled the contempt in the expression of the judge, who'd privately congratulated her on getting rid of a pompous jackass.

Her last customer, Mrs. Kruger, came and Jamie loaded the four flats she'd bought into her car.

"Thank you, Jamie." The elderly woman gave

her a check in payment. "The jam tastes different made with berries from the Little Blue Fruit Stand. I suppose that sounds silly."

"It isn't silly. Granddad used to say this place had a blessing on it."

"I believe it." Mrs. Kruger glanced at Brad. He was awake and blinking sleepily at the ocean. "Are you all right, dear? I understood you've had trouble with your neighbor."

"No worries—we've straightened it out," Jamie said. "It was a miscommunication over the property lines."

"I'm so glad. And you've gotten divorced? What a shame."

"Some marriages aren't meant to be."

"Gabe and me, we've had fifty-two happy years." Mrs. Kruger's attention kept moving in Brad's direction. "Do you think you'll ever get married again?"

"I don't know, Mrs. Kruger. Right now I'm focusing on my business," Jamie answered patiently. The motherly types who remembered her from childhood were interested in her romantic plans, though some of the younger wives were also inquisitive, but for entirely different reasons. Jamie had already learned a sour truth—a youthful divorcée was considered dangerous by some women, although her genuine friends weren't worried.

Mrs. Kruger's curiosity was transparent as she squinted at Brad Denning. "Is he a friend?"

"He's from the resort. He just stopped to sample

the berries." Jamie didn't want to say that Brad had needed to rest.

Disappointment clouded the kindly woman's features. "What a shame. Your grandfather prized a good gab. Gabe would come to get the berries for me, and they'd sit for hours talking baseball. Speaking of which, I should go and get that jam started."

Waving cheerily, Mrs. Kruger drove away and Jamie walked to the trailer. Brad was eating strawberries and his brow was less tense.

"We can go now, unless you'd rather hang out here," Jamie told him.

"You don't lock up?"

"There's no point. It's easy to break in and then I'd have to repair the latch."

Brad asked to be dropped at the resort entrance, saying it was only a short distance to his brother's apartment. Jamie didn't push; the man had the right to decide things for himself.

Later as she snuggled onto her smooth cotton pillowcase with Marlin purring against her on the bed, Jamie's mind wandered through the day's events. It was annoying that she kept thinking about Zack Denning. She'd appreciate it if he would stay on his property and leave her alone, but it was a reasonable bet that she'd have another encounter with his lordship in the near future.

The man hadn't given up. He was probably in a tactical retreat while he devised a new plot to get Granddad's land.

CHAPTER FOUR

JAMIE YAWNED AND glanced at the lit display on the clock. *4:00 a.m.* She relaxed, grateful she didn't have to get up and rush out to the fruit stand.

Gordon Chen had originally wanted his produce picked up in a single load, but since the resort restaurants needed strawberries for their breakfast menu, it had required her getting up at an ungodly hour to coordinate everything. She'd finally told Gordon it made too long a day for her. He'd offered a compromise; he would take direct delivery of the berries from a grower she trusted, and send two of his guys midmorning for the rest. The new arrangement was beginning today.

"Mrrroow?"

In the faint light she saw Marlin stretch and yawn a few inches from her face. If he wasn't such a lazy old guy, it might be scary to see those gleaming teeth so close to her jugular.

"I know you miss Granddad," she murmured. He let out a feline sigh as if he'd understood. She doubted her grandfather had allowed Marlin to get on the bed, but she didn't have the heart to banish him. He slept each night lying against her, snoring, his huge head on her shoulder.

Marlin was a typical cat—he knew a sucker when he saw one. *I'm lonely,* he'd practically screamed when he'd launched himself at her the day she'd arrived in Warrington, yowling for all he was worth. The man watching the house had taken care of his basic needs, but there was no substitute for affectionate company.

Petting him absently, Jamie thought about a design for a piece of cat jewelry, but wasn't sure it would work.

Mr. Peterson had called to tell her that four of her pendants had sold that weekend and that he'd be glad to take more. It was a victory. Mr. Peterson owned the finest art studio in town and had been reluctant to carry jewelry. If she hadn't been George Jenkins's granddaughter, he probably wouldn't have agreed; apparently, her persistence was paying off for both of them. She'd have to go through her stock to see what might work for him. And now that she'd have more free hours, perhaps she could concentrate on the higher-end market, which gave a better rate of return than regular tourist shops.

She drowsed another hour, then pulled away from a protesting Marlin, who settled into the pile of blankets with a sulky expression.

"Sorry, pal. I've got a business to run."

He closed his eyes and twitched the tip of his tail. Dressing quickly, Jamie took care of some household chores and dashed to the fruit stand. Deliveries were now scheduled for eight-thirty.

By ten o'clock, the Mar Vista restaurant staff had picked up their order and she was ready for business. The sun was shining and seemed to promise a clear day, although it could change in nothing flat. That was one of the interesting parts of living on the coast.

During a lull she discovered a cell phone under the edge of the trailer while tidying the area, the second since opening the stand. A customer had already claimed the first, and another had come by, saying his was missing and wondering if he'd dropped it there. Pleased, she phoned the number the man had left.

"Mine showed up," he said. "Darnedest thing, it slid between the driver's seat and the emergency brake and was nearly invisible. My ten-year-old unearthed it while scrounging for loose change."

"I'm glad you found it."

"Me, too. I've lost three and didn't want my wife to know there could be a fourth."

Jamie got off and checked the cell she'd found, hoping to retrieve its phone number, but the battery was dead.

Drat.

Then she remembered Zack Denning hunting through his pockets before using his vehicle radio.

Jamie gazed at the phone speculatively. It wasn't a gadget-packed iPhone, but a genius entrepreneur might be too busy for bells and whistles. She hoped the phone *was* Zack's; he'd hate owing her a favor, however minor.

After dealing with several customers, she dialed Mar Vista's office.

A woman answered. "Denning Enterprises. Trudy Lopez speaking."

"Hello, this is Jamie Conroe."

"Oh, hello, Ms. Conroe. How may I help you?" The woman's voice became rigidly correct.

"I found a cell phone at my produce stand and wondered if it could be Mr. Denning's. He seemed to have lost something when he was here." She almost mentioned it was when he'd tried to have her arrested for trespassing on her own property, but thought she should save her gibes for the man who deserved them.

"May I put you on hold while I ask him?"

"That's fine."

"I apologize for the delay, Ms. Conroe," Trudy said when she came back. "Mr. Denning did lose his phone and he'll be right there to see if it belongs to him."

"That's not necessary," Jamie replied hastily. "I'll send it with Gordon's guys tomorrow. They can return it the next day if it isn't his."

"It will be faster if he comes."

Jamie tensed. "I know he's got another cell phone to use in the meantime—he contacted his lawyer at my house after he was out here."

"Yes, he does have a spare, but—"

"So there's no reason for him to come," Jamie interrupted.

"Nevertheless, he should be there in a few minutes. Thank you for calling."

The woman on the other end disconnected without letting Jamie protest again, and she stuck her tongue out, annoyed. The tables had gotten turned and it was her own fault—Denning must have wanted an excuse to come over, and she'd provided one. Owners of fancy resorts didn't rush to a fruit stand because of a cell phone; they sent flunkies to do it.

On the other hand, knowing he had ulterior motives could level the balance of power.

She washed two baskets of strawberries and sat down to wait.

ZACK HAD BEEN deep in financial reports and purchase orders when Trudy came in and said that Jamie Conroe may have found his cell phone. The timing was amazing. He'd spent most of the morning mulling over how to approach Jamie. Somehow he *had* to get her onto the resort and make her understand what he was trying to do. He didn't know what was keeping her in that particular spot, but getting her to move that hideous trailer from sight was a top priority.

Despite Jamie's protests to stop him from coming, his misplaced cell phone was the perfect opportunity. With luck there'd be a free moment when he could invite her to lunch or dinner to talk about alternatives.

A young couple was at the stand when he arrived, dithering about whether to buy one or two boxes of strawberries, and if they should get organic. He admired Jamie's patience as they posed a dozen questions and finally left with a lone basket of fruit.

He gestured to the departing car with a smile. "Business would be easy if it wasn't for the customers, wouldn't it?"

Jamie put the money away and shrugged. "They're newlyweds. Figuring out how to buy things together is a part of marital adjustment."

It was a curious observation to make. According to what she'd told the sheriff, she was divorced and using her maiden name. Was she bitter? Relieved? Indifferent? Probably wise not to open that can of worms.

"You were very patient," he commented.

"Granddad used to say couples have to learn how to be married. He saw it when they came and shopped here, and how it changed as they grew together."

"He sounds like a smart man," Zack said, finding to his surprise that he meant it.

"Very." She reached behind the counter and took out a cell phone. "This must have fallen under the edge of the trailer and gotten covered up by the mat, but the good news is it didn't get as damp as it would have otherwise. The morning dew can be heavy."

He flipped the phone open. "I appreciate your call. I'll have to charge the battery to verify it's mine."

"No problem." She grinned wickedly and held out a bowl of gleaming strawberries. "You really should try one. They're something special."

She had him at a disadvantage, and knew it. If he kept refusing, he'd appear obstinate and childish.

"They look delicious." He took a large one. The sweet taste burst in his mouth and his senses sharpened with pleasure. How long had it been since he'd paid real attention to the flavor of food? The ambition to build Mar Vista had taken over everything else. Even when testing menu items, he'd analyzed the appeal for his customers, rather than enjoying Gordon's talent.

Her eyes danced and she offered the bowl again. "As they say about potato chips, it's hard to eat just one."

Swallowing his pride, he took a second berry. How should he introduce the subject of a dinner business meeting? If he'd wanted a date he would suggest it as a thank-you for the strawberries, or for locating his phone. But it wasn't that kind of situation.

"Please have dinner with me at the resort," he said, belatedly realizing that lunch wouldn't work because of her hours at the produce stand. "That way we can discuss things without disruption. I'm really not a morning person. I'm much more charming at night."

"We don't have anything to discuss, and I have no interest in your 'charm.'"

He winced. Apparently, aspects of his interpersonal skills were getting rusty. "I'd still like to talk. Plus, we have two fine restaurants which you supply produce for. Don't you want to sample Gordon's menu?"

He had her there. No one disliked Gordon.

"Of course I would, but I can sample his food whenever I please. Aren't both of your restaurants open to the public, not just guests of the resort?"

"Yes," he said smoothly. "But why not eat with me, as well?"

Negotiation 101—try not to ask questions that can be answered with a yes or no. Push for a more complex answer.

She shrugged. "As I said, we don't have anything to discuss."

Zack intended to stand there as long as it took to convince her. "Indulge me. At worst, it will cost you an evening, and you'll get a gourmet meal out of it."

JAMIE DIDN'T WANT to accept the invitation, but it would delay the inevitable. Zack genuinely thought he could change her mind, and wouldn't give up until she made it clear his pursuit was pointless.

"Okay," she agreed and was amused by the surprise on his face.

"Excellent. Our Sunfish Grotto is superb." There was a hint of triumph in his voice that warranted a hole punched in it.

"Not the Grotto. I understand your other restaurant is less formal, and I'd rather not have to get dressed up after working out here all day."

His jaw clenched. "If that's what you prefer. We'll do the Sunfish Grotto another day."

Like hell they would. They'd eat dinner. He'd propose his purchase. She'd turn him down flat and tell him to quit trying. End of the matter.

But she smiled pleasantly. "Does Thursday work for you?"

"Sure. I'll pick you up at seven."

He must think she was an idiot. No way would she let herself be dependent upon him for transportation. "I'll meet you at the restaurant."

"That wouldn't be courteous of me."

"This isn't a date. It's business."

Zack seemed to hesitate. Was he regretting his invitation? "Then how about coming to the office?" he suggested. "There's a parking lot for employees and it will have extra space. We can walk to the restaurant, or take one of the golf carts."

He was likely worried that she'd show up in Granddad's battered pickup and park by the Mercedes, BMWs and Acuras belonging to his customers. God forbid she get dust on one of them.

It was tempting to yank his chain by doing the opposite to what he expected. Granddad had left her a beautifully maintained 1940s-era Jaguar stored in the barn. Zack would probably love to see it in his customer lot, not tucked out of sight. She'd have to consider whether it was worth getting the battery charged...or was it so old it had to be cranked? Her knowledge of classic vehicles was woefully lacking.

"I'd be delighted to come to the office," she said, which seemed to make him suspicious.

With a small nod, he got into his car. Before he turned onto the paved road, she saw him halt and stare back at her, no doubt evaluating how he'd handled the encounter and what his next move would be. Too bad. She held the trump card because no one could force her to sell.

The next few days Jamie determinedly put Zack and their upcoming dinner meeting out of her mind. Her success at the Peterson Gallery was great incentive to focus even harder on her silver casting. She sketched several designs between customers during the day, and made good progress on the casting and finishing work at night before going to bed.

Brad Denning dropped by the produce stand every afternoon. He was comfortable company. At rare moments he spoke of his deployment overseas, mostly relating stories about the children he'd met. Yet from the shadows in his eyes, Jamie knew he had far darker memories he could have recounted. He usually walked back to the resort on his own steam, only once letting her give him a ride to the front gate.

When Thursday came, Jamie woke up and realized she hadn't checked Granddad's old Jaguar to see if it was running. It was just as well, since the Jag wouldn't operate the same as modern cars and she'd look ridiculous driving into Mar Vista, jerking and stalling. Her Honda would have to do.

At six-thirty that evening, she dressed in a simple skirt and blouse. For a minute she examined herself in the mirror. Her outfit wasn't the height of fashion, which was fine. The choice of a red blouse was deliberate; red was supposed to be a "power" color.

It felt odd driving through the gates of the resort. She'd spent her childhood summers on the uninhabited point sticking into the ocean, yet Zack Denning had managed to give Mar Vista the air of having been there for decades, instead of months. Then she hit a snag. She had no idea where the office was and there were no directions to the employee parking lot, just discreet signs for guest registration. In exasperation she finally asked one of the valet-parking attendants how to get to the business office. He gave her directions and she got there shortly past seven.

"My apologies for being late," she told Zack as he waited by the office door.

He wore a nicely fitted sports jacket, and she mused idly how many of his guests were single women on the hunt for a husband. He'd be a decent catch provided they didn't object to his love affair with Mar Vista.

"Not a problem."

Jamie decided it was best to keep him on the defensive. "Your employees must learn by osmosis how to find their parking area, since it isn't marked."

"I should have given you directions."

"What if FedEx has to make a delivery? Or someone else? Must they call and get directions?"

"Delivery folks have always found us."

"Maybe not," she countered. "Some of them could be wandering the salt flats, thin with hunger, thinking the office is a figment of the imagination."

His expression was so pleased that she wondered if he was up to something. "You might be right." He led the way to a golf cart, escorting her into the passenger's seat and settling behind the wheel. It was extremely quiet when he turned the key, and she figured it had to be electric. He headed away from the buildings, saying, "I'll give you a quick tour before dinner. That way you'll know where everything is located, so you won't get lost again."

They glided around the golf course as he pointed out various features.

"Trade magazines are predicting the course will eventually receive a top-one-hundred ranking," Zack enthused. "We went for a more natural type of construction, with only certain sections manicured. It plays just over eight thousand yards, and our ninth hole rivals the sixteenth at Cypress Point in Pebble Beach."

Jamie understood. Her father was a golfer and had played a number of the top courses in America and Scotland, so she recognized that Mar Vista's design was top-notch. Not that her dad could afford to golf at Mar Vista. The family had gotten together on a Father's Day gift for a weekend at Pebble Beach four years ago, but it was plain that Zack's resort was equally exclusive, and extravagantly expensive.

Zack directed the cart toward the buildings. But he didn't stop; he drove on to an airstrip a mile away, then to a series of paddocks and horse stables. Lately she'd seen more riders around, so she'd suspected he had stables. Granddad hadn't cared if people used his land as long as they respected his privacy and didn't litter, so the area was already a popular location for horseback riding.

Next Zack showed her a display of shiny bicycles for the energetically inclined. Afterward they went down a winding road to a private marina where guests could take kayaks or sailboats out into the cove, or moor their private yachts.

"I've tried to include a wide variety of activities for my guests," he said as they drove back. "All the rooms have a view, and we have plenty of carts for transportation, with frequent recharging stations around the resort. That's a big improvement on combustion engines running everywhere."

Jamie checked her watch. More than an hour had

passed since she'd arrived—Zack's "quick tour" was anything but. And it had the flavor of something he'd planned in order to prove the resort was of greater importance than her trailer and fruit stand. That was why her comments concerning the difficulty getting to the office had pleased him; they'd given him an excuse to take her all over his resort. She took a deep breath, trying to contain her frustration.

They approached a building not far from the office. *At last*. It had been a busy day, and aside from everything else, she was hungry. She climbed out and Zack led her through doors to an elegant lounge. There was a tasteful bar, but no sign of a restaurant. A side room had mahogany billiard tables with the air of a fine English country manor.

They went up a hallway…again no restaurant, only numbered doors. Zack stopped at one and opened it with an electronic card key.

"I thought you'd like to see one of our guest rooms."

That clinched it; he wouldn't have had the card key in his pocket unless he'd planned his tour.

Temper simmering, Jamie entered the well-appointed suite. It oozed luxury and had a private deck overlooking the cove. As for the bathroom, it was enormous, with numerous plush towels flanking a separate shower and bathtub. She'd visited nice hotels with her ex-husband, but nothing like this.

The reminder of Tim soured her mood further.

Apparently, her ex had been boasting that he'd reached a point in his career where he could pay for the very best on business trips. She hadn't understood why people from her old life kept bringing him up until Caylie Browning confessed that Tim was *asking* them to mention him to her. Since then Jamie had cut off contact with all of their mutual friends. Whatever Tim's game, she wasn't playing.

In the hallway, Zack took her arm. "I think you'll be impressed with the business center in the reception building. We'll go there next. You could virtually run an international corporation from our facilities. We also have pools, one of them heated, saunas that—"

Jamie yanked free. "You are an incredible jerk, Zack Denning. You invite me to dinner to discuss a business proposition that I'm not interested in, and instead you drag me all over your lavish resort to try and awe me into submission. No wonder you wanted to pick me up—you were going to keep me here at your mercy. But it wouldn't have worked. I'd have walked home rather than put up with this nonsense."

The bartender stared, but Jamie didn't care. She stormed out of the building, stopping only to get her bearings.

Zack caught up with her. "I'm sorry you see it that way," he said, his polished exterior obviously ruffled. "We can go to the restaurant now."

"Why do public-relations people believe that sort

of thing works?" she asked incredulously. "You're not saying you're sorry for being a jackass. You're saying you're sorry *I* see your behavior a certain way—implying that I'm seeing it the *wrong* way. That just makes people madder. You really don't get how rude you've been, do you?"

"I was simply—"

"Rude," Jamie repeated. She stalked toward the employee parking lot, with Zack following.

"Look, I apologize."

"Forget it. You can't impress me with the sixty unique offerings on the menu or caviar that drips from crackers or rare French wines. I don't want cheese specially flown in from some village in Tuscany or olives soaked in two-hundred-year-old brandy or whatever absurdity is currently a fad of the rich and bored. I'm done, with you *and* this place."

Her furious voice seemed to catch more than one ear. In the employee lot, out of view from the guest areas, several staff members quit chatting among themselves and hurriedly ducked into their cars.

"Please, Ms. Conroe...*Jamie*," Zack said. "We'll go straight to the restaurant."

Jamie groped for her car key and thrust it into the lock. "Oh, sure, with a detour past twelve more features of your precious resort."

"I assure you—"

"Don't bother. I refuse to sell my land, so there's

no point in us even talking, much less eating together. It's mine and you'll have to live with that."

"Be reasonable," he said through gritted teeth. "You run a seasonal fruit stand. This is a high-end resort. I can make it worthwhile. If you insist on keeping the property, I'll buy you a piece of land on the highway and move the stand there, so at least the beachside area will be visually appealing to my guests. And selling your product on the main road would increase your profits. Or I could pay for better signs and an attractive structure on your present site."

"What part of *no* don't you get?" Jamie snapped. She slid inside and slammed the car door. She drove out, senses on alert; angry drivers were often careless drivers and she didn't need the owner of a Mercedes blaming her for a dented fender.

The sun was bidding a glorious farewell to the day as she pulled into the garage. Fortunately, she had a large salad prepared from her leftover produce. She added a hard-boiled egg and grilled chicken and took it to the porch to eat and watch the sky.

The *gall* of the guy.

Jamie stabbed a spinach leaf, only to drop her fork in disgust.

The one positive was her speech to Zack, declaring she'd never sell, which had been the entire point of going to Mar Vista in the first place. Her jangled nerves relaxed. She'd wanted him to understand the land was hers, no matter what, and she'd said it in no uncertain terms and loud enough that some of his employees had heard it, too.

Mission accomplished.

She leaned back in her chair and began eating again, her good humor restored. It had cost her more than two hours, but was worth every minute.

CHAPTER FIVE

KIM SIGNED THE last letter her assistant had given her, tossed the pen aside and gazed through the window at her view of the Golden Gate Bridge.

It was noon on a Friday and she was done for the week. Naturally, there was always something she *could* do, but lately she'd scaled back her workload, handing portions off to her junior partners. There had to be an advantage to having her own firm, such as reducing her hours to a reasonable number. It would be tough to meet anyone and get married while working a ninety-hour week, much less have children. And even if she didn't ever have a family, what was the point if all her tombstone said was that she'd had a prominent law career?

The biggest barrier was that she didn't know what to do with time that wasn't filled with legal briefs or meetings or tussles in court. Sitting in her apartment wasn't appealing, and she didn't feel energetic enough to jostle elbows with tourists at Fisherman's Wharf or Golden Gate Park. A relaxing activity was more tempting, such as a weekend at a resort.

She stared at the phone and a piece of paper lying next to it with Mar Vista's number.

Why not?

She could certainly afford a few days on the coast, and Zack's resort was an unquestioned wonder. It had been years since she'd gone horseback riding or boating or taken a drive to see beautiful countryside. Actually, a drive sounded great—it would be easier on Brad than vigorous pursuits, and she'd love catching up with him. Zack had been so consumed by his fruit-stand worries on her last trip that she hadn't had a real visit with either one of the brothers.

She dialed and the phone rang once before being answered. Of course, a business run by Zack Denning wouldn't make someone wait longer.

"Mar Vista," said a voice with a faintly British accent. "How may I help you?"

"Hello, this is Kimberly Wheeler. Do you have a single room available for tonight through Sunday or Monday?"

"Yes, I would be happy to reserve one for you, Ms. Wheeler. Shall I also reserve a tee time on our golf course?"

"I won't be golfing. I'm flying in and will get there mid to late afternoon."

"I'll notify the airfield manager, Ms. Wheeler. Is there anything else I can do?"

"Not right now."

On her way out Kim asked her assistant, Chloe,

to call the airport to get her plane ready and file a flight plan. It wouldn't take long to pack and she might miss the worst of the commuter traffic if she hurried.

"I'll phone Mr. Denning to let him know you're flying in," Chloe said eagerly. She was enamored with Zack and undoubtedly hoped to speak with him personally.

"Don't bother. It's not a business trip."

"But wouldn't he want to know you're coming?" Chloe persisted.

Kim tried not to smile. "I'll contact him when I arrive. See you next week."

Two hours later Kim was in the air. A pilot's license was convenient for the rare occasions she needed to travel to see clients such as Zack Denning, but it was the freedom she loved.

She landed on the Mar Vista runway and the airstrip manager assured her the plane would be refueled, inspected and put in a hangar until she was ready to leave. In the meantime, another employee arrived to drive her to the reception area.

Okay, Zack might be obsessed with Mar Vista, but his idea of luxury was pretty nice. He hadn't cut corners in any area, including support staff.

"The resort must have created an employment boom in and around Warrington," she said as they left the airstrip.

"Yes, ma'am," the driver agreed courteously. "I

grew up in Warrington and we're pleased there are more jobs now."

"Do you enjoy working here?" she asked.

The man hesitated. "I suppose so," he said finally.

It was odd. The employees under Zack's supervision had always been more than satisfied. Then Kim remembered that when she'd come to meet with Jamie Conroe, his office manager had seemed unusually tense. Was something going on?

All at once she wrinkled her nose. She was going into attorney mode...or was she? Zack wasn't just a client; he was an old friend. Once she'd even thought they might make a life together. So she couldn't help being concerned. It was probably her imagination, anyway. Zack was a consummate manager, but with so many employees, there would inevitably be a few with personal issues and an occasional malcontent.

At the marble-and-mahogany reception desk, she registered and was ushered to her room.

"You said you weren't golfing, so we selected a room with a water view instead of the golf course," the bellhop explained. "Is that satisfactory?"

"It's fine."

When she was alone, Kim opened the French doors and stepped onto the small deck, looking at the shimmer of sunlight on the ocean. Rather than traffic noises, she heard the peaceful, distant tumble of waves and the call of a seabird as it swooped low.

She smiled and sat on a comfortable lounge chair.

This was a far better way to spend a Friday than working on a legal brief.

IT WAS ZACK'S custom to scan the list of reservations and arrivals each afternoon. He liked to greet old acquaintances, and would write a note of welcome to be delivered to their room. He'd been surprised to see a Kimberly Wheeler of San Francisco listed. He checked the address to be sure it was "his" Kim, then headed to her room. Why had she returned to Warrington? Was it too much to hope she'd found a legal loophole to get rid of Jamie Conroe's blue trailer?

On the way, he grabbed a courtesy basket of fruit, and when Kim answered the door at his knock, he practically shoved it into her arms.

"Hi. I saw you'd registered and thought you could use this to snack on. Have you come up with a legal maneuver we can employ? I'm not trying to cheat Ms. Conroe—I'll pay fair money. I just want her out."

"Wow," she said, waving him into her room. "I'm here for twenty whole minutes and you couldn't wait to find out if I flew up with news that I could have given faster by phone."

He ran his fingers through his hair and dropped into one of the easy chairs in the living-room section of the suite. "Sorry. Last night was a disaster."

"What do you mean?"

"I invited Jamie to dinner so I could make an

offer, either to sell the land or make it worthwhile to move that awful trailer to another location. At the very least, I wanted to convince her to let me construct a less offensive building."

"I hope you didn't use the words *awful* and *offensive* when you made your proposal, or is that why it was a disaster?"

"Hell, I didn't get a chance to make an offer. I was showing her the resort when she suddenly got mad and left."

Kim raised an eyebrow. "Suddenly?"

"Yeah. And now Gordon is upset since he fixed a special meal for her and she didn't get to eat it. He went to a lot of trouble because she'd refused to go to the Grotto, so he'd gotten it together to send to the Clam Shell."

"But isn't everything cooked in the same kitchen? He didn't go to any trouble, Zack. He was just upset because Jamie left."

"I know. It's just that…" Zack groaned with exasperation. He'd been holding it in all day. Confiding in Brad was out; it wasn't fair to bother him. And he couldn't say anything to Trudy—she'd already told him the employees were gossiping about an argument some of them had witnessed and he didn't intend to confirm the story.

"What happened?" Kim ordered.

"To start with, she wouldn't let me pick her up and insisted—"

"Smart lady," Kim interjected.

He scowled. "What is it with you? Are you starting an admiration society for Jamie Conroe?"

Kim sat down, and for the first time he noticed she was casually dressed. He hadn't seen her don jeans in years; she always wore suits in their business meetings.

"Look, Zack," she said, crossing her legs. "I know how hard it can be for a woman to make it in the world of men. Jamie obviously has good instincts and kept a measure of control in her own hands. I respect that. Now, what did you do when she got here?"

"Well, I'd suggested she come to the employee parking lot and she had difficulty locating it." The corners of Kim's mouth twitched and Zack ground his teeth. What was so damned funny? "Anyway, it seemed the perfect moment to take her on a tour."

"Did she know in advance that you were going to show her around?"

"No, it was just the right timing. Then she accused me of trying to awe her into submission or something equally absurd. I simply wanted her to understand how important Mar Vista is—to think of the jobs and tourist dollars we're bringing in."

Kim pursed her lips. "How long was this tour?"

"I don't know. She got in past seven, a little late, but that didn't matter. I guess it was after eight-thirty when she left."

"An hour and a half. That's some tour. Was it over or did you have more you planned to show her?"

"Not quite. I was taking her to see…" Zack's explanation trailed off and he groaned again.

He didn't need Kim to tell him he'd been an idiot. It was painfully clear now that he'd seen things from a different perspective—and he *had* been a jackass. Jamie Conroe and her ridiculous fruit stand had fried the circuits in his brain.

"Listen, Kim, could you go with me and—"

"Forget it, Zack. We're old friends so I let you blow off steam, but I'm not your lawyer this weekend. I'm here to relax. Maybe you and Brad and I can have dinner at the Grotto tonight, *if* you promise not to mention the fruit stand, *or* Jamie Conroe, *or* anything having to do with real estate and Mar Vista."

Zack opened his mouth, then shut it. What *were* people conversing about these days? Mar Vista had been his sole focus for so long he'd lost touch with the rest of the world.

Kim chuckled as if she'd read his mind. "We can debate politics, chat about our families, or even the mating habits of the pelican. You just can't bring up *you know what*. I'm a paying guest this visit and I get to call the shots."

Zack counted to ten. Kim had every right to call the shots, and he had no business expecting her to invent a magic solution for something that was his own fault.

He'd messed up royally and had a dismal conviction that he owed Jamie Conroe another apology.

FRIDAY AFTERNOON WAS busy at the fruit stand. Jamie had a steady stream of customers planning to make jam over the weekend. She'd ordered extra produce to meet the increased demand, and when four o'clock came she was still waiting for several people who'd requested her to hold berries and other items for when their work shift ended.

It kept her on her toes, particularly since Mar Vista employees were among her customers. A couple of them were actually swapping rumors about a verbal sparring match their boss had gotten into the evening before; she was pretty sure they didn't realize she was involved or they wouldn't have discussed it in front of her. She didn't want anyone to know she was the one in the conflict.

Worse, now she couldn't stop comparing the fruit stand with the chic elegance of the resort, which was precisely what Zack had hoped she'd do.

"Thanks for holding the berries," said one woman who came by around four-thirty. She wore a Mar Vista housekeeping uniform. Her shoulders sagged and she kept rubbing her neck.

"Looks as if you've had a long day," Jamie commented sympathetically.

"Yes, lots of people checking out and in, so we had a huge number of rooms to do. It wouldn't be so bad if…" The woman's voice trailed off.

"If?" Jamie prompted.

"It's nothing. I should be grateful to have a job, even if it isn't going anywhere. Well, I'd best get these berries cleaned. We're having a tea at my church tomorrow and I volunteered to make the strawberry shortcake."

"Mmm. Sounds delicious."

As the woman drove away, Jamie saw Brad Denning walking up the road.

"Hi. I'm later than usual," he said. "I didn't think you'd still be here."

"I don't have much regular stock left, but several folks are coming to pick up their berry orders."

Brad nodded. "Do you mind if I borrow your chair for a while?" Though he came by nearly every day, he always asked. He was good company, whether they talked or simply listened to the ocean waves.

"You're welcome to it. I'm leaving in an hour or so if you'd like a ride."

"Maybe." He slid into the chair next to her and leaned his head back, closing his eyes. Then he roused himself. "You totally discombobulated Gordon yesterday. That's Gordon's description, not mine."

"Yikes. Did I get the produce order wrong?"

"No, but he thought you were eating at the Clam Shell last night."

"Oh?" Jamie said warily.

"He'd cooked a special dish and you didn't come."

"I'll have to tell him I'm sorry I didn't make it."

She had an urge to ask when Gordon had been told she'd arrive. Seven? Eight? Nine? It hadn't occurred to her that he would prepare a particular dish, or that Zack would have mentioned she was coming. If she *had* known, she might have swallowed her outrage and gone to the restaurant anyway, though she wouldn't have been able to appreciate the meal after Zack's tactics. In some circles his actions would be considered smart business; to her they were just lousy manners.

Jamie pulled out her BlackBerry and keyed a quick text to Gordon saying she hadn't known he'd expected her and wished she'd gotten to taste his cooking. She didn't make any excuses or say why she hadn't made it to the restaurant.

Gordon was a nice guy, but this situation showed how complicated things got when other people were tangled up in your life. It wasn't that she wanted to be a hermit, but it was important to maintain her independence. And keeping a certain distance from others would help.

"I'm sure you missed some terrific food," Brad said, sounding half-asleep. "He's one hell of a chef."

Without a doubt. Jamie looked at her watch. Elegant people in elegant clothing would soon be headed to the Clam Shell and Sunfish Grotto dining rooms. Gordon would be up to his elbows getting ready, so he wouldn't read her message until later, but at least she'd sent it.

She hadn't seen the Grotto—Zack's interrupted "tour" hadn't gotten that far—so she could only imagine the restaurant's appearance and atmosphere. But it wasn't difficult; everything at the resort was tasteful and luxurious, in contrast to her brightly colored homemade signs.

Argggh. She had to quit making comparisons. Mar Vista had a completely different purpose than the Little Blue Fruit Stand. Zack Denning *wanted* her to feel garish and out of place compared to him. But she had every right to do business on her own land, a business that had been operating much longer than Mar Vista. Too bad Zack didn't like it. If Granddad's trailer was an issue, he ought to have done his research and chosen somewhere else for his wealthy clients to spend their money.

As BRAD HIKED back to the resort, he decided his muscles were improving. As uncomfortable as he was in Mar Vista's moneyed setting, it was helpful being in California. Walking the grounds was far more pleasant than using a treadmill, and the resort's well-appointed gym had weight machines that approximated the therapy equipment he'd used in Maryland. It was one of his better days, so he hadn't taken a ride from Jamie; the pain wasn't gone, but it was manageable.

Zack had stomped out of the apartment in the early morning, plainly disturbed...a condition most likely caused by Jamie Conroe. Something about her got under Zack's skin, and Brad wondered if there was an attraction his brother was trying to ignore. He couldn't tell what Jamie felt, but it wouldn't be remarkable if she reciprocated. Zack was a handsome devil. When they were teenagers, the girls had practically drooled over him, though his thirst for success had also been a draw for some of them.

Brad went in through the rear entrance of the administrative wing and stopped to greet Zack's office manager, thinking he could have used her efficient skills in his military unit.

"Hi, Trudy."

"Hey, Brad," she said. "Zack wanted me to pass on a message in case you came by—Ms. Wheeler is spending the weekend at the resort and suggested the three of you have dinner at the Grotto at seven."

Kim? What had brought her back to Mar Vista... though considering Zack's mood this morning, perhaps he'd needed her to deal with something.

Brad checked the office wall clock. He had time for a shower and a short rest. It would be great to see Kim, and he enjoyed watching her shift into lawyer mode, reminiscent of a general marshaling forces and directing battle. It was amazing that Zack had let her get away years ago, and an even bigger mystery how he'd kept her as a friend. In Zack's shoes Brad wasn't sure he could have managed it, but he was glad Kim still liked the Denning family.

At dinner he was surprised the conversation stayed away from business *and* by Kim's casual statement that she'd come solely for relaxation. She seemed to be aiming the remark at Zack.

"I know," his brother muttered.

"Just keeping you honest."

He glared, but didn't say more.

Brad almost snickered. Zack *had* to learn how to do something other than run a resort—he didn't even finish his meal, rushing off to investigate a minor problem the reception desk had discovered, leaving them to have dessert alone.

"That's Zack." Kim laughed, seeming unperturbed.

She'd chosen a raspberry-chocolate torte from the selection available and ate it, relishing every bite, without a single comment about the calories or having to "work it off."

It was unaccountably...hot.

"You want to do something tomorrow?" she asked when the last crumb had been consumed. Brad looked down and saw that he'd polished off his own pastry and had only a vague idea of how it had tasted. "I have zero leisure skills," she explained. "I need a friend to keep me on the right track."

"Zack isn't free?"

"You've got to be kidding. What that guy knows about leisure could be poured into a jar lid."

He grinned. "True enough. Okay, sure. Let's do something."

IN THE MORNING they ate breakfast together then took a stroll along the ocean bluff, soaking up the vistas of water and rocky shoreline.

"It's a fine piece of property," she said. "But

I wonder how many golf balls go into the water from here."

"The grounds manager says they designed the course so the balls wouldn't be hit as much in this direction, but it's still providing a business for some of the local kids. They collect the balls and sell them at the municipal golf course in Warrington. That takes me back. I did the same thing for years. That's how I got my second bike."

Kim laughed. "Did Zack do it, too?"

"Not exactly. I picked up the balls and he sold them on commission. It actually worked out well since I got more for the balls than if I'd peddled them myself."

"So he was already a businessman that young?"

"He's the only kid I knew who could open a lemonade stand in winter and make a profit. He labeled it Non-Caliente Lemonade."

"*Non-Caliente*. Isn't that a mixture of English and Spanish?"

"Yep. It basically means 'not-hot lemonade.'"

Kim started laughing and gasped. "In the winter he made a profit selling lemonade because it *wasn't* hot?"

"You bet. Of course, I have to admit it was first-rate lemonade, none of that powdered stuff."

"Zack has always been into quality."

Brad hadn't thought of it that way, but she was right. Zack had never tried to profit on the basis of someone else losing out or getting shortchanged.

He might charge top dollar, but the people who bought what he was selling got the best there was to buy.

It was nearly eleven when they started back toward the main buildings. "How about going for a horseback ride?" Brad asked. "We could bring a picnic lunch."

"I don't know...." Kim shrugged. "What if we take one of the resort's loaner cars and drive the coastline instead? We could get lunch wherever it looks interesting. That would be easier on your leg, especially after such a long walk."

"I don't need to be coddled," he answered shortly.

"I'm not coddling you, but you *have* had a rough recovery."

"I also don't need your pity."

"Dammit, Brad, you don't have to get your testosterone in a tailspin," Kim snapped. She stopped and drew an exaggerated breath. "The truth is I admire what you did over there."

"I was just driving down a road and got caught in an explosion."

"But you were there, being a soldier. That's a lot."

"Don't give me any medals and don't wrap me in cotton. I can ride a damned horse."

"I'm not wrapping you in anything," she said huffily. "I was just making an effort to be nice before you go back and get blown up forever."

Strangely, her irritable reply made him feel

good, because other people usually assumed his military career was over.

THAT EVENING JAMIE took a container with Mar Vista printed on the top from the refrigerator. She'd found an ice cooler on her front porch late the previous afternoon, with a pleasant note from Gordon explaining it was the meal he'd prepared for her. Apparently, he'd had it delivered prior to receiving her text message. She had eaten the appetizer and salad immediately, leaving the entrée for Saturday.

It was great to come home to a ready-made meal, especially since she was more tired than usual. For the second time that week, there'd been a mess at her produce stand—boxes scattered and one of the canopy poles knocked over. It was probably teens out joyriding, zooming too closely. Granddad had occasionally had the same problem and dealt with it by putting a chain between the posts at night to keep the behavior from becoming a regular thing.

Jamie took Gordon's entrée out of the container. It looked fantastic and, despite being chilled, was fragrant with garlic and other seasonings. That morning he'd ridden out with the truck to pick up the daily order, his friendliness making it clear he wasn't unhappy with her. He did seem on edge when it came to his boss, but she'd carefully avoided the pitfall of *that* subject.

While the food heated, Jamie sat on the deck overlooking the salt marsh and ocean. Her move to Warrington had turned her into a bird-watcher, and she enjoyed seeing the egrets and other wild-life that teemed in the marsh. It was an endless display, though she sometimes worried that Marlin would have a heart attack as he gazed at the feathered buffet.

The timer buzzed, and she went inside to take the entrée out of the oven, only to hear the doorbell. With a sigh, she opened the door and came face-to-face with Zack Denning.

"Yes?" she said curtly.

"I…uh…I came to apologize," he said. "I acted badly the other night."

Jamie examined his face, debating internally how to handle the situation. He sounded sincere, but he still might be hoping to buy her land. It was wise to keep her response simple.

"Apology accepted."

He looked at the pot holder in her fingers. "You were just about to eat. I'll contact you when it's more convenient."

Zack hurried down the steps before she could say "don't bother." His rushed exit had the flavor of an escape, and Jamie watched as he climbed into his vehicle. He glanced back and they stared at each other. It was an odd moment, charged with aware-ness…or maybe it was just her imagination.

After his Mercedes disappeared around a curve, Jamie looked at her worn jeans and faded T-shirt—

hardly her sexiest outfit. Yeah, it had to be her imagination. There was no way Zack Denning would find her the least bit attractive.

CHAPTER SIX

OVER THE NEXT few days, Zack had trouble sleeping, though it wasn't the resort keeping him awake…it was Jamie Conroe. And it wasn't just her slim figure bothering him. She was the damnedest woman, so stubborn she made a mule look cooperative. If she wasn't disrupting his plans, he would have admired her determination.

At least the night staff was getting extra focus, he reasoned as he walked through the laundry. It was 3:00 a.m. and everything was quiet. The employees gave him quick nods as they worked. He'd expected them to be more relaxed with him after several months, but admittedly, he didn't see the night crew too often.

"How are things going, Alice?" Zack asked one of them, a local woman he'd recently hired after several members of their cleaning crew quit.

"Fine, sir."

She kept folding the thick towels used poolside. Everything seemed to be operating well, but Alice's demeanor was a surprise; she'd proved chatty during her interview, a trait that had nearly disqualified her. He wanted a cordial staff, not employees who were intrusive on his clients' visits.

Zack continued his inspection of the resort's functions after daybreak, going into each department and speaking with the supervisors. He was shocked when the head of housekeeping hinted she might be resigning soon. When he'd recruited her, she'd been enthusiastic and had spoken of long-term goals and commitments. Now, less than a year into full-time operation, she was considering taking another position.

Damn. Losing Margo would be a blow; she was superb. He'd already had to replace his maintenance supervisor. Fortunately, Zack had convinced someone from a resort he'd once managed to come as a replacement. Zack mentally went through a list of people he'd previously worked with to see if there was a likely candidate for the housekeeper's position. Or maybe he could persuade Margo to stay with a pay increase or additional perk.

Aside from Margo's hints about leaving, he found nothing of obvious concern. In the kitchen, Gordon no longer seemed upset, which was a relief.

Zack spent the rest of the afternoon checking purchase orders and evaluating new merchandise for the shops. He added his endorsement to the various managers' recommendations.

Trudy offered to stay late, but he waved her out and reviewed financial records until midnight. Tired, he climbed the stairs to his apartment, his eyes slowly refocusing from staring at a computer screen for six hours. He had an uneasy feeling about Mar Vista, but couldn't pin down why. It wasn't simply Jamie's fruit stand, although that was bad enough.

In the apartment kitchen there was a note from Brad saying he'd be back in the morning, and Zack figured his brother had gone on a date, which pleased Zack. He'd been spending so much time on Mar Vista that he hadn't given Brad the attention he deserved. It made no difference that Brad didn't want the attention, preferring to pursue his personal rehabilitation plan.

Zack frowned. By his brother's own admission, he was being much more aggressive with his workouts than the doctors from Bethesda had approved. Granted, Brad knew his body better than anyone, but it was a worry. In any case, a date would be good for his brother.

Numbers danced across Zack's sight when he closed his eyes, and he envied Brad's activities for the evening. Zack's own social opportunities were limited; he couldn't date an employee, single guests of the resort often had an agenda, and he hadn't met many local women beyond his staff. That was, other than Jamie, and she hardly counted. Yet he kept remembering the healthy color in her cheeks and the curves that were often concealed by her farmer's overalls.... That was what enforced celibacy did to a man. It made him have ridiculous thoughts.

He sat in an easy chair and picked up a newspaper, needing to catch up on world events. He'd run into an old acquaintance visiting the resort who'd mentioned a humorous episode in the political arena. Zack had felt like an idiot, having no clue about the issue, and it underscored the fact that he'd lost track of normal conversational topics. Many of his guests were well-informed; conversing with them required being equally informed himself. He read until the words blurred and his head dropped.

Zack was jolted awake when the front door opened and he realized it was light outside. Brad stood in the living room, gazing at him with raised eyebrows.

"You weren't waiting up for me, I trust."

"No, fell asleep reading the paper. How was your date?"

"It wasn't a date. Jamie's having trouble with vandalism at the fruit stand. At first she thought it was joyriding teens, but it didn't end, even when she chained the road."

Adrenaline rushed through Zack's veins, waking him more effectively than caffeine. "Why the hell are you involved?"

Brad's jaw got squarer than usual. "Jamie was going to spend the night in the trailer to see if she could catch the culprits. I couldn't let her do that alone."

Zack's frustration mounted. Why was it his injured brother's responsibility? "If she's got a problem, she can call on her buddy at the sheriff's department," he snapped. "*You* don't have to deal with it."

"As far as I'm concerned, it's a Denning problem." Brad's expression was angry. "Mar Vista staff members could be trying to help their boss by attempting to drive her off the land. It's no secret that the two of you've been going at it. One of the staff even told me he saw you and Jamie having a fight in the parking lot."

"It was an argument," Zack said, almost growling, "not a fight, and I went to her house and said I was sorry."

"That doesn't mean your employees see it that way. Some are on edge and might decide a little sabotage will clear the decks. Maybe get their boss's notice. Regardless, I'm staying with her until this is sorted." Five long strides took Brad to the guest room. He pulled the door shut.

Zack slammed his fist on the chair arm. How *dare* Jamie insinuate that he or his employees had anything to do with her problems? What kind of man did she think he was? He would never condone such behavior. She was just making trouble for him and Mar Vista. He ought to take her to court. At the very least, he'd tell her exactly what she could do with her outrageous claims.

JAMIE DRAGGED HERSELF home and stood under a hot shower, hoping it would energize her. The night had proved a bust. After seeing vandalism every day for over a week, there hadn't been so much as a bent blade of grass while she was watching.

She hadn't planned to tell anybody what had happened—she could handle her own problems—but Brad had found her fastening the chain across the road on Sunday evening and hadn't bought her vague explanation. He'd pushed for details and had apparently deduced her intentions when he saw her overnight bag. He'd simply shown up—a chivalrous marine—to stand guard with her.

This vandalism wasn't like the sort that Granddad had written about—it was too calculated. The vandal had started throwing mud on the chairs, knocking over canopy poles and tossing spoiled fruit onto the canvas. They would have had to bring the fruit with them; she didn't leave any stock behind in case raccoons or squirrels got at it.

The timing also seemed suspicious, occurring so soon after the dispute she'd had with Zack. Still, it was unlikely that he was to blame, though she had to admit that some people would do whatever it took to protect their interests.

Whoever was guilty, she had to stop them. She would identify the culprit and report him to Curt. If they'd guessed she was there, perhaps it would break the pattern for good. Either way, the problem would be solved. And while she appreciated Brad's staunch desire to help, it wasn't needed.

The water in the shower grew cold and Jamie

hastily stepped out. It was time to dress and run to meet her suppliers. She filled a cup with leftover coffee and rushed to the stand. Wednesdays usually weren't as busy; given half a chance, she could grab a few catnaps.

Once at the stand, she barely refrained from snapping at one farmer who'd forgotten three things she'd ordered. He apologized and promised to return shortly. The Mar Vista truck arrived for its pickup, and when they left, she irritably got busy arranging vegetables on the display.

Gravel spun several minutes later as Zack's Mercedes SUV ground to a halt next to the stand. It was déjà vu—he looked as pissed as the first day she'd met him.

Fine. Bring it on. Lack of rest left her cranky enough to relish a new argument with the jerk.

Zack strode toward her. "How could you tell my brother it's *my* fault you're having problems? I'd never let my employees think vandalism is okay, even on an atrociously tacky old trailer that should have been hauled to the dump years ago. I should sue you for slander."

"Watch out, Mr. Big Shot!" she yelled back. "You might get contaminated by my trailer and get hauled to the dump with it. As for slander, you can stuff it. I may have wondered whether one of your employees was getting their kicks out here, but I didn't say anything to Brad. And if you're so pure of heart, why did your brother come up with the idea all by himself?"

Zack looked taken aback. "Brad knows I wouldn't condone anything like this. But if it will reassure you, I'll send word that the fruit stand is off-limits for Mar Vista employees. They won't even be allowed to shop here."

She planted her hands on her hips. "That's just like you and your grizzly-bear, heavy-fisted management style."

"I do *not* have a heavy-fisted management style."

"Really? Informing people where they can and can't shop isn't very friendly. And accusing innocent people of criminal acts is as heavy fisted as it gets. You should have learned that when you tried to get me arrested for being on my own land."

He opened his mouth, closed it, then opened it again. "I have nothing to do with any vandalism, period. And leave my brother out of it."

"I tried to leave him out of it, but he's a nice guy, something you certainly don't have in common with him. He showed up last night and wouldn't leave."

"You—"

A car turned down the drive and she gestured at it. "If you don't want anyone else to see you unglued, you should leave."

Face taut with anger, he stomped to his car.

Jamie went back to arranging her displays. Fatigue still dogged her heels, but she felt better having harangued her nemesis.

ZACK CLENCHED THE steering wheel as he drove back
to Mar Vista. He'd put a memo out to his employees to stay away from the fruit stand. Naturally,
he couldn't actually tell them they couldn't shop
there—hell, he'd seen Trudy hiding a basket of fruit
that must have come from the trailer. But he could
send a stern message otherwise.

Yet as he parked by the office, Zack couldn't stop
thinking about what Jamie had said. Much as he
hated to acknowledge it, she had a point. Perhaps he
should just ask his staff to report anything strange,
instead of blasting off a warning.

Inside he attempted greeting Trudy normally.

"Howdy, boss," she said. "I see you got through
the financials. I did check them, you know."

"It can't hurt to take a second look."

"Of course." Her voice was unusually stiff and
he wondered what was wrong.

"Uh, Trudy, I need to send a message to the staff.
There's been some vandalism at the fruit stand.
Could we ask everyone to keep an eye out and re-
port if they see anything questionable?"

"Sure. I'll write a draft and get it to your desk
ASAP."

"Thanks. Even if I don't want the trailer in its
present location, Jamie Conroe is a…a neighbor.
It's right for us to assist if we can."

Trudy bobbed her head and bent over her computer while Zack went into his office.

A steaming cup of coffee sat ready for him.

Whatever was on Trudy's mind, it hadn't impacted her efficiency. He didn't expect his office manager to fetch coffee, but Trudy seemed to think it was a matter of course. Within five minutes, a beep on his computer alerted him the memo was ready.

To the Mar Vista Staff:
Our neighbor, Jamie Conroe, has been troubled by vandalism at her fruit stand lately. We can help by being alert and reporting anything that might lead to catching the guilty party. Thanks to everyone.

Zack went to Trudy's desk. "That's perfect."

A small smile transformed her features to their typical good cheer. "I'll get it printed and sent to everyone."

"Great."

"Did you finish your inspection?"

A chuckle escaped him. "To tell you the truth, I didn't even start it. I'll do a quick run now."

"Daily inspections may no longer be necessary, you know. You have an excellent staff."

"Could be," he agreed. "But I have a lot riding on Mar Vista and it's my job to make it work."

"It's… Never mind." Her cheeks had gone pale. "See you later."

He suspected she wasn't feeling well. *Again.* Lord, what a mess it would be if she was pregnant.

As he began his morning route, Zack's thoughts

went to the fruit stand. Trudy's message would surely demonstrate his lack of support for any negative actions. Not that he believed his employees would do such a thing. The locals liked Jamie, and though his management staff didn't have a history in the area, they surely knew he would never sanction scare tactics.

None of that fixed the problem of Brad spending nights on guard duty. His brother had suffered severe damage to his bones and muscles; if Brad ended up confronting an intruder, he could be seriously injured. That left few options. Jamie clearly intended to continue keeping watch at the trailer, and Brad wouldn't let her do it alone. And now that he'd had a chance to think, Zack was disturbed about it himself.

As much as he'd rather keep away from Jamie, he'd have to go in Brad's place.

JAMIE FINISHED FOR the day, drove into town to make her deposit and hurried to the house to grab a bite and a nap. She set her alarm for seven-thirty, figuring it was best to get to the trailer before nightfall. She had hidden her car the previous night around a bend in the road, so unless somebody was spying for hours, they shouldn't guess anyone was on-site.

And hopefully, tonight Brad would realize she was perfectly all right by herself. It wasn't as if she meant to challenge the culprit. She had better sense than that; she just planned to take pictures with a camera that worked in low light. If somebody came, she'd focus through the trailer's window and begin clicking. They wouldn't know she was there or that she'd gotten the evidence to hand over to the authorities. She'd explained all that to Brad before he'd gone back to the resort, so he'd see the sense of staying home.

When the buzzer on the clock rang, it jarred every nerve. More than anything she wanted to remain curled up in bed with Marlin, who'd landed next to her three seconds after she'd slipped under the blankets.

"I gotta go," she muttered to the cat.

She dressed in black so she'd be less visible in the night, and filled Granddad's old stainless-steel thermos with coffee. On the way out she grabbed the sack of food she'd packed to pass the night. The irony couldn't be escaped—as a kid she'd begged her grandfather to let her sleep in the trailer above the beach and he wouldn't let her. Now that she *had* to do it, she'd rather not.

Still, once she was there, the trailer was pleasant and warm with memories. She carefully checked and covered possible holes that could let out light, so she could read or watch the personal DVD player she'd brought with her.

At about nine, she froze. The sound of a vehicle stopping, followed by soft footsteps on the gravel, raised her hopes. With any luck she'd photograph the perpetrator and be able to go home to sleep. Quietly she switched off the lamps, pulled the heavy curtain aside and began clicking.

Knock. Knock. Knock.

Her hand jerked and she almost cursed.

"What?" she hissed at the door.

"It's me," a voice whispered.

"Brad, I told you I'm fine by myself," she said as she opened the door.

But it wasn't Brad; it was Zack.

"What are you doing here?" she demanded.

"The only way I could prevent Brad from coming was to take his place."

Jamie tried to shut the door but he blocked it with his foot. "I said I don't need anyone. I'm doing this by myself."

"I'm here for my brother's sake, not yours."

"What is it with you Dennings? Can't you take no for an answer?"

"Jamie, I'm here for the night whether you like it or not. If necessary, I'll stay out here—how are these chairs for sleeping?"

She rolled her eyes. "You can't be serious. All *right.* Since you aren't being reasonable, you'll have to move your car behind the trees around that curve in the road. No one will come if they see someone is here, and I want to catch whoever's doing this."

While he was gone she considered locking the door and refusing to answer, but apparently there was *one* thing the Denning brothers had in common—pigheadedness. Zack would spend the night outside, and she'd never get any evidence.

After several minutes he returned.

"Remember that it's your decision to spend the night in a tacky trailer," she said, letting him in. "Don't blame me if it makes you grumpier than usual with your staff."

Zack seated himself. "Very funny. So, what's going on? Are you sure it's intentional vandalism?"

"I assumed it was teenagers joyriding, but they're pitching mud and rotten fruit on the chairs and smearing it on the canopy. It could still be teens, yet it feels too deliberate, and it's practically every night. That doesn't seem like kids."

"It couldn't be animals?"

Jamie shook her head. "I don't leave anything here overnight. I either use my leftover produce or donate it to a women's shelter in Warrington. Besides, animals could leave muddy footprints, but they wouldn't throw globs on the walls."

"Has there been major damage?"

"Mostly petty annoyances so far."

He set a large paper bag on the table.

"I didn't know what you'd prefer," he told her. "So I brought two orders of Gordon's daily special in case you haven't had dinner yet."

She stared at him suspiciously. What did he expect to gain by bringing food? Still, it would be silly and wasteful not to eat.

She waved a finger as she joined him at the table.

"Dinner or not, I won't discuss selling my land. Got it? And if somebody tries anything, you let me handle it my way."

"Understood."

ZACK RESPECTED JAMIE'S resolve to be self-sufficient, however impractical it might be, especially since it could be multiple vandals attacking the stand.

"All I'm doing is taking pictures for the sheriff through the window," she continued. "I'm not going to confront anybody."

Smart.

Jamie ate and settled with a book, offering him a choice of reading or the DVD player. But Zack was restless and studied the trailer's interior—it was in good condition, clean and comfortable, which surprised him. It wouldn't be a top pick for a claustrophobic, but it was rather nice. He looked closer and could tell the cabinets and various features were custom-made, another surprise. Everything fit together quite ingeniously, including a kitchenette and table.

Zack rolled his shoulders and realized that for the first time in eighteen months, he wasn't buried in purchase orders, financial portfolios, blueprints or other activities to support Mar Vista. There was only a quiet, cozy space and a woman who annoyed him more than anyone he'd ever known.

Yet Jamie wasn't annoying him at the moment.

A faint fragrance drifted around him—it wasn't

perfume, just vanilla and strawberries and something uniquely feminine. Jamie wore sweat-suit bottoms that clung to her curves, and her T-shirt bumped out in all the right spots. It was an exquisite reminder of how long he'd been living a monkish existence.

A stack of games was tucked on a shelf, and Zack decided they could be a much-needed distraction.

"How about a game of Scrabble?" he challenged.

She shrugged and tossed her book onto the bed.

Two hours later, Zack looked at the score in confusion. He hadn't played in ages, but he used to be decent at the game. Jamie was better, and a fierce competitor; if only her intelligence wasn't paired with so much stubbornness.

"Chess?" she asked and he nodded.

She played chess as expertly as Scrabble, but he managed to back her into a stalemate. He might have won if he hadn't been sidetracked by Jamie's quirky expressions as she pondered her moves… that, and her innate femininity she couldn't entirely hide.

"I have a chess set my grandfather carved at home," Jamie said, packing up the game. "Dark green jade for one player, and jade that's almost white for the second. He used to keep it in the trailer, but I got worried that pieces might get lost."

Shortly after midnight Jamie stretched and peeked out the window to see if anybody was in view. "I want some air," she said, picking up her camera and slipping through the door. Zack followed as she led the way to a sand dune above the water. It was out of sight of anyone approaching the trailer.

The night was bright and still, the Milky Way a glorious canopy above them.

"It's perfect, isn't it?" Jamie whispered. The moonlight shone on her face, revealing awe as she gazed at the beach.

Other concerns slid away. The sea foam seemed to glow with a light of its own, and the waves curled into the shore in an endless rhythm. Stars glittered and Zack found himself searching for the familiar constellations, Orion's Belt and Gemini and the Big Dipper. It had been years since he'd looked at the stars in any special way; he couldn't even recall when the different constellations appeared.

"I haven't taken time to enjoy how beautiful it is here," he admitted, though there was a chance Jamie would twit him about it. He waited, but she just sat in companionable silence.

"My grandparents met on this beach," she said at length. "My grandmother was an artist who came here to paint. Ironically, Granddad couldn't fully appreciate a painting."

"Because he was color-blind." Zack remembered Jamie mentioning that the first day they'd met.

"Yes. But he could sculpt, and he asked if she would model for him, sitting on the sand with the wind blowing in her hair."

"So she said yes, and that's how they fell in love?"

Her laugh was low and musical. "No. Leah didn't want to be carved into stone or wood or metal, but she did want to be carved into Granddad's soul. She loved him from the instant they met, though Granddad said he was too old for her—he was thirty-eight, and she was twenty. Her parents were opposed to the relationship and her sister said she was crazy, but Leah was strong and followed her heart."

"Why do you call her Leah instead of Grandmother?"

"I didn't know her. She died seven years after they were married, and Granddad always called her Leah. He never got over losing her so early and loved her for the rest of his life." Jamie was silent for a moment before sighing. "Where have true-blue men like that gone?"

She didn't sound bitter, just sad. The moonlight silvered her skin and hair, and her scent mingled with the freshness of the ocean breeze. Zack wasn't usually the fanciful sort, yet he couldn't stop thinking that she reminded him of a fairy tale...a water dryad who'd appeared from the waves rolling into shore.

Instinctively he pulled her close, his lips moving over hers.

She felt good and tasted better.

JAMIE'S HEART JUMPED and a surge of desire swept through her, only she couldn't allow it, so she shoved Zack with her elbow and shimmied backward.

"Is this a new strategy to get my property?"

He stared at her and she could have sworn he was bemused—as if a hardheaded businessman could get bemused over anything except a hot stock purchase.

His jaw hardened. "That was the last thing on my mind. Are you such a cynical divorcée that you can't accept that somebody finds you attractive?"

"Huh."

She got up and marched to the trailer. Cynical? She wasn't cynical; she was careful—especially around a man whose career and business were his sole priorities. Zack Denning seemed oblivious to everything except his resort—so even if she wanted romance, it wouldn't be with someone like him.

In the trailer she climbed onto the upper bunk, pulled a blanket over her and pretended to be intent on her book when he came inside.

Neither of them said a word. Later when she heard noises outside she slid down to snap pictures through the window, but it was just a herd of deer wandering by.

Zack peered out, too, then lay back on the lower bed.

Jamie couldn't sleep between listening for a potential vandal and hearing Zack's steady breathing. She didn't think he'd use seduction to get what he wanted, but his kiss was suspicious when she knew any physical charms she possessed were well disguised by her hands-off clothing.

Jamie finally dropped off near dawn and woke when the first farmer arrived. She crawled from the bunk. Zack was gone; he'd probably escaped to his fancy resort.

She juggled the deliveries and Mar Vista produce order, sneaking gulps of coffee from her thermos and bites of food from her sack of groceries. The containers from the meal Zack had brought were gone. Had she thanked him for dinner? Probably not—she'd gotten too annoyed about him coming to begin with.

She drowsed between customers—the coffee might have been decaf for all the good it did her.

Brad got there late in the morning. "How did it go?"

"The same as the night you were here. I hope they've given up. This could get old." Jamie put her palm over her mouth as she yawned.

"Shall I tend the store while you take a nap?" he offered. "I don't have many demands on my time. I exercise, I eat Gordon's cooking and I sleep. That's it. I'd love being useful for a change."

Jamie hesitated, yet Brad wasn't his brother and they'd become friends. Letting him watch the stand wouldn't threaten her independence, and after the way he'd phrased the suggestion, it would be churlish to refuse. "That would be great. I'll nap in the trailer and you can get me if I'm needed."

"Go home if you want."

"The trailer's fine."

She went inside and lay in the bunk Zack had used. It smelled faintly of a man's aftershave. She recalled the brief moment on the dunes when he'd kissed her...sensation streaking through her body until she was doused by cold reality.

It was almost enough to make her question her choices over the past couple of years, which was doubly annoying. She was content and happy living in Granddad's house with Marlin as her companion—a hot kiss notwithstanding, Zack Denning wouldn't be nearly as much company as a persistent feline.

She resolutely turned over and pushed the thought away.

KIM USUALLY LOVED the busy bustle of San Francisco, but by Wednesday following her return she was pacing her office between meetings with clients. The accusations she'd thrown at Brad echoed in her ears; she should have been more sensitive to his pride. And just as bad...how could she have tactlessly mentioned the possibility of him getting blown up forever? Her father and uncle were both former naval officers and she was proud of their service.

Well...it was easier to take it in stride now that her dad and uncle were retired and out of danger. She remembered being afraid a lot when she was a kid and she'd had nightmares for weeks when her uncle was injured at an embassy. It was one of the reasons she gave to organizations that supported military families and veterans.

So, if she was being honest, she was furious at the idea of Brad going back into harm's way. And she had no doubt it was exactly what he planned to do once he sufficiently recovered; he was determined to save the world.

Furious?

Kim pressed her lips together.

Make that scared.

Still, she ought to apologize. Brad was a decorated marine and a friend. He deserved respect.

Kim went to her desk and opened her calendar on the computer. If she rescheduled her appointments, she could fly to the resort again on Friday. She wouldn't mind another relaxing weekend—it had gone okay after she'd laid down the law to Zack. He was even more consumed with his goals than in college, and that was saying a lot. Back then he had barely paid attention to anything else, except in bed, and once he'd even broken off foreplay to call the hotel where he worked. That was the beginning of the end, particularly when she'd figured out he was discussing something that could easily have waited.

She hit the intercom to tell Chloe to reschedule everything for Friday…and Monday as well, in case she chose to stay longer.

CHAPTER SEVEN

AFTER A SECOND night at the fruit stand's trailer, Zack's mood was grim when he returned to Mar Vista. Nothing had happened—not even a lone deer had passed the trailer as far as he could tell.

There'd been only a pained silence between him and Jamie. They'd talked enough to make an agreement about taking turns sleeping, but that was it. He'd brought dinner from the Mar Vista kitchen again, and she'd stiffly thanked him. Strangely, the awkward silence just made him more aware of her.

During one of his spells on guard, he'd stared at Jamie while she slept. She'd looked pixieish with her fist tucked under her chin and her body curled into a sweet little ball. The memory alone made him break into a sweat, and he held on to his control with bleak determination.

He parked at the office and hurried in to begin his own workday.

"Hi, boss," Trudy greeted him.

He signed the items she had waiting before catching sight of a pregnancy magazine sticking out from under her purse.

Trudy's gaze followed his, and she cleared her throat nervously. "Yes," she confessed. "I'm finally having a baby at the ripe old age of thirty-seven."

He almost let out an agonized "how can you do this to me," but restrained himself. Jamie had suggested he'd be grumpier than usual after spending nights at the trailer, also describing his management style as grizzly-bear heavy-handed. It had offended him and he'd dismissed it at the time, but now it hit him that lately he *had* been like a bear with a sore paw.

Trudy was watching him, her posture defensive.

"Congratulations," he said, swallowing his dismay. "You and Rick must be excited."

Trudy relaxed. "Thanks. We're pretty over the moon. We'd given up hoping, but coming here seemed to make the difference. Don't worry. I plan to stay through to my ninth month and I'll have someone fully trained for the period I'm out. I'll be back. I want a career *and* to be a mom."

"That's great," he attempted to say in a natural voice. He escaped to his office and groaned.

So, Trudy was going to have a baby.

It wasn't the end of the world. There were other office managers who were efficient, though he'd appreciated working with Trudy Lopez more than anyone else he could remember. In practice she functioned as his second in command and...he *should* consider redefining her position and pay scale to assistant manager. Not that there was much point in doing it now.

She may have said she planned to come back, but he couldn't count on it. More than one of his employees had chosen full-time parenting over a job. It was a choice he'd respected, disappointing as it had been sometimes to lose a good worker.

To make things worse, when he opened his email he saw several notes from his mother that he'd missed reading. He scanned them—she wanted to know what was going on with her two sons.

Zack tapped out a reply. He was fine. The resort was doing well and was frequently filled to near capacity. No, he hadn't resolved the issue with the fruit stand yet, but was sure it wouldn't be a problem. Most important, Brad appeared to be gaining in strength and was walking a lot.

Zack reviewed the phrases he'd typed—they were terse and his mother might try to read between the lines to find a hidden meaning.

On the other hand, she *always* tried to read between the lines, and he didn't have the oomph to tinker with his language.

He finished by signing, "Love, Zack," and hit the send button.

Months ago he'd asked Trudy to handle some of the status reports to his mother. She'd given him a what-planet-are-you-from look and told him that mothers didn't deserve to be staffed out. She was right, of course.

God, he was bushed, and spending nights with Jamie at the trailer didn't help. Hiring someone to go in his place was an option, but it didn't seem right.

He put his head against his leather executive's chair. It wouldn't hurt to rest his eyes for a while.

A KNOCK AT the door took Brad away from the breakfast he'd assembled from bits and pieces in Zack's kitchen. His brother didn't cook much. He relied on the Clam Shell or Sunfish Grotto for most of his meals.

Brad answered and saw it was one of the resort employees.

"Mr. Brad Denning?"

"That's me."

"A guest asked me to deliver a note to you."

"Uh, thanks. Let me…" He groped in his pocket for a tip, but the employee stepped backward.

"The guest was quite generous, sir. Have a good day."

Brad sat at the table and took the note from the Mar Vista stationery envelope.

Brad, just arrived for another weekend. Any chance we can get together? Kim.

Odd.

Prior to flying in to meet with Jamie Conroe, Zack said Kim had visited once, for Mar Vista's official opening. Yet now that Zack's legal needs were decreasing, she was visiting more often. Why? She was beautiful and talented with her own successful law firm, so it was hard to believe that a minivacation at Mar Vista was the sole reason, especially as she was coming to this *particular* resort.

Back when she and Zack had been a couple, Kim was the one who ended the relationship. Maybe she was rethinking her old decision and hoping Zack was ready to settle down now that he'd accomplished the goal he'd worked toward for so long.

Brad hadn't detected any romantic feelings for Zack on Kim's part, but he was better at spotting enemy patrols than amorous intentions. The biggest question was his brother's interest in Jamie Conroe—the woman knew how to punch Zack's buttons in a way Brad hadn't seen before. Not that he and Zack had spent much time together in the past ten years, but they'd regularly corresponded by email and there'd never been a hint of a woman who rattled Zack the way Jamie did.

So, what *did* his brother feel for Jamie?

Zack had vehemently insisted on taking over sentry duty at the trailer, his ego prodded by the idea that employees from the resort might be involved with the vandalism. Brad also suspected it was partly to keep *him* from a potential hazard...which was hardly necessary. Injured or not, his training as a marine would beat out Zack easily. Yet was there another reason Zack wanted to go? Lust?

Brad deliberately focused on his eggs, rather than

Kim. The situation bothered him. He liked Jamie, but he'd hate for Kim to be disappointed by his brother again.

ON FRIDAY JAMIE'S energy flagged more than ever from the lack of sleep, but coffee and willpower kept her going. In a midday lull she contemplated another night in the trailer with Zack Denning. It was bad enough to spend the hours listening for possible intruders—spending them confined with Zack in a small space was worse. If only she could convince him not to come.

Inspiration struck and a surge of adrenaline shot through her. Jamie snatched her BlackBerry and a slip of paper where Zack had written his cell number. Quickly she typed a message. Thx 4 coming but tired & think it's over so won't go 2nite. For good measure she sent the same note to Brad's cell phone. It was a harmless white lie. Besides, the vandalism likely wasn't linked to Mar Vista, so it wasn't Zack's problem.

Since she'd opened the stand for the summer, she had seen a steady increase in the number of customers who came shortly after 3:00 p.m.—Mar Vista employees getting off their shift. It was something different from Granddad's experiences, and she was learning to adjust how she stocked the stand. But it was uncomfortable because she couldn't help over-hearing their conversations about Mar Vista. One woman was particularly vocal whenever she came, and was even more fervent that afternoon.

"I'm surprised Mr. Denning doesn't check every table in the restaurant after we've set it," she griped. "So he can be sure we got the folds in his precious napkins right. One of these days we'll see him out there with a ruler, measuring how far the plate is from the edge and if the silverware is aligned in a precise ninety-degree angle."

"The pay is decent," her companion offered.

"Sure, but we'll never get into management."

"Why not?" Jamie said without thinking, then kicked herself. It wasn't her concern and she didn't want to get drawn into Zack's business.

"Mar Vista management always comes from outside the area," the second woman explained. "When they replaced the maintenance supervisor, they went clear to Atlanta, Georgia."

"Oh."

Jamie didn't know what to say, so decided it was safest to say nothing. "Did you want anything else?" she asked instead.

"No, this is it for today."

There were several more customers before Jamie closed. She wanted to get back while it was light, and had barely enough time to deposit the receipts and return with a sack of food. Admittedly, she was a bit nervous about being there alone, but she refused to give in to fear. She'd lock the trailer door and could contact the authorities on her cell phone if someone showed up. In any case, she was keeping a low profile, so nobody would know she was there; she'd parked even farther away, behind a grove of trees.

She pulled out the sandwich she'd made at the house and sat at the table to work on jewelry ideas. Lately her imagination had been running wild with concepts that ranged from natural subjects to fantasy figures. One gallery had advised her to specialize in a single motif, such as the ocean. But Jamie didn't want to be limited; she'd rather be identified by the quality of her designs and execution.

It wasn't quite dark when tires crunched quietly past the trailer. She frowned. A vandal wouldn't come so early. A few minutes later, there was a soft rap on the door; she held her breath and stayed absolutely still. Zack was being anal, double-checking to make sure she hadn't come to the trailer. Couldn't the guy accept a text message as final?

"Jamie Conroe," a voice said outside. "I'm not leaving, so if you want pictures of destructive scumbags doing their thing tonight, let me in."

She waited mutely, only to hear loud music begin to play. "I'll have to amuse myself," he called. "Ella Fitzgerald is my favorite."

Jamie lunged to the door and jerked it open. "Turn it off," she ordered. "I'm supposed to be undercover."

His grin was triumphant. "I knew that would work, though I hate to stifle Ella."

"Brother," she exclaimed. "Why are you here? I sent you a text."

"Yeah, but it's strange," he answered. "I could swear your message said you *weren't* coming to the trailer, yet here you are."

"I was being polite," she countered. "This isn't your problem and I don't need a man to take care of me." She stomped to her seat and swept the drawings into her portfolio.

Zack eyed her sandwich lying on a napkin. "Is that your dinner?"

"I haven't had a chance to go shopping since this started. It'll be fine and you can have half."

He raised a hand. From his forefinger dangled a bag. "I've got sandwiches, too. Grilled garlic chicken with portobello mushrooms and Gordon's wine and Fontina cheese sauce, on freshly baked sourdough rolls. Are you *sure* you prefer a slice of lunch meat slapped between two dry heels of bread?"

The scents emanating from the bag were tantalizing, and Zack looked at her with the same challenge she'd employed when offering him strawberries. The glint in his eyes was lazy and sexy and made her gulp.

"Sounds appetizing," she said.

He handed her a paper box, and inside she found a crusty roll piled thick with chicken. Portobello mushrooms stuck out from the edges and a drip of sauce hung ready to drop, so Jamie gave it a swipe.

Zack stared as she licked her finger, and she felt like saying she hadn't meant anything provocative, but kept her mouth shut. It was safer.

Jamie set out a plastic container of strawberries after they'd eaten the sandwiches, and Zack smiled faintly as he swallowed a juicy berry. Unwilling to work on her designs with him nearby, she doodled until he suggested another round of Scrabble.

They set up the board and Jamie tried to form words from the letters she'd drawn, yet playing a game with Zack was almost as tense as ignoring him. It was crazy to let him disturb her this way. At most he wanted a quick tumble under the sheets. She wasn't his type and she was glad of it, no matter how attractive he might be. And it wasn't as if sex was that important; with her ex-husband it had been second-rate at best, so she didn't miss it any more than she missed the rest of her marriage.

If only she could stop remembering Zack's kiss on the sand dune. However brief, it had…curled her toes.

Jamie gazed at the Scrabble board without really seeing it. She had to get hold of herself. Even if Zack denied it, he must wonder if an intimate association could help him get rid of the produce stand. He was wrong. Nothing could make her sell, especially to a man wanting to build exclusive guest rooms over the soil where her grandparents had met and courted. Granddad had trusted her to take care of the land, or he wouldn't have left it to her.

Zack took the first watch, so she climbed into the bunk at midnight and closed her eyes, but sleep didn't interest her. Questions ran wildly through her head, such as did Zack do certain *other* things as well as he kissed?

After a couple of hours she pretended to wake up so he could get some rest. Maybe he wasn't fooled, but he didn't say anything as he lay on the narrow mattress and turned his face away.

Jamie leaned against the wall and concentrated on the sounds outside the trailer. Ocean waves murmured; a gentle breeze rippled the canvas awning; an owl hooted in the distance. But then she bolted upright at a soft pattering on the roof. Zack sat up, too.

"I think it's a raccoon," she said.

Zack yawned and settled back. "We have to be careful at the resort. We've put springs on all the doors so they shut automatically and even installed special screens on guest patio doors and balconies so someone can't accidentally leave them ajar, allowing little bandits to explore the rooms."

"Has anyone blocked the screen and let one in anyway?"

"Yup." His voice was sleepy. "We give discreet warnings, but one guest thought it would be entertaining to get a video of raccoons in their room. His wife nearly sued for divorce on the spot. The raccoons peed on her designer silk scarf and made off with a five-carat diamond pendant. And I hesitate to say what they did to her Prada shoes and purse."

His gravelly laugh did peculiar things to Jamie's stomach and she reminded herself it was the enforced intimacy that was boosting her awareness. As a counterbalance she pictured an evening with Tim, then stopped cold. She'd rather deal with unsettled nerves than rehash the dead past.

They traded watches at 3:00 a.m., and she woke two hours later to see Zack crawling into his bunk. Since it was light outside, there was no point in staying awake, so she dropped asleep again.

Jamie's eyes were gritty when she finally dragged herself out of bed, and she scowled when Zack greeted her cheerfully. She poured two cups of coffee from her thermos, thinking that for someone who'd claimed he wasn't a morning person, Zack was in a mighty good mood.

"I've got an idea," he announced.

"Then don't let it get stale," she grumbled as he drank from the steaming mug.

"Lord, this is tasty," he said appreciatively.

"Granddad's recipe. So what's your big idea?"

"You should come to dinner tonight at the resort."

Jamie choked and coffee sprayed onto the table. "*That's* your brilliant plan? Correct me if I'm mistaken, but didn't we already run that one over with a golf cart and beat it to death with a club?"

He handed her a paper towel. "The way I see things, it's incredibly unlikely that my people are involved. But either way, if we're seen eating together it will demonstrate solidarity."

Oh, great. More time with Zack. Yet as much as it hurt to admit, his idea had merit. Jamie nodded slowly as she mopped up the spilled coffee.

"Excellent," he said. "But you might try keeping your temper in check so people are convinced we're friends."

"What? You've got a lot of nerve implying I'm a powder keg ready to ignite. You're the one who roared in here the first day with a full head of steam."

"You were… I *thought* you were trespassing."

"So if you make a stupid assumption, acting like an overbearing, uptight jackass is justified?"

"Uptight is a matter of opinion." He put on his shoes and jacket before going to the door, throwing a parting shot over his shoulder. "And I *am* picking you up at your house, to enhance the show of friendship. I'll be there at six."

She would've followed him out and continued the argument, except she heard a truck arriving with one of her deliveries. Probably Burt Friesen; he was always first. Rushing to put on her shoes, she stepped out to see Zack drive by with a friendly wave as though they were best buddies.

"Morning, Jamie," Burt said. "Wasn't that the owner of Mar Vista?"

"That's him," she murmured as Burt lifted boxes from his pickup. "He came by and we had a cup of coffee." Which was the truth—just not the complete story.

"I heard he was upset that you'd set up business here, so I guess it's not an issue anymore."

Jamie did her best to smile. "We've worked it out."

"That's nice. We all need good neighbors."

Good neighbors. That was a joke. Zack Denning was a pain in her neck along with a few other places, and she didn't know what to do about it.

ZACK DROVE A section of his normal daily-inspection route and then headed to the office. His energy was running high—the argument with Jamie had put him on his toes. However tired and grouchy, her wit was unimpaired. All the same, it seemed as if everything was a battle with her. Of course, he could have been more tactful, but triggering her temper was fun.

He found Kim at the tennis courts, zipping her racket into a protective sleeve. There was a faint sheen of perspiration on her forehead and the glow of a vigorous workout, but no sign of a play partner.

She waved. "Hey, Zack."

"Don't tell me you were practicing against the backboard. I doubt Brad is up to a round of tennis." Even as Zack said it, he hoped his brother hadn't tried to keep up with Kim. Brad was closemouthed regarding his condition, but his persistent limp told Zack enough.

"The tennis coach just left. Is there *anything* you don't provide at Mar Vista?"

"I hope not," he said. The coach's job included playing with guests in need of an opponent, but he generally wasn't on duty until 9:00 a.m. He must have come in early. Hardly a surprise—most men fell over themselves to accommodate such a beautiful woman.

She examined him from head to toe. "What's going on—did you sleep in your clothes?"

He shrugged, deciding he ought to shower before encountering another guest. "It's a long story. I'd better get going. See you later."

After cleaning up, Zack went by the front desk and had them make a reservation at the Sunfish Grotto for six-fifteen.

"Yes, sir. By the way, the new koi fish for the serenity garden have been released in the ponds."

Pleased, Zack went to see the exotic newcomers drifting in the water. He still wasn't sure the Japanese-style garden was right for Mar Vista, but the guests weren't complaining. At night the low lights and hidden corners offered privacy to couples who didn't want to walk the ocean bluffs or find other romantic locations.

He hadn't shown Jamie the garden, and he likely wouldn't be doing so anytime soon. Whatever Jamie believed, he played fair. And it wouldn't be fair to show her so much as an extra blade of grass, because she'd have to stay to protect her silly fruit stand. Besides, pretending to be on cordial terms with him would stretch her minuscule patience to the limit without provocation.

Why did she charge through the world with her fists ready? His dad would call her a worthy opponent, but while Zack admired self-reliance, her determination to take care of herself and fight all comers was unusually strong.

Soon after three he got a text from Jamie. It wasn't a cancellation, but she was reminding him that she'd prefer going to the Clam Shell. He'd wanted to show off the Grotto, but he could take her there another evening. It was a reasonable request; she would barely finish at the fruit stand in time to get home and be ready for their public meal out, so it should be her choice where they dined.

BRAD THOUGHT IT was curious that Kim was back at Mar Vista so soon, but he was glad to see her. The awkwardness he'd expected from their quarrel never materialized. Kim simply hugged him and suggested they explore the art galleries in town.

The resort had loaner vehicles for guests, but Zack had tossed him a set of keys the day he'd flown in, saying he hardly ever used his car, so Brad might as well. Like everything with Zack, his ride was quality—a sleek, sporty BMW. He didn't know many jarheads who could afford a Beamer, and he pictured his own vehicle, a twelve-year-old SUV, stored behind his parents' garage. It was somewhat beat-up, but it ran smoothly and had come with no monthly payments.

"You haven't been into Warrington before now?" Brad queried as he parked on the central shopping street in town. "Zack said you came to the grand opening."

Kim grinned. "You know Zack—I was lucky to have a minute to eat, much less do sightseeing."

It was true, and who would understand Zack better than Kim?

The community seemed to be flourishing, particularly the businesses catering to the tourists. Off the main street they strolled into a small art studio, where Kim was taken with a sculpture of seabirds, though she did a double take when she glanced at the identifying information.

"Too pricey?" Brad asked.

"It's not for sale, but check the artist's name."

Brad read the placard explaining it was a piece by a George Jenkins. "So?"

"That was Jamie Conroe's grandfather. The same name, at least."

He read the placard again. It was dated 1952. "You think it's the same guy?"

"Anything's possible. The decor in Jamie's house is exquisite. I thought she must have completely re-done it after her grandfather died, but maybe not." Kim turned to the gallery attendant. "Was this a local artist? I heard there was a George Jenkins who used to live near the new resort."

"Yes, ma'am. It's the same man. He didn't sell many pieces in Warrington, but he gave this one to my aunt in the 1950s."

Next they went across the street to a picturesque café. Brad ordered the mocha latte for Kim and regular black coffee for himself, along with two slices of blackberry pie. According to the sign out front, it was the "most delicious pie in the county."

Kim shook her head as she sipped her foamy concoction. "It's odd that we saw a sculpture by Jamie's grandfather. He was quite talented."

"Not so odd." Brad swallowed a bite of pie. It *was* delicious, and much more his taste over the elaborate dishes they served at Mar Vista. "You wouldn't believe the flukes that occurred overseas. I once had two guys assigned to my unit who were cousins—they hadn't seen each other since they were ten. But Jamie's grandfather *was* an artist, so it's really not a coincidence to find his work in the same town where he lived."

"I guess you're right. Listen, Brad. One of the reasons I came up this weekend…" Her voice trailed off and Brad wondered what the problem might be. As a rule, Kim was more articulate than most people.

"Yes?" he prompted.

She took a deep breath. "Saying that stuff about you getting blown up was terribly insensitive of me."

He began laughing. It was the best chuckle he'd

had in ages. "Good God, Kim. If you think *that* was insensitive, you ought to hear the things we hurled at each other in the hospital."

"It's not funny," she said stiffly.

"You don't have to tell me, but if I didn't laugh, I wouldn't see the point of going on."

"Well...I wanted to apologize and I'm relieved it didn't offend you."

"Actually, I liked it. You can't know how tiresome it is to be around people always walking on verbal eggshells. You forgot to watch your mouth and it was a treat."

IT WAS AFTER five when Jamie was able to stash the remnants of the day's stock in the truck. She dropped the receipts into the night deposit at the bank and got home shortly before six. A long hot shower would have been nice, but instead she ducked in and out in nothing flat.

"Be there in a second," she called as the doorbell rang. She pulled a robe on and dashed to peek out the front window. It was Zack. She opened the door. "Come in. I only got home a couple minutes ago and I'm hurrying as fast as I can."

"Don't rush," he assured her, though his voice was rough, making her aware that she had nothing on under the old pink terry.

Jamie hurried to her bedroom. She sternly reminded herself this was not a date; she and Zack didn't even like each other, though it hadn't kept her from imagining how he looked without clothing.

Hmm.... No time for lustful fantasies. She searched her closet for something suitable to wear—the kind of outfit you wore to dinner with a friend or for an informal business meal. Her aqua T-shirt and tan A-line skirt would have to do. A pair of silver earrings her grandfather had cast years ago completed the outfit.

She went into the living room and found Zack on the couch, defending himself against Marlin's determined advances.

"Did you get my message about going to the Clam Shell?"

"Yeah." He lifted Marlin from his lap, but the feline promptly jumped back onto Zack's legs.

"Come on, boy," Jamie urged, luring the cat to the floor with a handful of treats. "Sorry. He got spoiled last winter when I was here all day, so now he's hungry for attention."

Zack stood and brushed himself off. "Doesn't he know when people don't want him on top of them?"

"You don't have experience with cats, do you? If someone doesn't want them around, that person becomes their favorite target."

"You're kidding."

"Not a bit. It's part of their twisted feline sense of humor. I love cats, but I admit that dogs are easier animals to get along with."

"I wouldn't know."

"You wouldn't?" Jamie broke off in amazement. "You've never had a dog *or* a cat, even as a kid?"

"No. Mom was allergic to pet dander or something, and I don't have time for an animal now."

What an insight to the guy's life, and he didn't even seem to know what he'd missed.

"Are you ready?" he asked.

"Sure."

Zack's hand on the small of her back was just a polite gesture as they left the house, but it sent electric currents up and down her spine anyway.

CHAPTER EIGHT

As JAMIE SANK onto the butter-soft leather of the Mercedes passenger seat, she reminded herself to keep a friendly appearance.

Friends. Pals. *Buddies.*

What a joke. Fortunately, it didn't have to be genuine; they just had to make it look good.

Zack drove into the parking lot and parked in the most visible spot, near the parking valet.

"Hello...Brian," he said as they passed the valet, his pause nearly imperceptible as he glanced at the employee's name tag. Jamie had already noted the Mar Vista staff wore tags identifying them for guests—and apparently for their boss.

"Good evening, Mr. Denning," the valet replied.

"Brian, have you met our neighbor, Ms. Conroe?"

The man barely blinked. "She may not remember, but I knew Jamie when we were kids and she was visiting her grandfather."

"Of course I remember you, B.B.," Jamie said, using his old nickname and giving him a wink. She was surprised by his lack of expression. Brian Berk had been one of the funniest boys Jamie had ever met; he'd told the stupidest elephant jokes and made them hilarious. "Is your sense of humor still getting you in the dog house?"

For a moment Brian's bland mask slipped and he grinned. "I swear I wasn't the one who painted the dog blue."

"No, but you were the one who added the eight ball."

"Hey, I was twelve and the paint wasn't toxic." All at once Brian looked at his employer apprehensively. Perhaps he wasn't supposed to be too informal with the resort clientele.

Zack smiled easily. "Someday I'll have to hear the whole story. I hope you have pictures."

"I...er...think my mother has some," Brian stuttered.

"She's probably saving them to embarrass you when your kids are old enough. There are a few my own mother is holding over my head, even though I keep reminding her blackmail is illegal."

"That would be Mom's speed."

Zack extended his arm and they shook hands. "We'd better go so we can make our dinner reservation."

The Clam Shell might be the resort's casual restaurant, but it was elegant enough in Jamie's opinion. At least she wasn't too underdressed. There were people in evening clothes, but also men in shorts and women in jeans—designer jeans, to be sure, but still jeans.

"Evening, Sean." Zack greeted the maître d' without the hesitation he'd shown with Brian. No doubt he ate there often enough to know the restaurant employees.

"I understand you're eating in tonight, Mr. Denning."

"Yes. Sean, this is Jamie Conroe, one of Mar Vista's neighbors. Jamie, this is Sean Deacons. He keeps things running at the Clam Shell."

The maître d' stepped forward and bowed. "Ms. Conroe—our chef has spoken of you."

"I'm sure he has," Zack inserted casually. "We're fortunate to have Jamie coordinating the purchase of organic produce for our restaurants. She's brought the quality to an exceptional level."

The maître d' led them to a section of tables on a low platform and Jamie figured Zack had chosen the location for its visibility. Sean would have held Jamie's chair for her, but Zack beat him to it.

As Jamie looked around the restaurant, she noticed various employees covertly watching their boss. Whether it was curiosity or concern that he was inspecting their work, she didn't know. The comments from the woman at the fruit stand implied he was a micromanager and a nitpicker of major proportions.

A server came with the menus and Zack introduced them with rare charm.

Once the employees got through gossiping about

the evening, Jamie guessed she'd practically be seen as a member of the Denning family.

She opened the menu and studied it, recognizing some of the dishes that Zack had brought the past few nights. Prices were conspicuously absent—asking the cost would probably be considered gauche at Mar Vista's rarefied strata.

"How nice to see you, Zack," a woman said, stopping by the table, a tall man next to her.

"Cheryl, Linc." Zack stood to shake her hand and that of her husband. "Welcome to Mar Vista. I noticed your names on the reservation list."

"Oh, yes, we got your note. Our investment manager told us he'd visited your resort, so we had to see it for ourselves," the man explained.

"Terrific." Zack turned to Jamie. "Let me introduce you to my neighbor and friend, Jamie Conroe. Jamie, this is Cheryl and Linc Augustine. I've known them for fifteen years. We met when I was working at a resort in Pennsylvania."

The woman gave Jamie a swift visual inspection, blatantly assessing her. Jamie lifted her chin, thinking of cats circling and trying to decide who was alpha in the crowd. Well, she didn't have to be top cat, but she wasn't settling for bottom of the heap, either.

"Nice to meet you." Linc shook her hand; unlike his wife, his eyes were filled with frank appreciation. Not that he seemed the type of guy who strayed—he simply wasn't blind to other women.

"Could we get together tomorrow, Zack?" Cheryl asked. "We'd love a personal tour of Mar Vista. From what we've seen, it's everything you intended it to be. Linc is already planning our next visit."

"It would be an honor for such old friends," Zack assured her. "I enjoy showing it off to people."

"I can vouch for that," Jamie said with a straight face.

Zack coughed and picked up a goblet of water.

Luckily the Augustines moved on at Sean's urging, who was waiting to seat them.

"Thanks a lot," Zack muttered, sitting and gulping the rest of his water. "I almost choked to death."

Additional guests strolled by and Jamie marveled at how well Zack remembered them, especially when he seemed to have trouble recalling the names of some employees. Of course, Mar Vista did have a large staff, and they'd only been up and running for a few months. With turnover, there also could be new people he hadn't met yet. At the thought, she pressed her lips together. She was making excuses for him.

"Sorry for the interruptions," he said. "I should have gotten a different table. You haven't even had a chance to study the menu."

She shrugged. "That's okay. How do you know so many of your guests?"

"I've managed at a number of resorts and you get to know the people who visit on a regular basis.

That's why they're here—because they know me. I hope they'll return because of Mar Vista itself."

Jamie thought she saw a hint of concern in Zack's expression and she supposed it was natural for him to be worried for his investment. It sounded as if he'd been planning Mar Vista for a long time.

Or he could be playing on her sympathy and wasn't concerned in the slightest.

Lord. When did she get so cynical? Zack had suggested she was a bitter divorcée, but he was wrong. Her view of the world had nothing to do with her divorce; it was from years of contact with Tim and his kind. Her ex-husband had attracted similar-minded people—men and women who cared less for kindness and honesty than for profit and winning the game. It would take a while to shed the excessive caution she'd learned from being around them. Still, it had proved an education on how some people operated—a lesson she shouldn't altogether forget.

"Pardon me, Mr. Denning." It was the maître d'. "Mr. Chen asked if you were available to step into the kitchen."

"Certainly. Jamie, do you mind?"

"No problem."

She read the menu while she waited. Everything looked fabulous, with the unique flair she'd expect from a top chef. But Gordon also wisely offered a range of familiar dishes for the less adventurous. Nearby diners, studying the menu as well, were joking about the notation on certain items, stating they could be prepared with organic products upon request.

"Only in California," declared one. "What does our daughter call it—the land of bean sprouts and gurus?"

"And Disneyland," the wife added.

"That's right."

Despite their humor, the couple opted for organic ingredients when they ordered their meal. It made sense; there was a growing focus on eating healthier, and she felt a flash of satisfaction, knowing she'd helped get the best produce to Gordon's kitchen.

Jamie looked around the restaurant again. In an upper section she saw a circular dining area with broad windows overlooking the cove to the south of the resort. She didn't expect to be back, so it would have been nice to sit there, but the more public location was best.

The evening was going the way it should.

Zack was making sure as many guests and employees as possible knew who she was, and that their relationship was friendly. If their conversation occasionally had an edge to it, she doubted anyone had noticed. Once the news got out, the problems at the stand might go away. And once she got Zack to accept that she wasn't selling Granddad's land, there would be little need to see each other. Life in Warrington would be much simpler, the way she'd planned it to be.

ZACK HURRIED INTO the large kitchen that was the hub for two restaurants and a banquet hall. Gordon directed the various chefs and circulated food similar to a maestro conducting a symphony. Patiently he waited until the chef saw him.

"Sean mentioned that Ms. Conroe is here," Gordon said, hurrying over. "I know she's favorable to spicy food. Would she be agreeable to me preparing something off menu for her? And for you, naturally."

Zack had the distinct impression that "and for you" was an afterthought. At a guess, he was still earning his way back into the chef's good graces.

"I'll ask, but I'm sure she'd be pleased. The same for me."

"Send word with Sean."

In another moment, Gordon was in the flow of his kitchen while Zack departed in relief. There was no disaster to address. He hadn't told Gordon that he'd invited Jamie to the resort in case the arrangement fell through. An unhappy chief chef made an unhappy kitchen.

"Major crisis?" Jamie queried as he regained his seat.

"Not even a small one. Gordon wanted to know if you were interested in eating something off menu. It's a compliment. He'll usually make a special for the day, but not for individuals."

She appeared uncomfortable for some reason, but simply nodded. "That would be great."

Signaling Sean, Zack said to let Gordon know they'd be pleased to have whatever he chose to prepare.

The wine steward brought the bottle Zack had ordered that afternoon and poured their glasses. Jamie sipped from her goblet and made a low sound of approval. "This is a Sonoma Valley wine, isn't it?"

"One of my favorites. Mar Vista carries a selection from around the world, but we specialize in California wines."

"Brad says you both grew up in Virginia. How did you end up in Warrington?" she asked.

"The weather is better on the West Coast for a year-round resort—no hurricanes or heavy snow. I scouted locations for a decade before I found this one."

"Hawaii's climate is even better."

"The land is too expensive and staying in the continental United States makes us more accessible for short stays. Besides, the California coast has character, and I didn't want a typical location."

"Define *typical*."

As the conversation continued, Zack was relieved by how the evening was going. Kim came in after seven and was seated several tables away. She waved at them, but deliberately fixed her attention on the nearby clamshell fountain made of iridescent glass.

"Isn't that your lawyer?" Jamie asked, obviously tensing.

"Not right now," he answered with a wry chuckle. "Kim informed me in no uncertain terms that she's here to relax and I'm not allowed to discuss anything legal. She did the same thing last weekend."

"She comes up that often?"

"No, just the past few weeks. I'm glad she likes the place. She isn't a golfer, but we offer other recreation."

A half smile played on Jamie's mouth and he wished he knew what she was thinking. The woman could give lessons to Mona Lisa with her enigmatic expressions.

It was strange. Feature for feature, Jamie was no more attractive than Kim. Yet when he looked at his former lover, he felt only a warm friendship. Jamie, on the other hand, was making his blood rush in a southern direction with the speed of a heat-seeking missile. Was his desire for her simply because she was so different from the women visiting the resort? No artifice, no attempt at sophistication, just annoying and stubborn. Her uniqueness had to be the explanation, along with his lack of a social life for so long.

"Mr. Denning?" It was the maître d'. "I have a message from the front desk."

Sean gave him a sheet of paper; there'd been a mix-up in reservations and they were asking how he wanted it handled. He almost excused himself again, then changed his mind.

"Please tell the desk to take whatever action they feel is appropriate."

"Certainly, sir," Sean answered, clearly surprised, and Zack realized that ordinarily he would have charged in and dealt with it himself. In fact, he almost had. It was an odd shift and he wondered why he didn't feel his usual fierce need to supervise the situation.

Jamie raised her eyebrow when they were alone. "I don't mind if you have to take care of something."

"No, it's minor. They can figure it out. Anyway, I'm sure our appetizers will arrive soon."

THE APPETIZERS WERE delicious, though it was hard for Jamie to relax and appreciate the food. She couldn't forget they were on display, and how could she be comfortable with Zack in any case? More than anything she wanted to get everything resolved and stop having him around.

His explanation for Kim Wheeler's presence sounded genuine; he'd been too chagrined. Besides, Jamie had a strong suspicion as to why the attorney was visiting Mar Vista…Brad Denning. The funniest thing was that neither Kim nor Brad nor anyone else seemed to have a clue what was going on. They were either in love, or very close to it, and nobody was admitting a thing to anybody, including to themselves.

"Why are you smiling?" Zack asked warily.

"Was I?"

"Yeah, it's a cat-who-sneaked-into-the-cream kind of smile."

"Really?" Jamie's smile widened. "I thought you didn't know about cats. You told me you'd never had a pet."

"I know enough to recognize that smile," he retorted.

She laughed. "I was simply enjoying the appetizers. These egg rolls are terrific. Have you tried the Thai peanut sauce with them?"

"Not yet."

Jamie drank more wine, her gaze drifting again to Kim. She felt an age-old urge to play matchmaker between the lawyer and the healing marine, but it wasn't her business and what could she do anyway?

KIM DIDN'T MIND dining by herself, but it was frustrating knowing Brad could be sitting across the table from her.

While he'd insisted they go horseback riding that afternoon, she could tell he was in pain but she couldn't say anything.

The trip into town had been more enjoyable than the horseback ride, and she'd managed to apologize to him, even if he hadn't thought it was necessary. As for having dinner together, he'd excused himself. Perhaps it was because he was too tired from the ride, or from pride over the question of who would pay…a question tangled by his brother owning the place. Honestly, she'd never fully understand the male ego.

After ordering her dinner, she went to the powder room and found Jamie Conroe there, dabbing a spot on her skirt with a towel.

"Hi, Jamie. Don't worry. I'm not at Mar Vista as an attorney."

"That's what Zack said."

Kim looked to be sure the attendant couldn't hear. "Brad mentioned you've been having problems with vandalism. Are you okay?"

"I'm fine. It's nice of you to ask."

"He—he was worried whether—that is, if someone at Mar Vista…"

"I'm sure it isn't," Jamie assured her quickly.

"What did the sheriff's office say?"

"I reported it and they drive by as part of their patrol, but they can't stay and guard the place. That's why I'm trying to gather evidence myself."

Kim suspected Zack and Jamie's very public dinner was a different kind of effort to stop the vandalism, but that subject was off-limits in case it was misconstrued as a lawyerly inquiry.

"By the way, I saw a wonderful seabird sculpture in Warrington by your grandfather," she said. "Is his work for sale anywhere?"

"Probably not. Most of his pieces sold as soon as they went on the market. I'm not sure how many he completed over the years. Art was a hobby by the time I came along. He enjoyed trying various mediums, such as silver. The earrings I'm wearing are some he made for my grandmother."

"May I see?"

Jamie obligingly removed one and handed it to her. The delicate design was distinctive and had been crafted and finished with equal care.

"He was quite an artist. Did he do much jewelry?"

"No. He sculpted, which is where the silver casting began, but he preferred working on larger pieces."

"Is silver casting what you do?" Kim asked, returning the earring.

"Yes. I became interested because of Granddad and took classes in college."

"May I come over and see your work sometime?"

Jamie grinned. "Sure. Give me a call and we can meet up."

"I'll unblock my number so you know it's me," Kim said, remembering Jamie didn't take calls from shielded numbers, and wondered why she was so careful. Of course, more and more people screened their calls, particularly if their cell-phone plan had limited minutes.

Jamie dried her hands. "I'd best get back."

"Talk to you later."

ZACK HAD WATCHED uneasily when Kim headed toward the powder room at the same time as Jamie, almost jumping up to stop her. Fortunately, he realized it would draw undue attention from the dining room, and if Jamie came out and saw them talking, she'd go ballistic.

The salads arrived as Jamie returned to the table, her expression unruffled, so he kept his mouth shut about her potential encounter with Kim.

The food that Gordon kept sending out was extraordinary. Each course seemed to have a culinary influence from a different part of the world, some quite spicy, which didn't faze Jamie in the least. In fact, she even ate an extra serving of the fiery sauce that came with the chicken dish.

"Your mouth must be coated with asbestos," he finally commented. His own use of the sauce was far more modest.

"I love bold flavors—I sometimes have to remind myself that subtle is good, too."

"I'll have to keep that in mind," he said without thinking.

She glanced up and flushed slightly.

Dessert came, a tiramisu confection of custard and whipped cream layered with sponge cake.

Jamie stared at it. "Gordon has an inflated idea of the size of my stomach. I'll have to take most of this home."

She managed a third of the dessert, then Zack signaled the server to have the kitchen put it in a container.

Jamie checked her watch. "I'm pretty beat. Do you think we can call it a night?"

"Of course."

He stood and held her chair. At the door, Sean handed her a box. "With the chef's compliments."

She beamed. "I don't want to interrupt Gordon, but will you tell him it was fantastic?"

"It would be my pleasure."

As they went to the SUV, Jamie waved at Brian, who discreetly gestured back at her. For a powder keg, she made friends easily.

Once in the Mercedes, there was silence as Zack drove her home.

"Well, thanks," she said, climbing out before he could open the door for her. "After our show tonight, I don't think there's a need to keep watch any longer. And it will be awfully nice to spend the night in my own bed."

"Agreed. The trailer isn't as bad as I thought it would be, but it's not king-size, either."

"Right."

She closed the door and hurried into the house. Suspicious, Zack drove a short distance down the drive, parking out of sight before sliding out and heading toward the house. There was a spot where he could see the place without being too obvious. Sure enough, within minutes Jamie came through the door, carrying a tote bag. She didn't go to her car, but hiked in the direction of the beach.

With his longer legs, it wasn't hard to catch up.

"What happened to sleeping in your own bed?" he demanded.

Jamie gasped and spun around. "Cripes," she exclaimed. "Did you have to scare me half to death?"

"Apparently I do. Why are you hiking out to the trailer?"

"Whoever is doing the vandalism might have figured out that someone is guarding the stand because of the cars."

Zack made an exasperated sound. "You said spending the night in the trailer was unnecessary. Good Lord, Jamie, the message that we're friends is already rampaging through my staff at the speed of light. With so many employees from Warrington, the word will spread there almost as quickly."

"And what if the vandalism isn't related to the resort?" she countered. "I'm protecting my business, the same as you would. The same as you are now, since I know you don't want it getting around to your high-toned guests that some of your employees might be vandals. But you've done enough. I'll handle it from here."

She kept walking, so he had no choice except to keep up.

Her remark had startled him. He'd never truly looked at it from her standpoint…yet it *was* a business. Tiny compared with Mar Vista, but hers. He'd only seen its temporary nature and the fact she could make more money if she moved to another location, up near the highway. Her stubborn refusal to leave had seemed unreasonable, but Zack had to admit that if he was selling vegetables for a living, he'd rather do it with a million-dollar view. As it turned out, that view was worth more than any amount of money to Jamie since her grandparents had met on the beach. He sighed.

On Monday he'd have to talk with Rick about having hedges installed on the shared property perimeter. It would be an expensive solution, and less than optimal, but it seemed to be the only option.

His shoreline purchase had a permanent hole in it.

CHAPTER NINE

JAMIE MARCHED ALONG the path that had served for decades as a foot route from Granddad's house to the beach property. Admittedly, after passing through the gate a few hundred feet from the house, she was now cutting across Denning property, but Zack didn't seem to be complaining about *that* at the moment.

"Go away," she told Zack when he kept following her.

"If you're keeping guard, so am I."

She ground her teeth and kept walking. She'd debated whether she should wait before heading to the trailer, but dinner had taken longer than expected and she hadn't relished the idea of going in the dark. Besides, Zack *had* left; she'd checked to be sure. He must have returned and watched the house from a vantage point. Stubborn ass.

"Where does this path come out?" he asked.

"Close to the place where we were parking the cars those first couple of nights. I used to walk back to the house this way if Granddad was busy and couldn't take me."

"So you could sneak a little TV, right?"

"'Fraid not. Granddad didn't like television and never had one in the house. I felt funny bringing one in, but I'm an old-movie buff and enjoy history programs. Of course, Granddad..."

"Yes?"

"Nothing." Jamie didn't want to finish what she'd started to say...that her grandfather had never been truly alone. He'd said once that he could hear Leah singing to him from heaven, and he would rather listen to her than a silly box. Other people might have thought he was crazy, but not Jamie.

The sun was dropping low, casting a rosy light across the landscape, and Zack pointed to a crane winging across the clearing. "That's amazing. Out here you feel a million miles from civilization. How did your grandfather get all this land?"

"He bought it," she said. "Piece by piece. It wasn't expensive back in the forties and fifties, and he purchased some of it from the county."

"Why? I mean, did he have a purpose for so much land, or did he just want to keep people away from his home?"

"It was partly that, but mostly he wanted to keep it natural. The salt flats aren't an official bird sanctuary, but they've wanted to create one for a while, and Granddad thought it would help if these parcels weren't developed. But when he got older, he also wanted to leave something to David and me. Selling a portion was the only way he could save the rest."

Zack nodded thoughtfully. "Since your name isn't Jenkins, I'm guessing your mother was his daughter. She's…gone? Is that why he left it to you?"

"Oh, no. Mom is fine, but my parents didn't need it, and Mom told him to give what he had to us. She has some of the paintings and sculptures and Leah's jewelry as remembrances. To be frank, Mom was never crazy about living here. I guess it was lonely for a girl growing up without a mother and having an eccentric father."

"You don't mind calling your grandfather eccentric?"

"Granddad would've been the first to admit it. Mom adored him, but her feelings toward Warrington are another matter. My brother feels the same."

"You seem to like it well enough."

Jamie had never really thought about it, but she *did* like Warrington. It was home to her happiest childhood memories, and the person who'd understood her best.

"My mother wanted us to know Granddad as individuals, so they sent me here each August, while David came in July," she said slowly. "The month with Granddad was what I looked forward to all year. I played and dreamed to my heart's content. It's when I thought anything was possible."

"You don't think so any longer?"

"Life can get in the way of dreams."

"If you let it."

That was fine for him to say—apparently Zack Denning didn't let anything get in the way of what he wanted.

She stopped. "Look, you should go back. I can handle this. There's still time for you to get to your car before it's completely dark."

"No."

"I'm not a child," she said in frustration. "You wouldn't even know there was vandalism if it weren't for Brad walking out here every day. And you wouldn't have gotten involved *then* if he hadn't been recovering from his injuries."

"Maybe, maybe not, but I'm involved now. I won't let you stay alone in the trailer as a target."

Throwing her hands up in disgust, she wheeled and stomped ahead. The last thing she wanted was to spend more time with Zack, *especially* in private. Her gut churned, her nerves teetered on the edge of a cliff, and she resented feeling that way about a guy she didn't even like that much.

They were getting close to the fruit stand, so Jamie walked more quietly, sliding around to open the door and get inside, Zack close behind her. She didn't turn on the trailer's battery-powered lights at first, but used a flashlight. Zack seemed as tense as she was, helping her double-check the spots where light could escape and making sure they were securely covered.

Inevitably they kept bumping each other in the small space until she finally said, *"Sit."*

"I'm not a dog."

"No, you're a pain in the ass."

"Gee, and I thought we were starting to get along." Zack gently tugged a lock of her hair, and she was abruptly aware of the heat from his long, hard length.

She swallowed.

Brad had mentioned his brother ran for exercise, and it was obvious Zack didn't have a flabby inch from the top of his head to the bottoms of his feet. Many businessmen ignored fitness, yet however much he was obsessed with his resort, Zack stayed in shape.

Great shape.

Jamie fumbled until she found a light switch. The glow from the LED lamp was softened from being in a recessed cove over the table and she tried to inch around Zack without touching him.

"Uh…how about another chess match?" she suggested.

He smiled lazily. "That's one possibility, though I had more vigorous pursuits in mind."

Don't do it, her protective instincts warned.

Do it, screamed her body.

Protective instincts began losing the argument as Zack pulled her close and kissed the corner of her mouth. The light fabric of her skirt did nothing to conceal his response and the bulge pressed to Jamie's abdomen sent heat deep into her core.

"Zack, I don't think…"

"Good—don't think." His kiss deepened and he eased the hem of her T-shirt up and over her head.

It was annoying, but not enough to make her stop him. Zack shifted around the tiny space and bumped his head on the upper bunk, then cracked his knuckles on the curved wall of the trailer as he tossed her shirt.

"*Ow.* Stop laughing."

"I wasn't."

"You were thinking about it."

Fair enough, she *had* thought about laughing, or a small chortle, at the very least. They tumbled together to the mattress on the lower bunk and she was grateful it was made of space-age foam, thick and cushioning.

Jamie unbuttoned Zack's shirt and spread her fingers across his chest. It wasn't the most romantic setting in the world, yet her pulse seemed to pound in rhythm with the ocean waves tumbling and crashing in the distance. He wasn't moving fast enough for her, so she unhooked her bra and felt his breathing become harsh as he stared in the faint light.

"Jeez, Jamie. You've been hiding some great… scenery."

She was glad he approved, but she couldn't admit it aloud. Not to Zack, a man from a world she'd rejected.

He's temporary, a voice whispered in her mind.

It was almost enough to make her stop, but his thumbs flicked her nipples, sending rationality reeling.

Her last sane thought was that she really hoped he had protection....

Jamie woke slowly, disoriented at first. The LED light over the table was still on, dimly illuminating the sleeping area. She was utterly relaxed...until she realized Zack held her snugly in the narrow bunk, one leg tucked between hers, his chest rising and falling in the steady rhythm of sleep.

One thing was certain: Zack was a generous lover, taking the time to discover the things that pleasured her most. What was that old line—it was nice to know what the shouting was all about?

Shouting? *Hmm.* They'd been making enough noise that their presence wouldn't have remained a secret to anyone outside the trailer.

Yet it was difficult to care at the moment.

Her body was going limp again, too replete to do anything else, and Jamie thought idly that this was the bunk in which her grandparents had spent their honeymoon, visiting Yellowstone and the Tetons, as well as points along the old Route 66. It wasn't the same mattress, of course. Granddad had updated everything, creating a strange mixture of sentiment and practicality.

Nevertheless, it was in this trailer where he and Leah had made love and conceived her mother.

It ought to feel weird to be here with Zack, but it didn't. Granddad had understood biology and the sex drive and he wouldn't have objected…as long as she wasn't doing something stupid. He *would* have taken issue with her marriage, but not with outrageous pleasure.

Sorrow shot through Jamie. She should have realized Tim was a mistake the first time he'd refused to visit Warrington with her. In the beginning, he hadn't tried to stop *her* from going, but Granddad had looked askance each time she showed up without her husband. He must have guessed something was wrong. Then later…Tim hadn't wanted her to go, either.

Jamie determinedly pushed the thought away. What was done was done. She had rich memories of her grandfather and he had still entrusted her with his house and the place where he'd met Leah, despite any conclusions he'd come to about her marriage.

She yawned, debating whether or not she should try to stay awake and listen for possible vandals. But the camera was sitting ready and she could get to it in a minute if she heard anyone outside.

Besides, she felt sleepy and satisfied and…

A BIRD CHIRPING caught Zack's waking attention. With the interior of the trailer shielded from letting out light, it also wouldn't let morning sunshine enter. There was only a low glow from the light

Jamie had switched on the previous evening. But the bird was announcing the dawn and his body was rested in a way it hadn't been since this whole mess had begun.

Hell, he hadn't felt this good in longer than he could remember.

Jamie's head lay on his shoulder, her hair in streaks and waves on his chest. From her steady breathing he guessed she was still asleep. Making love with her had been incredible. He might have expected the tight space to hamper them, but they'd managed very well...very well indeed.

Abruptly Brad's face rose in his mind.

His brother came down to the trailer and visited Jamie every day as part of the walk he'd chosen for his physical therapy. And it was obvious from things both he and Jamie had mentioned that he spent time with her once he got here. Not to mention the fact that Brad had been determined to help when the vandalism started.

What if Brad was interested in Jamie Conroe? Yet even as his guilt rose, so did his desire. Somehow he'd have to keep it in check.

In her sleep, Jamie sighed and her arm slid across his chest and down his abdomen before it stopped. His body hardened and he tried to focus on Mar Vista, on his parents, on George Jenkins, on anything except the softness of her skin.

It seemed forever before her eyes opened.

"Good morning," he said.

"The same to you." She sat up and started putting on her bra. While obviously not entirely comfortable, she wasn't haranguing him for what had happened.

"I'm sorry," he finally said.

Her eyebrow rose. "For what?"

"For…this. I haven't been thinking straight the past few days. I realized a while ago, a few minutes ago I mean…well, that you and Brad might be—God, he's been through hell and I'd cut off my arm before I'd mess things up for him."

Her eyes widened as she stared at him, her breathing growing quicker, and even in the low light he could see an angry red rising in her cheeks.

"Who the hell do you think I am?" she demanded. "The good-time girl for the Denning family? You wouldn't have gotten to first base if I'd cared for Brad in that way."

"Uh…" Lord, he'd messed up big-time. She would have slapped him down hard last night if she hadn't wanted the same thing—anything else belonged in a Victorian novel. But it didn't solve the problem of whether Brad was interested in *her*.

"Okay," he said. "I'm not thinking clearly this morning, either, but—"

"Boy, is that the understatement of the year."

"Look, Brad likes you and he's here a lot. He might have developed feelings you're not aware of."

Her mouth dropped open. "Are you nuts? Anyone with half a brain could see that Brad is crazy for Kim Wheeler."

Brad...and Kim?

No, it wasn't possible.

"If—if Brad has feelings for Kim," he stuttered, "then why hasn't he done anything about it?"

"Because Brad is a man of honor," Jamie retorted. "Which is a condition you should try to get acquainted with. He'd never make a move because of the history you and Kim have, and don't bother denying that you've been lovers. I figured it out the day the two of you showed up on my front porch."

"It was back in college," he protested. "We lived together for a couple months, and she was the one who broke it off. Brad knows that."

"So what? You're awfully good friends and Brad would never chance getting between you, *especially* if she was the one who ended it. He probably wonders if you still have a shot at happiness together."

"I'm only interested in friendship with Kim. But Kim and Brad? I can't wrap my brain around it."

Jamie shrugged. "They're mismatched, but Kim's got it bad for him, too."

"You're crazy."

"Really? Why else is she suddenly feeling an urge to fly to Mar Vista...now that Brad is here? She knew it was nice before he arrived and didn't come except for that one business trip to meet me. Not that she's admitted it to herself. They're both nuts for each other and doing everything in their power to believe they're just friends."

Jamie glanced around on the floor, then tugged her lacy black briefs from under his knee, ignoring his nude state and the obvious signs of his renewed arousal. As she bent over to pull them on, the smooth curve of her bare hip made his blood pressure rise.

Zack had never thought of himself as a hip man—breasts, yes, and there was something about a woman's waist, but with Jamie, everything was a turn-on. He closed his eyes and concentrated on controlling his response. After opening his big mouth, she certainly wouldn't tolerate an attempt to coax her back into the bed.

Jamie picked up her cell phone and checked the screen. "It's after seven. You'd better get dressed and back to Mar Vista. My deliveries will be starting in less than an hour. You were here yesterday, too, and while I don't mind people thinking we're friends, I'd just as soon they didn't start speculating about what else might be happening."

And neither did he; his business was his business and it was hard enough to keep it that way in a resort atmosphere with employees forming an oddly isolated community.

So, he began the search for his own clothing. Jamie slipped out the door while he was dressing. Obviously she didn't have the same fascination with watching him cover up his nudity that he'd had for her. Or if she did, she wasn't going to indulge it.

He finished rapidly and followed her out the door. She was straightening a few display shelves, the wet early-morning fog drifting around her.

"Anything happen out here that we didn't hear in the night?" he tried to ask casually.

She turned, her face still annoyed. "Everything is in place."

"That's good." He groped for his keys and pulled them out. If he hurried, he could get back to shower and change before his daily rounds.

Jamie unexpectedly grinned and cocked her head. "Excuse me, have you forgotten that you insisted on walking here from my house, dogging my every footstep?"

Zack groaned. His SUV was more than a mile away, up Jamie's long driveway. He *had* forgotten that he would have to hike back. Something about Jamie Conroe short-circuited his brain.

There weren't going to be any morning rounds that day. *Again.*

LATER THAT MORNING Brad glanced at Zack's bedroom door. It stood open and the room was empty. His brother had spent four nights with Jamie, helping to guard the fruit stand, and his mood was definitely suffering.

Brad had told Kim about the damage and the attempt to catch the culprit, but he'd skated over the fact that his brother was spending nights with an attractive woman in a very small trailer, however innocent the reason. If Kim wanted to rekindle anything with Zack, having questions about his interest in another woman wouldn't make a good start.

The front door opened and in came Zack. "Hey, big brother," he said. "Have a good night?"

Brad blinked at Zack's unexpected good humor. "Probably better than yours since I slept in a full-size bed."

"Yeah, that trailer is awfully small."

"You seem chipper. Did you catch the vandal?"

"No, not a sign, though I doubt we would have noticed. We both dropped off and didn't stir until after daybreak. You can only go so many days without sleep before it nails you."

Brad nodded. A solid night's rest could explain Zack's improved mood. "Maybe they've given up."

"Yeah. I'm hoping that after seeing us at dinner, the word will get out. Even if it's some local yahoos, which I'm sure it is, knowing we're solid has got to make them think twice about coming back."

Brad began the stretching exercises the physical therapist had recommended doing before attempting something more strenuous. It did seem to help. He planned to walk several miles before meeting Kim at the harbor. She wanted to take a sail on the little cove below the resort before flying back to San Francisco.

"It's too bad that you planned your dinner with

Jamie while Kim was here," he said. "Otherwise, you could have eaten together."

"Why didn't you guys meet up for dinner?"

He shrugged. "I got onto Skype with a few of the guys from my old unit."

"Oh, that's great. I'd better shower and get to work."

Zack disappeared behind his door and Brad headed out for his walk. As usual, he would swing by the fruit stand. Lately he'd been making the circuit twice a day, morning and afternoon; it meant he was getting stronger. The guys he'd talked to from his unit hadn't asked about him returning to active duty and he didn't know the possibilities himself. Pushing his limits was the only way to find out.

AFTER THE MAR VISTA staff picked up their produce, Jamie posted a sign saying she'd be back soon and asked customers to put any money in the metal box. Fortunately, Sunday mornings were slow. She had to hike back to the house and get the truck to refill her water reserve. As she was fastening the sign to the canopy pole, Zack's SUV rolled up.

"Hi," he called. "I figured you'd need your truck, so I came to give you a ride."

The crumb. How dare he do something so thoughtful?

But it *was* convenient and refusing would be ridiculous, so she grabbed her tote bag and slid into the passenger seat.

"I'm staying home tonight," she said, forestalling anything else he might say. "Nothing's happened and everyone will have the whole day to talk about us having dinner."

Yet she almost laughed at her own words.

Nothing had happened?

Nothing, except ending up in bed with the last man she'd ever expected to "know" in that way. The fact that it had been incredibly pleasurable didn't change the fact it was a mistake, and it would be dumb to chance another night with Zack in the tight confines of the trailer. Sure as anything, they'd wind up between the sheets again. Zack's arousal as he'd watched her get dressed that morning showed he wanted more, and her body was clamoring for another round, as well. But if she slept at home, there was no risk of making the same mistake again.

Zack pulled up in front of her house. "Are you sure you won't be heading over there at nightfall?"

"Are you trying to convince me I should?"

"No, I don't want you doing anything reckless."

She slid out of the seat. "Too late," she muttered.

"What was that?" he called through the half-open window.

"Nothing," she snapped. "Thanks for the ride."

"You don't sound grateful," he taunted.

"Go eat a golf ball."

"Just being neighborly. I'll overlook your bad mood."

Boy, did he think he was clever. A caveman, covered in hair and crowing at the sun because he'd nailed the girl.

With a wave, he drove away, and she hurried to the house. As long as she was home without having to walk, she might as well change her clothing. Filling the tank on the back of the truck wouldn't take long, so she'd get back to the stand without much delay.

As the morning wore on at the trailer, Jamie realized she could have ordered more stock for the day, but that was okay. Finishing early was terrific and she drove into town gratefully. There was time to run errands and still clean the house, maybe even work on her jewelry. No crowding into a dark trailer with the windows shut so she couldn't even hear the ocean clearly. No spending it with a sexy guy who was the opposite of what she wanted, *if* she even wanted a guy in the first place. Which she didn't.

Around eleven, Jamie crawled into her freshly laundered sheets and turned out the lights. An hour later she was still staring through the bedroom window at the stars and listening to the distant murmur of the ocean.

After her divorce, one of her girlfriends had rushed to give her advice, saying she needed an "interim lover" before looking for a permanent partner. Jamie had smiled, while privately rejecting the idea. Her plan had been to opt out of romance altogether, yet she'd ended up with an interim lover after all.

And she didn't have any illusions—Zack was

temporary. Sure, they had a physical combustibility that put Ma O'Leary's cow and the Chicago fire to shame. But beyond lust, they didn't have a shred of common ground aside from the piece of land he wanted, and she would never sell.

Jamie threw back her blankets. Maybe a cup of warm milk with sugar and vanilla would help her sleep.

At the big windows overlooking the salt flats and ocean, she sipped the milk and tried to relax before going back to bed. Marlin rubbed around her ankles, yowling a complaint. Cats liked predictability and the past four nights had unsettled his expectations of the world.

Back in bed, Jamie patted the pillow. Marlin finally jumped up and stared at her in the gray darkness.

"Right," she agreed. "I was unfaithful to you. Another male spent the night in my bed, and I've got to admit, he knew what he was doing."

Marlin yawned.

"Yeah, I suppose you have no interest in that side of life since you've been fixed. Otherwise I might try to find a sweet little feline number at the animal shelter to keep you company."

Jamie rolled over, punched her pillow and stewed. When Zack had kissed her the first time, she'd wondered whether he might be thinking getting close to her would help him get what he wanted. The possibility still couldn't be ruled out, at least subconsciously on his part. Zack Denning was a man who made professional and financial achievement his top priority. Even if she did want a relationship with someone, it *wouldn't* be with someone like him.

CHAPTER TEN

SEVERAL DAYS LATER Jamie decided that sleeping in her own bed had made little difference to the amount of rest she was getting. She was spending entirely too much energy thinking about the way Zack had touched her. Of course, her sexual experience was mostly limited to her ex-husband, which wasn't much to judge by. On the other hand, Zack might have set an unreasonably high standard. Though it was hard to be sure since he'd given her the first genuinely explosive orgasm of her life; it might not seem so incredible a second time.

On Wednesday evening when she heard the clock in the living room chime midnight, she groaned— she'd been in bed for hours without a minute of sleep. The idea kept sneaking into her head that she ought to give herself another night with Zack and prove to herself that sex with him wasn't such a big deal. If she ever changed her mind and decided to make a future with someone, then it wouldn't be fair to have Zack as an impossible standard.

Idiot.

Jamie punched her pillow, and Marlin jumped from the bed, thoroughly offended at being disturbed.

The prior winter had been so nice—no land-dispute complications, no customers or lawyers, and best of all, no men or churned-up emotions. Was it any wonder that Granddad had lived as a hermit most of the year? It now seemed utterly sane the way he'd sold vegetables for a few months, spending time on the land he cherished, and afterward retreated to his house while the world rushed on without him.

She yawned and tucked her hand beneath her cheek, finally drifting to sleep.

When the phone rang, jolting her awake, it felt as if she'd barely closed her eyes. Lifting the portable handset, she stared blearily at the caller ID before answering. It was her father. Much as she loved him, she'd have preferred more sleep.

"Hello, Dad."

"Hi, sweetheart. Did I wake you?"

Jamie glanced at the clock. "It doesn't matter. I have to be up soon to go to the fruit stand."

"That's why I called at this hour. I know you aren't a morning person, but you told us you were going out to the stand early these days. Of course, I guess I could have called you later, when you were at the trailer…though I'd hate to disturb you when you're helping a customer."

There was a tone in his voice that his family knew well. Her father was terrific, but quite capable of anxiously hemming and hawing around a subject without ever getting down to it.

"What's up?" she asked.

"It's… Well…you see, Tim called yesterday. Your mother and I decided we should let you know."

Lord. Jamie had hoped Tim had gotten the message that his calls weren't welcome since he'd finally stopped his incessant attempts to contact her directly.

"What did he want?"

"To ask how you are. He said he didn't want to bother you, but hoped we could fill him in."

Jamie closed her eyes and counted to ten. She didn't blame her parents for being confused over the end of her marriage; she'd never explained what a jerk Tim had turned out to be.

"What did you tell him?"

"That everything was fine. It is, isn't it?"

"Absolutely. I'm quite happy about the move here."

And, aside from total confusion concerning a particular man and his effect on her libido, it was the truth. The vandalism was a bump in the road, nothing more. As for her libido, she'd deal with it…though admittedly, it was a lot easier to abstain from sex when your experience with it was indifferent at best.

"That's wonderful," her father said. "We've been worried with the house being so isolated. Not to mention the fruit stand out on the dunes and you there all day by yourself with people coming and going."

"There's no need to be concerned," she assured

him. "And I'm not alone out here any longer. There's a big new resort next door and lots of high-toned people who are always around." She didn't want to mention Zack or Brad, because if Tim called again, her folks would probably get chatty and pass on any information they'd heard. "Look, Dad, Tim shouldn't be calling you. We aren't married any longer."

"Even if a marriage ends, that doesn't mean people stop caring."

"I know. It's just…" Her voice trailed off. She'd planned to say it was her business and she didn't want anyone else mixed up in it, but her father wouldn't understand. Divorce was relatively rare on both sides of the family and they were all trying to make sense of how to handle the changed relationships.

"Yes?" The anxious note in his voice had returned.

"Nothing. Don't worry about me. I'm doing great."

They chatted a few minutes longer before saying goodbye, and she hung up the phone in relief. It was her own fault—in order to protect her pride, she hadn't told her family the real reasons she'd ended her marriage, so there was no point in getting uptight that they didn't understand. But if Tim kept contacting her parents, she'd have to explain.

Stretching, she jumped out of bed and made a decision—sleep deprived or not, she would be in a good mood today.

At the fruit stand, she chatted with the farmers as they unloaded boxes. She washed berries for sampling and greeted Brad when he arrived. It was barely past eight-thirty, but Brad Denning was military and she'd always suspected that marines rose before dawn and bench-pressed trucks for light exercise.

"Isn't this a fantastic day?" she asked, waving at the brilliant blue sky.

"The best," he agreed.

Brad didn't stay long and said he'd probably see her on his second circuit. She admired his determination and wondered if he anticipated a return to active duty. From what he'd said, he was eligible for twenty-year retirement—though talking about retirement seemed odd for a man who couldn't be more than forty. Brad wouldn't settle for coasting his life away, so if he retired, the challenge would be finding something else worth his dedication.

Not that it was her business.

It was when Zack dropped by that Jamie's cheerful mood faltered.

"Any more problems?" he asked.

"No. It's been fine."

"That's great." He looked distinctly uncomfortable. "Um, should we discuss the other night?"

"There's no need," she said quickly.

"It might be a good idea."

"And men say *women* have a burning need to rehash everything. I don't." The last thing Jamie wanted was to discuss *anything* with Zack, especially the other night. Her brain was reeling from the internal debate; she didn't need an external one.

Zack's gaze narrowed. "You can't tell me you take…uh…sex casually."

"No, though unlike you, I can say 'sex' without hesitation."

"I was trying to be sensitive. It's a buzzword for some women."

"Not for me," she lied. It wasn't a huge lie; it was more like stretching the truth. "And to be honest, I'm glad you didn't employ the phrase 'making love' or a euphemism such as 'going to bed together.' I don't need euphemisms and it wasn't making love. It was sex—a mistake we both made in the heat of the moment. We don't have to beat it to death with conversation."

He frowned. "I wouldn't necessarily call it a mistake. And even if it was, I'm at fault for initiating it."

She rolled her eyes. "Give it a rest. I was there, too, and unless you slipped something into my drink, I can take responsibility for my actions. Cripes, how long has it been since you had sex?"

"It's… Well, not since we broke ground, and I'm not sure when before that."

"That explains it—I was a drink after a long drought. No wonder it seemed hot." Privately, Jamie thought the idea was depressing, but she wouldn't admit it out loud. She'd never thought of herself as strikingly attractive, but she defied any woman under a hundred to be indifferent to how a man like Zack Denning saw her.

Zack shook his head. "It was more than that, or what I'm trying to say is that it wasn't—"

"So it wasn't hot?"

"It was hot, but *not* because it had been a while."

"Hmm. How can you be so sure?"

"Because…" He stopped when a car drove into view.

Jamie lifted her chin. "I have customers coming. Maybe we should wrap this up and—"

"I'd still like to talk about the land."

The remnants of her pleasant mood fled. "At the risk of sounding repetitious, I'm not selling."

"Yes, I know. But there may be other options to discuss. I could have some other signs painted, or even bring in a stand that would fit better."

"I really don't…" The car stopped and passengers spilled out. She sighed. "I'll give it some thought. Just leave, will you?"

The cheerful family careened toward the stand.

"Want some caramel corn, mister?" one sticky-faced youngster asked Zack, holding out his bag. He was around six years old, a darling age in Jamie's opinion, but Zack looked as if he were being confronted by an alien offering to suck out his brains.

"No. Uh, thanks." Zack backed away and glanced at Jamie. "We'll talk later."

His discomfort couldn't have been more obvious, and it occurred to Jamie that he probably didn't spend much time around kids. On his "tour" he'd explained the resort had facilities for children, including licensed nannies to provide child care, but it was primarily geared toward adults.

Children... A faint, melancholy ache went through Jamie,

She was still determined not to tie up her life with anyone, but that also meant kids weren't in the equation. Tim hadn't wanted a family and she'd given up hoping he'd decide otherwise, so when they'd divorced, getting pregnant was the last thing on her mind. If she ever considered another relationship, she'd most likely want children, which was another reason not to get romantic notions about Zack. Colicky babies and luxury resorts didn't exactly fit together. But then, she doubted marriage fit into his plans, either, so she had nothing to worry about, romantic notions or not.

ZACK DROVE AWAY from the Little Blue Fruit Stand in frustration. Damn, why had he admitted how long it was since he'd been with a woman? And he should have waited to talk about the land. To go from discussing sex to business was probably as crass as a guy could get. But he'd let himself get short-circuited again. Jamie had on a worn pair of jeans that showed her curves and a snug T-shirt that reminded him all too well how great she looked without it.

For days he'd been trying not to think of making love to her, yet this morning he'd had a sudden urge to talk, and not only about the fruit stand. Why *hadn't* she contacted him to discuss what had happened between them? She was right; that was what men expected women to do…beat a subject to death, or at least into abject submission, particularly when it came to relationships and intimacy.

Across the golf course he saw his brother, and it reminded him of what Jamie had said about Brad and Kim.

Was it possible they felt something for each other? He knew they'd crossed paths over the years. If Brad came through San Francisco he usually called Kim, and when he'd been stationed at Quantico in Virginia, she'd stopped to have dinner with him on her vacation. Hardly the courtship of the century, or if it was, it would take a century to get anywhere. Yet, Kim *was* visiting Mar Vista more often now that Brad was here; her name was on the reservations list again for the coming weekend.

Hell, he didn't have time to think about Brad and Kim at the moment. He was giving another personal tour to old friends that morning, and going to the fruit stand had taken most of the time he'd planned to spend reviewing purchase orders.

Lifting the microphone on the SUV radio, Zack signaled the office.

"Hey, boss," Trudy greeted him. "I thought you'd be here an hour ago."

"I got sidetracked. You checked those orders, right?"

"I always do."

"No issues with any of it?"

"Nope."

"Then send the approvals through."

"Sure, boss. Anything else?" Trudy's voice sounded brighter. Maybe her morning sickness had improved—so far it hadn't caused much disruption to the office, and he was trying to be genuinely happy for her and Rick. They were a terrific couple, and if having a baby was something they wanted, he shouldn't begrudge them that.

"Nothing right now. Talk to you later. I've got some folks I'm meeting."

"Have a good morning."

He signed off and headed to the restaurant where he was picking up Don and Nina Courtland. Strangely, the prospect of spending time with them seemed dull, but it was probably because it was the fourth tour he'd given in a week. Still, he was wondering if there were more important things to do than showing off swimming pools.

JAMIE FINISHED THE DAY, trying to restore her good humor. For a woman who'd accused her neighbor of being a grizzly bear, she had to admit to being quick on the draw herself lately. Zack, in particular, knew how to push every button she possessed, but he hadn't managed to push them that morning. Maybe it would get easier now that the sexual tension had been released. She hoped so.

Brad showed up as she was stowing the leftover produce in the back of the truck. It was his fourth loop of the day, and he'd pushed so hard, there was a yellowish-gray tinge to his face. The source of *his* restless tension wasn't a mystery—he'd mentioned that Kim was coming the next day. There was something both sad and hilarious about watching two people who'd been in love for years and didn't have a clue how they felt.

"Want a ride?" she asked as she finished her final tally.

He hesitated, pride obviously warring with good sense. "Sure," he said. "To the gate."

"Is there any chance you cook?" she said as they climbed into the truck cab. "I've got more leftovers than usual."

"I can knock together a meal."

"Good—grab one of the paper sacks in the back when you get out."

At the main entrance he did as she'd suggested and limped down the road; she wished he'd let her drive him to his door, but the man was too stubborn.

That evening she cast a pendant she'd been working on and was pleased when she examined the finished piece later that night. It should work well for the art gallery. If it sold quickly, she might make more. She'd thought of casting unique designs, the problem being that they'd have to be very high priced. But she could make limited runs and number them.

Things were getting back to normal. Zack obviously wasn't through with his efforts to change things at the stand, but she could deal with it. She might even agree to new signs, yet she wasn't sure about retiring Granddad's trailer. It was a tradition.

With so much falling into place, she should have fallen asleep easier, but it was well after midnight before she drifted off. For someone getting up by six, it was an awfully short night. Even so, she drove to the stand that Friday morning with renewed determination to relax and keep a good attitude. She was confident she'd be successful—as long as Zack didn't show up.

As she drove over the dirt road, she looked at the trailer and slammed on the brakes.

It was a mess.

After days of nothing happening...now this. The canopy was knocked down but the fabric was spread out, showcasing a sloppily spray-painted Get Out. Some of her display boxes were thrown aside and broken, as if someone had backed a car into them.

She parked and walked around the trailer, feeling sick. The chairs were gone.... She found them thrown over the rise on the beach. Spoiled fruit was smeared over everything, and when she went inside the trailer, she found it was smashed on the walls there, as well. That was the worst part and tears stung. It seemed a particular sacrilege, to invade a private space and make it the target of such nasty venom.

Jamie decided sadly that cleaning the interior would have to wait until she'd taken care of the more visible damage. First, she had to hide the spray-painted letters on the canopy before her deliveries started arriving. Fingers trembling, she snapped several pictures with her phone for documentation. Then she cleared away the debris and half rolled and folded the awning so she could shove it out of sight.

Setting her jaw, she collected the scattered chunks of wood that had formed the foundation of her display trays and put them in a pile. She might not be an expert carpenter, but she could probably reconstruct them.

She was glad she'd gotten the canopy's spiteful message hidden immediately, because Burt Friesen arrived as she was raking up the rotten fruit.

"What happened?" he demanded.

"Oh." She tried to shrug as though it wasn't a big deal. "Some teenagers must have gone wild last night. I should have put the chain on. They were probably drunk and out joyriding."

"Let me help."

"Thanks, but I can handle it. Besides, you have more deliveries to make."

The other farmers came soon after, requiring the same dance around the truth. Corey Tappen brought the last loganberries of the season, then insisted on retrieving her chairs from the beach. While Jamie had been determined to take care of it herself, she couldn't help being grateful. The chairs might be made of plastic, but they were solid and awkward to move.

But she wouldn't let anyone do anything else and tried to sound brave and cheery as she sent them on their way. Next she sorted out the Mar Vista goods before getting back to her cleanup. She'd have to jury-rig something for displays, and would have to work fast if she didn't want Gordon's guys to see this.

"Hell." Brad's voice growled behind her as she was wiping the sides of the trailer with a bleach-soaked paper towel to kill the odor of spoiled fruit.

"You can say that again," she agreed.

"What can I do?"

"It's okay. I can handle it."

"I said, what can I do?"

A resigned laugh rumbled in Jamie's chest. "Can you figure out how to make a display?"

While she finished cleaning, Brad used the tools she had in her truck and repaired enough of the wood racks for her to get by for the day.

"How about the canopy?" he asked as they moved strawberries and vegetables into place.

It was a shame to let Brad see the spray-painted message, but the awning was important since it protected her stock from the sun. His expression grew dangerous as he read the words scrawled on the fabric.

"I'm sure it isn't anyone connected with Mar Vista," she said hastily.

"They're the only ones who want you gone."

The inescapable logic bothered her, but she couldn't believe it was the work of Zack or his employees. And there was logic *against* it being connected to Mar Vista, too. Zack was already installing a high hedge down the critical section of his golf course, separating it from the public road and the view of her signs and the trailer. The company providing the mature shrubbery and trees had brought in cranes and specialized digging equipment, but the resort staff was coordinating the effort.

And so far the Mar Vista grounds workers had shown no sign of anger; in fact, they'd waved and smiled and some bought fruit for a snack. The grounds manager, Rick Lopez, was among them. He had explained that he'd designed a layered effect to make the hedge look like a natural area of thick native growth, even sketching his ideas for her. He'd seemed pleased to have someone show an interest and had incorporated a suggestion she'd offered.

"I don't think it's anyone from the resort," she repeated to Brad.

There was little they could do about the spray paint on the awning. Jamie scrubbed off the rotted fruit and sprayed the fabric with a mild cleaning solution, and Brad helped get it up and pulled taut. She was pleased to see that no one could read the Get Out once the canopy was in place.

"Thanks, Brad," she said as the Mar Vista truck pulled in. Everything looked the way it should.

"Gotta pay for my breakfast," he said with a grin as he accepted a bowl of strawberries. He sat and ate the fruit before starting on the second half of his long walk. Since she was busy with customers at the time, they only waved at each other when he left.

Once she was alone, she bagged extra bits of debris before going inside to begin the painful cleanup there.

"Jamie?"

It was Zack's voice, and Jamie's shoulders sagged. What did he want? She didn't have the energy to deal with him, but she had no choice.

ZACK GLANCED AROUND and called Jamie's name again. Her truck was here, so she must be, too.

The trailer door opened and she slid outside. There was a smell of bleach and he was reminded of the first day they'd met, except today she was wearing cutoffs rather than her overalls, despite the morning's cool air. Her long legs were displayed down to the most disreputable pair of tennis shoes he'd ever seen. Damn, she looked hot.

"Yes?"

"Listen, I've been thinking about what you said." Yet even as he spoke, a carload of customers drove into sight. "I'll wait." He made his way to the chairs and tried not to listen to the chattering group of women. They were on a drive from the city and thought the stand was *soooo* charming. Some recalled visiting years before and asked about George Jenkins; Jamie started explaining about her grandfather.

Zack leaned his head back and closed his eyes. His thoughts turned to Jamie's comments about Kim and Brad. How could he have been so blind, and how could he let them see that he was okay with them getting together? In fact, he thought it was terrific, but that wasn't the kind of thing you could blurt out to either your brother *or* your former lover.

That morning, while sipping cold coffee in the SUV and staring at the horse stables, it had suddenly occurred to him that Jamie might have an idea. She was prickly, but she seemed to understand people in a unique way. And she'd seen what was happening with Brad and Kim when they hadn't even recognized it themselves.

It was also a good excuse to see her. He didn't like the way their conversation had gone the day before. Maybe he could salvage it in some way.

CHAPTER ELEVEN

JAMIE ENJOYED THE group of women who'd stopped, and wouldn't have minded if they'd stayed longer and given her time to think before talking with Zack.

Judging from the expression on his face, she doubted he knew about the vandalism. With a little luck it would stay that way, at least until she'd figured out what to do. He was so busy that Brad rarely saw him, and she'd promised Brad that she had no intention of staying at the trailer again. It wasn't unreasonable to hope Zack wouldn't get the news for a while.

Whoever was doing the damage must have figured out she was watching, so they'd waited until she was lulled into believing it was over. She couldn't take up residence in the trailer for the rest of the summer, so she'd have to devise another plan.

"Got them squared away?" Zack asked as she put the money into her cash box.

"Yep. Some of the women remembered me from when I was a kid, though I can't return the favor. They said that once a year they leave their husbands

to fend for themselves and take a weekend trip together. They must have a strong friendship—there
were five of them in that tiny Volkswagen."

"That would be one way to test it," he agreed.

"So, what's on your mind?" she asked. "Sex or
my land?"

"That's direct."

"Shock value. It throws people off guard. I should
market the concept to the navy."

"What if it isn't sex *or* the land?"

"You mean you're actually expanding your conversational topics?"

A peculiar smile played on Zack's lips. "Bleach
has an odd effect on you. You're using it today, and
were the day we met. You run in bigger verbal circles when the stuff's in the air."

"You should see Marlin when he's high on it. He
goes nutty, same as some cats do for catnip, except
it puts him in a bad mood. Granddad used to say
he was a mean drunk."

"Kim told me he was a mutant."

It was an odd conversation, and she did feel light-
headed. The bleach could be the cause, or the lack of
sleep, or the sexy guy sitting there that she shouldn't
be with again, or the fact that someone had trashed
her business and she didn't have a clue why, except
that she was an unwelcome neighbor to the afore-
mentioned sexy guy's resort.

The chairs usually sat next to each other, but

Jamie pulled the empty one around so it was farther away and faced Zack.

"You haven't offered me strawberries yet," he said in a mock aggrieved tone.

"There's a bowl there. You know how to help yourself."

He ate a couple while her mind raced in circles. Whatever Zack wanted, he was almost as bad as her father at getting to the point.

"I was thinking of what you told me about Brad and Kim," he said finally. "The idea of them getting together is terrific, if a little weird. I don't know how they'd work it out, but that's their business."

"Right."

"Do you really suppose Brad imagines he'd come between me and Kim?"

Jamie frowned. "He probably hasn't consciously thought about it that way. I'm guessing he just thinks the two of you are connected, so he won't let himself see how much he's attracted to her. He might even believe you still have feelings for each other."

"How do I let Brad know it's okay if they hook up?" Zack asked.

"Have you considered the direct approach? Simply tell him."

"Uh…we don't talk about things like that. That is…I wouldn't know where to start."

In spite of the morning's trauma, the humor of the present situation struck Jamie. Zack was so uncomfortable at the idea of a heart-to-heart chat with his brother that he was practically stuttering at the prospect.

Jamie rolled her eyes. "Try 'Hey, Brad, I think you and Kim would be a great couple—have you thought about getting together with her?'"

Zack shifted in his chair. "I can't leap into a conversation that way. How about you drop some hints to him? He's here a lot."

"Coward."

"It has nothing to do with that," he claimed with injured dignity.

"No, it has to do with being a man."

"Brad would be more comfortable talking about it with you than me," Zack insisted. "Women find it easier to talk about romance, and that would put him at ease."

"You can't resist those stereotypes, can you?" Jamie asked, amused all over again. The guy would do anything to escape a discussion about emotions with his brother.

"Whatever. Will you do it?"

"No." His face fell and she sighed. "Brad needs to hear it from you. He won't believe it otherwise."

Zack sat back in frustration and stared at the ocean for a few minutes. Jamie closed her eyes so she wouldn't be tempted to watch him and remember the wrong things. Instead she thought about how to catch the creep who was trashing the fruit stand.

"I know," Zack exclaimed, breaking into her thoughts. "Kim is coming up again today."

"Yeah, Brad mentioned it." Jamie didn't add that Kim had also called *her,* arranging a time to come see her jewelry.

"Let's all have dinner together at the Grotto. If you come as my date, it automatically pairs up Kim and Brad. Nothing *has* to be said—they'll both just know."

"Is that your answer for everything?" she asked, stalling to consider his idea. "Have dinner?"

"Food is an age-old remedy. In this case, it couldn't hurt for everyone to see us together again, either."

It wasn't a bad idea, although she still didn't believe anyone on his staff was involved in the vandalism. Even so, like he said, it couldn't hurt.

"Maybe."

"However, it really should be at the Sunfish Grotto. Casual dining won't send the same message to Kim and Brad as something more formal."

As much as Jamie hated the idea of dressing up, and wasn't sure what she'd wear, he was right. Two people on a date would likely choose the most elegant and romantic location available, even if they were double-dating. She didn't know if there was a protocol when former lovers were involved, but relationships weren't her forte in the first place.

"Okay," she said. "When did you want to do it?"

"If Kim agrees, how about tonight at seven or eight? I'll call her office, or text her. When is best for you?"

"Eight," Jamie replied, thinking of everything she had to do. Purchase a security camera—one that was sensitive enough to film at night and had a motion sensor. Maybe she'd buy two, put them in unobtrusive locations. All she wanted was evidence of who was attacking the stand; she'd give the video to Curt and he could handle it from there. It was what she should have done in the first place. If she had, her feelings for Zack Denning wouldn't have gotten so complicated.

"Jamie?" Zack caught her attention. "You look a million miles away. I was saying that I'll pick you up at seven forty-five. Do you dance? We've got a band at the Grotto on Friday evenings."

"I dance." Maybe when she went to buy the camera, she could shop around for something to wear. After she finished cleaning the trailer's interior she'd leave the box to collect the money and run into town.

ZACK WAS ANNOYED with himself as he left the fruit stand. The plan to have dinner at the Sunfish Grotto was fine, but he hadn't dealt with other important matters. Ironically, Jamie had given him the perfect opening with her crack about sex or land, but he hadn't been able to focus.

At the moment he was going to play golf with someone who wanted to invest in Mar Vista. He'd have to find a nice way of refusing the investment funds, or of saying he'd consider it without discouraging the guest from returning in the future.

It was a nice endorsement having a financial whiz interested in putting his money into the resort. But Zack wanted to make it on his own, without investors who'd try to control how he managed the place. He'd accepted his parents' investment funds only because it was so important to them to help.

Anyway, he didn't need investors. He was putting extra on his loan payments, along with building a healthy contingency fund. With the way reservations were filling for the months ahead, a time could come when he'd have to turn away customers. Before Mar Vista had opened, he'd had the lobby decorated for Christmas so pictures could be taken to promote the holidays. Amazingly, they were already a third booked for December—in June. Things looked better than he'd ever hoped they could.

Still, it would be wise to promise that he'd consider an investor rather than give a straight no. It made sense to keep his options open.

KIM QUICKLY SIGNED two letters and handed them to her office assistant. She was in a hurry, hoping to get to the airport before the noon traffic rush.

"Maybe we should change the return address to Mar Vista since you're going up so often," Chloe suggested with a barely concealed smile.

Kim pressed her lips together, unaccountably annoyed. She knew she'd surprised Chloe by planning yet another weekend in a row at Mar Vista. Admittedly, it was out of character, but stepping outside the box could be a good thing.

"Is something going on...romancewise, that is?" Chloe asked. They'd known each other for so long that her assistant sometimes got personal; it would have been a problem except she was strictly business when anyone else was present. Kim was well aware that some people still expected a higher degree of professionalism from a female attorney than they did from a male.

"If you're asking whether Zack Denning is still single, the answer is yes...as far as I know," she said. "I'm simply going up there to relax. I haven't gone on vacation in over three years and can't take one this summer, either. Mar Vista is great for short breaks."

"Uh...sure." A hint of pink brightened Chloe's cheeks; when she'd first met Zack she had acted like a lovesick puppy.

Kim had decided to treat herself to another trip after discovering flaws in a new client's paperwork. The Parkers had passed the contract to her, mostly as an afterthought, since their previous attorney had already approved it. They hadn't been happy about going to a new law firm, but their lawyer of thirty years was retiring and closing his office. Their attitude had improved radically after she brought the problems to their attention and they were now recommending Wheeler and Associates to everyone.

The firm was getting so many inquiries she might have to recruit another associate.

Changing the pace by going to Mar Vista *was* proving helpful, with the added bonus of seeing friends. The previous Sunday, she'd had lunch with Zack before going boating with Brad. Leaving later in the afternoon had been the only hard part; given a chance, the resort could feel like a second home. In fact, she'd been given the same suite on each visit, and when she'd mentioned it to Zack, he'd said it was policy, unless a guest requested a different room or it was otherwise occupied.

No question, Zack knew what he was doing when it came to the resort, however badly he'd handled things with Jamie Conroe. She wondered if they would ever resolve things—both parties were firmly entrenched in their positions.

Poor Zack—he was so passionate about Mar Vista, and Kim had to admit the fruit stand *was* an eyesore; his high-profile guests would also likely see it negatively. She assumed the land dispute had gotten pushed aside because of the vandalism. And, according to Brad, Zack had gotten his nose out of joint at the suggestion that one of his employees could be involved.

Men and their pride. Zack and Brad were both overly endowed with the stuff.

"Mr. Denning hasn't called recently," Chloe commented with a hint of disappointment in her voice.

"You must be handling his legal issues while you're at Mar Vista."

"Fortunately, there haven't *been* any legal issues," Kim said. And it was true—the problem with the fruit stand didn't have a legal resolution, which kept her out of it, thank heaven. She'd tried discussing it with Brad, but he'd gotten a little funky on the subject. It had to be hard for him, since he'd become friends with Jamie, but felt loyal to his brother.

Kim distractedly told Chloe she'd see her in a few days and hurried downstairs to hail a cab.

SHORTLY AFTER TWO that afternoon, Brad drove to Mar Vista's airstrip to meet Kim's plane. A resort employee could have picked her up, but Zack had wanted one of them to meet her. He'd asked Brad to do it since he had a commitment with another guest.

Brad was happy to meet the plane, but it was annoying. If his jackass brother wasn't careful, he'd lose his chance with Kim; she was too smart to waste time on a guy who was always too busy for her.

And now, between running the resort and helping with Jamie's troubles, Zack might go into work hyperdrive just as Kim was here again. At least Jamie wasn't sleeping in the trailer anymore and *was* seeking another solution.

He didn't know what kind of bastard would commit the kind of vandalism he'd seen at the fruit stand. It was violence of its own sort.

He leaned against the car and watched a speck in the sky until it turned out to be a bird, then another, and then another—this one turned out to be a Cessna. It seemed to hover lightly in the air before coming in. It was Kim, and as with everything she did, she landed with incredible grace.

The plane taxied close to the hangar and an employee rolled steps to the side of the plane.

"Hi, Brad," she exclaimed on spotting him. "Good to see you."

He was glad that she didn't seem disappointed that Zack wasn't meeting her.

"Same here," he answered. "From your expression, I'd say you have the world by the tail."

"I had an especially good week. You look as if you're doing better."

"I'm working on it."

"But something's bothering you."

Had she always been this perceptive?

"Yeah," he agreed. "Jamie Conroe's fruit stand was hit again, worse than ever, and someone wrote a get-out message on the canopy she uses for shade."

"Cripes. What can be done?"

"She's working on a solution. I told her to call if I can do anything to help." Brad didn't add that Zack had also gotten involved.

"I'm going over there tomorrow to…well, for girl stuff," she said with a smile. "I'll talk with her, too."

"Crap, I shouldn't have mentioned it. You deal with problems all week and deserve a chance to relax."

"That doesn't mean I stop caring about my friends."

"Of course not, but Zack is right about people needing a place to get a reprieve from real life."

She laughed, a low musical note he enjoyed hearing. "It's nice that you can see some point to Mar Vista."

"Give me a break," he protested.

"Okay, okay. I'm just having fun. You picking me up was a nice surprise. I didn't figure on seeing you until dinner."

"What about dinner?"

"Zack sent me a text saying he hoped we could all eat at the Grotto at eight. Didn't you know?"

That must be what Zack had scribbled on the note he'd left on the kitchen counter. Brad hadn't been entirely sure what it said. Maybe he shouldn't go. Kim and Zack ought to have privacy, or at least what passed for it in a public restaurant.

"I should probably stay home," he suggested. "That would give the two of you a chance to catch up with each other."

"No way," Kim protested. "I come up here partly to visit old friends, and not just one of them. If you don't go, I won't, either."

Kim also had a graceful way of including everybody, and he had to admit it was a more appealing prospect than eating alone.

AT FIVE O'CLOCK, Zack dragged himself in from the golf course. He'd played not one, but two rounds with guests—one in the morning, and another in the afternoon. Now that he wasn't an employed manager of a resort, some folks figured he was a man of leisure.

"Hi, Trudy," he said as he came into the office and slumped into a chair.

She regarded him sympathetically. "Maybe we should make a schedule," she suggested tentatively. "We could block out specific periods when you're free to spend time with guests."

"Good idea."

"It will ease up soon," she said. "Right now it's a novelty."

Zack knew that, and since he'd invited the interest of his various friends and acquaintances in his future resort for years, he could hardly complain that they were excited by its realization.

"There's another possibility," Trudy said. "Have you thought of hiring a second golf pro to go out with guests when they want someone and you're busy?"

"Good idea. You know, Trudy, it's obvious you think like a resort manager. I've thought about making you an operations supervisor or something of the kind, but don't know if you're interested now that you're starting a family."

Trudy's eyes opened wide. "I would, though there are a number of things we'd have to discuss first. But I thought you were determined to do it all yourself."

"I guess I was, but…things change."

Yes, things change, including him, he thought. Over the past weeks, Zack had been shifting his way of handling resort matters. He still wasn't entirely sure why, but the look in Trudy's eyes when he brought up this latest idea suggested he was on the right track.

"There's a note from Brad on your desk. He left it there this morning."

Lord, that was how he and his brother had to communicate now: exchanging notes. He *had* to slow down enough to spend time with Brad, though not while Kim was here—instead, he'd encourage the two of them to spend it together.

On his desk was a sealed envelope with his name printed in the neat block letters Brad used, much more respectable than his own scribbles. He opened the letter and his blood began to boil.

Damn. Damn. *Damn.*

He charged out of his office.

Trudy was startled. "Something wrong, boss?"

"Tell you later," he snapped as he strode through the door and dived into his SUV.

Damn that woman. He'd *been* at the fruit stand

that morning; it couldn't have been more than an hour after she'd finished cleaning up the latest mess from the vandals. Why the hell hadn't she told him?

It was tempting to gun the accelerator, but he held to the resort speed limit until he squealed to a stop by the fruit stand.

Dammit.

Jamie's truck was gone.

He headed for her house. Sure enough, there was her truck. He stomped up the steps to pound on the front door.

Faint footsteps came from inside, and the door opened after a pause. "Good grief, Zack," Jamie said. "Is the house on fire or something?"

"Why didn't you tell me the stand got trashed?"

Jamie shrugged. "It wasn't your problem in the first place. I'm taking care of it."

"Not my problem? Why in hell wouldn't you think I'd care for any other reason, if only as a neighbor? And we've definitely become closer than that."

Her lips thinned. "I don't need your concern. It's very nice and manly of you, but it's up to me to protect my own business. You don't need to worry— I'm not sleeping at the trailer anymore, and this time I mean it."

The words were strangely disappointing, but he couldn't stop to analyze it at the moment.

"Then what *are* you going to do?" he demanded.

"What I should have done in the first place. Whoever's involved must have figured out I was watching. So I've set up a couple of security cameras. They have motion sensors and will record whatever happens. Whatever evidence I gather, I'll pass on to the sheriff."

It was a sensible idea, though he had another concern. "What about here at the house? The jerk who's doing this might not stop at the fruit stand."

"I'm perfectly all right in my own home," she said. "Don't get any ideas—you are *not* staying with me."

Her face was angry and so stubborn he couldn't believe it. "Why are you so hell-bent on doing this by yourself?"

"It's *my* business."

"That's not an answer."

"Look, it's about self-respect and being able to stand on my own two feet. There's enough victim mentality in the world, people who think they have to rely on someone else to come along and fix things. I'm not going to do it anymore and I'm not going to let anyone push me around."

Zack ran his fingers through his hair, tense with the frustration Jamie always seemed to provoke. He supposed her attitude was healthy enough—in fact, it sounded like rhetoric from a consciousness-raising seminar. The concept was fine, but she was carrying it to a ridiculous length. No one could do everything completely on their own.

He tried to calm down. "Look, Jamie. I'm not asking you to become a doormat. I'm just saying that whoever is doing this isn't very...nice."

"Wow," she interjected. "I wouldn't have known that if you hadn't come along to tell me."

"Quit trying to sidetrack the issue," he retorted. "This is a bad person and *no one* should have to stand up to that alone."

"What if someone was targeting your resort?"

"That's different."

"Because you're a man?"

Okay, she had him there. But it wasn't the same for men and women, if only because some bad people targeted a woman, figuring she was more vulnerable. Besides, if someone was trying to hurt the resort, he wouldn't hesitate to bring in the police or security guards...okay, she was doing that, too... but it still wasn't the same.

"This isn't just nasty-minded vandalism," he said, ignoring the male-female issue. "Brad says someone spray-painted a get-out-of-Dodge-type message on the canopy."

"Crap, I hoped he wouldn't mention that."

"I haven't seen him all day, but he wrote a very detailed note. I just found it on my desk or I would have hauled my ass over here earlier."

She cocked her head and gave a strained grin. "Do you talk like that to your refined guests?"

"If they were doing what you are, I might."

"And they would probably say the same thing I am. Keep your nose *and* your ass out of my business."

Zack barely restrained himself from kissing the obstinate expression from Jamie's face—then he *would* be guilty of using a male ploy to influence the situation. But how could he make her see sense? It scared him to think that whoever was vandalizing the fruit stand could go after the house...or Jamie. She needed someone with her.

"You'd better go home and change," she advised. "We've got a pretend dinner date in a few hours and no one's going to buy it, least of all Kim and Brad, if you don't play the part. Try being suave, sophisticated and romantic, instead of bullheaded and angry."

"Me bullheaded? That's the pot calling the kettle black."

Some of the tension was easing between them, but Zack wasn't about to forget the main issue. They'd take it up again, after their dinner with Brad and Kim.

"I'll be here shortly after seven-thirty."

"I'll be ready."

He drove away, torn between conflicting emotions, among them a surprising disappointment that they wouldn't be sleeping in that hideous blue trailer together another night. The enforced intimacy had turned into something quite pleasurable. And he'd enjoyed being with Jamie, even *before* spending the night in the same bed.

They could be friends if she didn't have so many sharp edges. Then again, she might say he had just as many edges after the way he'd handled their land dispute.

The land dispute.

He hadn't found the time to give *that* issue the thought it needed. There had to be a solution that worked for both of them.

JAMIE WATCHED ZACK's vehicle disappear down her long driveway. She didn't like the way his words had made her feel, or the reminder that Granddad's house was isolated. Her dad had even mentioned the fact. It had never bothered her before. Upon first moving in she'd considered a security system, but quickly dismissed the need; now she had to admit to wishing she had one. But there was no way she'd admit that to Zack, who obviously didn't have a clue how important it was for her to stay independent.

She refused to explain her marriage or the anger with herself for taking so long to divorce Tim.

Somewhere inside, she'd known better. Tim's attempts to tear down her confidence were so typical. Why hadn't she seen that, instead of making excuses for him? While violence hadn't dominated their relationship, she should have left the first time he twisted her arm. But she hadn't. She'd stayed and become more and more overwhelmed.

It gave her a load of sympathy for women in similar circumstances. Walking out was tough. Thank heaven she hadn't also had children to consider.

One thing she was sure of: she never wanted to feel so powerless again. If it took being stubborn and determined to take care of things by herself without help, then so be it.

CHAPTER TWELVE

JAMIE LOCKED THE front door and checked the windows and other doors before heading to the bedroom. It wasn't paranoia; it was simply good sense, something everyone should practice. *Common* sense. Being independent didn't mean being reckless.

Now she had to get ready for dinner at a fancy restaurant.

After setting up the camera at the trailer, she'd thought about returning to Warrington to buy an appropriate outfit for the Sunfish Grotto. If it was as fancy as she'd heard, something casual wouldn't cut it. But a spate of customers had come and she'd finally decided it wasn't possible. The problem was that left only one possible gown for her to wear... the green one in the back of the closet. That dress was a reminder of her past life, and her old feelings of vulnerability.

She lifted her chin and firmed her spine. If she wasn't going to let an ex-husband overwhelm her, or a vandal, or even a sexy guy like Zack, she sure wouldn't let an *evening dress.*

Deciding to give herself the full treatment, Jamie ran a bath in the deep, old-fashioned tub and added lilac bath salts. Only a few. She disliked heavy scents and used no products with fragrance otherwise. Who needed a dozen cheap perfumes in laundry soap and such? But she did enjoy a faint lilac scent on occasion, so she sank into the tub and closed her eyes with pleasure.

After a long soak, she washed her hair and let it dry while she painted her nails and smoothed silky cream over herself. That kind of pampering had been rare lately and it felt incredibly good, though it evoked a memory of Zack running his fingers over her skin and kissing her almost everywhere.... No, best to forget that.

She chose her sexiest black lingerie—lacy briefs and a bra that had always made her feel confident. Instead of panty hose, which she hated, she slipped on stockings with garters, then swept her hair back to fall in waves down her shoulders.

Now, the dress.

Fortunately, it wasn't the kind to get rumpled easily, so she slipped into it, half hoping it might not fit anymore. The soft fabric slipped easily down her hips and brushed her ankles. Stroking it smooth, she turned to the full-length mirror and stared at her reflection.

She couldn't recall why she'd bought the dress in the first place, but it brought out the auburn tints in her dark hair and made her eyes seem a deeper blue.

The color complemented the light tan in her skin and hugged her figure in the right places, leaving bare shoulders and just the right amount of cleavage.

She looked good. Her ex-husband and the past be damned. Whenever she had a chance to wear this dress in the future, she'd grab it.

Zack would soon be arriving, so she quickly touched up her hair, mussed from pulling on the gown. Since she'd bought the dress for a Christmas party, she'd picked out a velvet wrap in a darker green to go with it, which would be welcome for the cool coastal evening. It clung sensuously to her skin.

Hmm. She turned back and forth in front of the mirror. A bit of jewelry, perhaps? No necklace, she decided, only Granddad's earrings.

Zack's rap at the door came as she was putting them on, and she hurried to let him in.

"Hi," she said, her eyes widening as she looked him over. He was wearing formal clothes that fit so well they must have been tailored for him.

"You look wonderful," he told her.

"Thanks. So do you."

He was ignoring their previous argument, though he did ask if her doors and windows were locked.

"Of course they are," Jamie answered sweetly, picking up her handbag and securing the front door, as well.

There was a BMW sports car in front of the house.

"That's my car, but I've been loaning it to Brad,"

Zack said. "I told him I had to steal it back for the evening. I didn't tell him I was coming to get you. I just asked him and Kim to be at the restaurant for an eight o'clock reservation."

"You're betting on the shock value to wake them up?"

"Might as well give it a shot."

The posh car increased the elegant aura of the evening. Once at the restaurant, Zack turned the Beamer over to the parking valet—Brian wasn't working that station—and escorted her to double-wide mahogany doors with Sunfish Grotto carved into the rich wood. The doorman held the doors open, while a concierge inside asked if he could take her wrap. She slid it off and saw Zack's eyes widen as his gaze swept over her from head to toe.

"Wow" was his single comment, and Jamie restrained a smile as they walked through the foyer and into the restaurant.

As chic as the Clam Shell had been, the Sunfish Grotto overshadowed it. There were fountains and hidden lights, tables secluded by discreet plants, lit aquariums and architectural features. The dance floor was flanked by an aquarium filling an entire wall, with waving plants and lazy fish.

Zack saw her looking at it and said, "During the day it's lit from the top by natural light, as well."

"It's beautiful."

"So are you."

A maître d' approached them. "Mr. Denning, your brother and Ms. Wheeler are already seated."

"Thank you, Dennis," Zack said. "May I introduce you to Jamie Conroe?"

"Very pleased to meet you, Ms. Conroe. Is this your first visit to the Sunfish Grotto?"

Jamie had a feeling he knew it was, but smiled anyhow. "Yes. Zack has been telling me how special it is, and now that I'm here, I can only agree."

"Yes, miss. I hope you enjoy your visit. Let me show you to your table."

Zack slid his arm around her waist as they followed the maître d', and a pleasant thrill went up her spine at his touch. Although they were playacting the "date" portion of the evening, Jamie could sense his pride at being her escort and a flash of old-fashioned feminine power went through her. It wasn't something she'd experienced in a while and she'd forgotten how fun it could be.

ZACK WAS STUNNED as he walked with Jamie through the restaurant. He'd known she was pretty, even the first day they'd met, though it had been masked by a smart mouth, her oversize clothes and an obnoxious trailer. It wasn't long afterward that he'd recognized her sexy appeal and felt a growing desire. Now, seeing her in a sensuous gown intended to send a man's brain reeling in foggy appreciation, he wondered how many complex layers were beneath

Jamie's surface. Why would she hide in overalls and sell strawberries over more glamorous pursuits? Of course, she'd probably accuse him of male stereotyping if he said anything.

"I hate to admit it," Jamie said, glancing at the creamy linen and sparkling stemware, "but this place is even more than you described. I used to dream of living in a home where entire walls were aquariums, just like your dance floor."

"You don't want that any longer?" he asked. If things had been different between them, he would have tried to convince her to forget dinner and spend the evening making love on the king-size bed in his apartment. Who needed food if you could have Jamie Conroe for every course from appetizers to dessert?

"No," she said. "Aquariums are wonderful, but now I want lots of windows and access to the outdoors. It's lovely visiting a place like this, though."

Zack blinked and dragged his thoughts away from his bedroom. They went around a row of plants and came to a private dining alcove created by walls of softly lit stained glass. An artistic mermaid on one side peered at a sunset on the other. Though it had added to the expense, Zack had asked the architect and interior designer to create numerous private spaces within the Grotto. Each was unique, and people were already reserving their favorites.

Kim saw them first, her eyebrows lifting slightly in surprise. "Hello, Jamie."

Brad looked at them also, his surprise more pronounced.

Zack pulled out a chair next to Kim's and held it for Jamie before seating himself. The maître d' bowed slightly and departed.

"I'm glad the two of you could have dinner with us," Zack said, choosing his words carefully.

Brad's brow creased, but he said nothing while Zack and Jamie exchanged a look. The four of them studied the menus, yet before they could order, a wine steward brought a bottle to the table.

"This is the selection you made earlier, Mr. Denning. Is it still acceptable?" He showed Zack the label.

"It's fine. Brad, taste the wine, will you?" he asked. "I want to take Jamie to the dance floor and see if her gown twirls as well as it looks."

"Of course," his brother answered in a stiff voice.

"Is something wrong with Brad?" Jamie whispered as they retraced their earlier steps.

"I don't know. We haven't had a chance to talk much lately. Right now I'm hoping he's reassessing his assumptions about me and Kim."

The band was playing one of Zack's favorite arrangements. It was an exquisite composition, yet he smiled humorously as he pulled Jamie into his arms.

"Is something funny?" she asked.

"Not really. The music is a piece I particularly like, that's all."

"And that's amusing?"

"It's called *Air on G String* by Bach. My band director in high school thought it would get the boys interested in practicing more. Unfortunately, he didn't realize the parents of the teenage daughters would object."

Jamie nodded. "Because it got the boys thinking about girls wearing G-strings."

"You got it." He gathered her closer. She was soft and silky and smelled faintly of lilacs. For a moment he had a peculiar conviction that he'd built the Grotto for the sole purpose of dancing with Jamie. Foolish, perhaps, but the Sunfish Grotto had been designed to create mood, so it shouldn't be a surprise that he'd been drawn under its spell.

BRAD SCHOOLED HIS expression, but he was annoyed.

What was Zack doing, messing around with Jamie? Sure, play a game for the staff. Put on a good show for the town and even the tourists, but a romantic display in front of Kim? And what about Jamie—what if she got the wrong idea? She was probably too levelheaded, yet it still seemed unfair.

"Sir?" the wine steward said. He'd poured a glass of the wine and was waiting for approval.

"Oh." Brad tasted the wine. "It has a sour taste. Is that normal for this particular vintage?"

The steward seemed startled. "No, sir, it is *not*. I'll take the bottle back and bring another."

"It's good you tasted it instead of me," said Kim when the steward had gone. "I'm not a connoisseur."

"Neither am I, though Zack has tried to educate me. He doesn't drink much, but says he'd rather have one good glass than a bottle of anything lesser."

Kim smiled. "My grandfather was an alcoholic, so I was always glad that neither of you were big drinkers."

Brad remembered her talking about it one late night when he'd called and Zack was at work. She'd been sad over her grandfather's early death from years of alcohol abuse and he'd mostly listened, her voice a pleasant change from the loud chatter of the men in the recreation hall.

"Would you like to dance?" he asked.

She hesitated for an instant. "I'd love to."

They made their way to the dance floor, where they saw Zack and Jamie turning slowly on the floor, along with two middle-aged couples.

"It's been years since I danced," Brad said in a low voice.

"Me, too, but I suppose the band will survive."

He held her carefully and moved onto the dance floor. She was obviously worried about whether the movements would hurt his leg, but the slow pace was comfortable.

"I'm not spun glass," she teased after a couple of minutes. "You can hold me tighter."

The words surprised Brad, along with the playful smile she cast at him. If he hadn't known better he would have said she was flirting. Hell, he was a lousy judge of women—it couldn't mean anything.

As they danced, Brad thought about switching partners to give Kim a chance to dance with Zack, but they didn't meet up in a way that made it possible. It was almost as if his brother was avoiding them on the dance floor. The band was starting a new piece of music by the time Brad was close enough to Zack to say anything.

"Zack, I shouldn't be selfish and keep Kim to myself," he said in a casual tone. "And you shouldn't do the same with Jamie."

A rueful expression crossed Zack's face, but he graciously bowed and agreed to the partner exchange.

"Have you figured out what to do about the fruit stand?" Brad asked Jamie after a moment.

"Yes," she answered softly after casting a quick glance around, probably to see if there were listening ears. "I've installed security cameras with motion sensors. They should pick up anything that happens out there."

"That's a good idea."

He was relieved; Zack wouldn't feel he had to watch the stand with Jamie, and she'd be safe.

They danced in silence for a few rounds, then Jamie glanced over at Kim. She and Zack were chatting amiably.

"It's nice that Kim has been able to come to Mar Vista so often," Jamie said. "She must enjoy it here, though seeing friends probably makes it even nicer."

"Zack and Kim go way back," he said.

"Hasn't she known you almost as long? Or maybe I misunderstood."

It was true; he'd met Kim only a month after she and Zack became acquainted, but they'd met *because* she was dating his brother. Of course, they hadn't been a couple for a long time and...well, his friendship with Kim *had* survived on its own.

When the music ended, Zack reclaimed Jamie and they moved away. Kim regarded them with a pleased smile.

"They seem to be getting along exceptionally well," she commented.

As Zack's lawyer, it was natural that she was concerned over the fruit stand and property issue.

"Yes, though I don't know how it will end," Brad murmured. "Jamie is very attached to the land. She told me it's where her grandparents met."

"No wonder it's special to her."

"I suppose the place you meet your future love is always memorable. How about you and Zack? Where did you two meet?"

Kim didn't seem to mind the question. "At the hotel where he was working, naturally. I went for a job interview and was surprised to discover the assistant manager was another college kid, same as me."

"Zack went up through the ranks like a speeding bullet. Did you get the job?"

"It was offered, but I got a chance to clerk for a lawyer, so I chose that instead. Zack would never have gotten involved with an employee, so if I'd gone to work for him, we would have become friends without the detour into romance." She tilted her head back and looked at him. "Bet you don't re-member where you met me."

Brad chuckled. "I do, as a matter of fact. You were hanging around the parking lot waiting for Zack. I was in town and he asked me to pick you up so we could all have burgers together. We ate alone because someone in a drunken stag party pulled the fire alarm at the hotel, and he couldn't leave. You had a jalapeño turkey burger with chipotle-flavored sweet-potato fries."

"I'm impressed."

"It's not every day a jarhead meets a gorgeous woman with adventurous tastes in food."

"Watch it, marine. I thought you said your social skills were rusty from being on active duty so long."

Strangely, Kim was acting completely normal and didn't seem to mind the possibility that Zack and Jamie had become a couple. And more than once her manner was flirtatious, or at least that was how it appeared to him. His social skills *were* rusty, but it was pleasant to be reminded that he was more than a soldier…and particularly nice to remember he was more than a recuperating patient.

Strangely, he'd always felt Kim was special. If there wasn't anything between her and Zack, then maybe...

No. Brad pushed the thought away. It was impossible. Who knew how long it would be until he'd recovered enough for active duty, if ever? The doctors seemed to think it was possible, but he was cautious about getting his hopes up. At the moment, he was a Marine Corp officer who wasn't physically fit to serve. What did he do in the meantime? He certainly couldn't be with Kim—she had a flourishing law practice with everything going for her. She didn't need a banged-up jarhead around.

OVER ZACK'S SHOULDER Jamie watched a large fish drift through the aquarium bordering the dance floor and wondered whether the wall-sized tank was fresh or salt water. Salt, she decided, noting the starfish hiding in the corner.

The dappled light from the aquarium provided most of the illumination on the dance floor, creating the ultimate romantic atmosphere. Or maybe it was just atmosphere, and Zack was responsible for the romance.... No. Jamie reminded herself it was an act.

After another dance, Zack looked down at her. "Should we go back to the table soon and order something?"

"Probably. I ate a snack around six, but it's wearing off."

"A snack? Did you think I wouldn't feed you for hours?"

"You never know. There must be a few places at Mar Vista I haven't seen yet."

He laughed and swung her around in time with the music.

It was amazing to think they were able to tease each other after having had a roaring argument earlier in the afternoon. Considering their history, they would probably be having another battle before long, but at least they'd set aside their hostilities in order to put on a good show for Kim and Brad.

Zack held her hand as they walked off the dance floor and back to the table.

"Did you notice that Brad either didn't notice us leaving, or didn't care?" he asked as they reached the table. "They're still dancing."

"Good."

"How about having dinner again tomorrow night, or even Sunday, since Kim has reservations through Monday? Same time, same place, but just the two of us. That should enhance the idea that we're a couple and show Brad that he's welcome to pursue a relationship with Kim."

Jamie sighed. One thing always led to another. Maybe it was inevitable that she would have to do something to keep the charade going once she'd gone along with it. Not that she minded, exactly. Brad was a terrific guy and doing something for him seemed worthwhile. She didn't want to examine any other motives more closely.

"Tomorrow night, then," she said. "But we'd better go to the Clam Shell."

"Why not here?"

"Because this is the one dress I've got that's suitable for this kind of fancy restaurant. I don't mind wearing things over again, but not two days in a row."

"That gown is gorgeous on you, but you don't need something long and fancy to eat here."

"I'll…think about it," she said, wondering if she'd lost her mind. It was hard to deny the appeal of coming back to the Sunfish Grotto. How many places were there like it in the world? "I'm not sure what I expected here—a lot of wood and leather and plants, I guess."

"We have some of that, but calling it the Sunfish Grotto opened up the imagination. There's even one table where the alcove is stone and there's an aquarium along one side at the top. It's part of the dance floor's tank, which makes it easier to maintain."

"You must have someone who does nothing except tend fish tanks."

"Close to it. He's also responsible for the fountains and ponds in the gardens."

"Hi, you two," Kim said as they came back to the table. "Hope we didn't keep you waiting."

"Go dance some more," Zack offered. "We'll order appetizers and might even leave some for you."

"I don't think we should go anywhere," Brad advised Kim. "He used to eat more potato chips at family picnics than the rest of us put together."

"Ha," Zack rejoined. "I'll never forget the time Brad introduced me to tacos. He told me the sauce wasn't hot and squirted a whole packet on mine. I swear he did it thinking I'd end up giving it to him."

"And did you?" Jamie asked with a grin.

"Not a chance. I ate every flaming mouthful."

"I thought you liked spicy food," Kim said.

"Not when I was eight."

Jamie pictured the scene: the small kid perspiring as he stubbornly consumed the taco with his eleven-year-old brother watching. It was an insight to the determination Zack had, even as a child. No younger-brother complex for him.

The server came, bringing them menus, so there was a lull in conversation as they studied their options. They each chose a main dish, and Zack added several orders of appetizers.

"This place is a marvel," Kim said as the menus were carried away. "I like it more every time I see it."

"The Grotto is my favorite part of the resort," Zack said. "At least of the parts we constructed. The whole area is fantastic. Maybe I'm biased, but this has to be one of the most beautiful sections of the California coastline."

Jamie felt the same. Warrington had been a popular tourist town for years, which accounted for its many art galleries and quaint restaurants. The town didn't lack motels or bed-and-breakfast establishments, but Mar Vista was the only high-end option and it was unquestionably boosting the area's economy.

"I couldn't believe it when I found this land for sale," Zack continued. "It was exactly the place I've imagined since I was ten years old."

"Exactly?" Kim teased.

"Okay, maybe Disneyland was more what I pictured at ten. But this is what I've wanted since I was at least fifteen."

"Most boys think of fast cars or being a famous sports figure at that age," said Jamie. "Why a resort?"

"Our mother got sick when we were kids," he explained. "She almost died, and after she got well, she couldn't seem to get her energy back. Dad splurged and took her on a vacation to a spa retreat, someplace where she would be pampered."

"Did it help?"

"We could hardly believe it when she came home," Brad said. "She was…*Mom* again."

Zack nodded. "It took Dad a while to pay off the credit cards, but it was worth every penny. I kept imagining what kind of magical place could do so much, and it seemed a marvelous thing to design and build. Especially if I was the one who made it happen."

"You wouldn't believe how into it he got," Brad

added. "He even made model buildings and tiny swimming pools with hot tubs. It was very eclectic, with a sky rail and everything from South Seas elements to a dash of Mad King Ludwig's castle."

Zack laughed. "Hey, I was ten. I tried to get it passed off as a science-fair project, but my teacher didn't buy it."

The story made sense to Jamie, and explained Zack's passionate zeal regarding Mar Vista. In a way she'd looked for a retreat to recover from her marriage. She couldn't have afforded a place that pampered her, but she'd created her own little oasis in Granddad's house.

"You never talked this way when we were in college, Zack," Kim said curiously. "I figured the resort was simply part of your overall business plan."

Zack raised an eyebrow. "Give me a break. I was a *guy*. A college student with an image to protect."

"Right, and twenty-year-old guys don't talk about ideals, just success. Male pride strikes again."

"I don't mind talking about it now."

Kim lifted her water goblet and made a small gesture with it. "That's because you've accomplished everything you dreamed of and more. Case in point—this goblet is fine, lead crystal, right?"

"It had better be."

Jamie hid a smile.

Zack's resort was a truly amazing place and she could see how helpful it could be for someone who was ill or traumatized, or just needed to recover their spirits for another reason. But from what Zack had said about paying off credit cards, it sounded as if his family hadn't been wealthy when he was a kid.

"Could your parents have afforded a place like Mar Vista?" she asked without thinking.

Zack seemed startled. "What do you mean?"

"It's nothing," she said. "Forget it."

"No, I—"

The wine steward came to the table and spoke to Brad. "Sir, I've chilled another bottle and apologize for the poor quality of the first. Would you like to sample it?"

"Sure."

Brad tasted the wine and gave his approval. The wine was poured all around, and shortly after that, the first of Gordon Chen's fabulous appetizers made it to the table.

Jamie noticed that Zack seemed distracted, then he shook his head and rejoined the conversation.

CHAPTER THIRTEEN

A VAGUE DISQUIET nagged the back of Zack's mind, but he pushed it aside. At the moment it was more important to focus on the evening. The server set small fine china dishes in front of them for the appetizers. Jamie put a stuffed mushroom on her plate, cut off a piece and ate it.

He swallowed hard as she delicately licked her lips. Was she being deliberately provocative? She saw him staring and raised her eyebrows. The next time he was sure she was doing it deliberately, as she followed the bite with an inscrutable little smile.

"This is incredible," she declared. "Can you believe what Gordon does with a mushroom and a bit of cheese?"

"Downright sinful," Kim agreed.

Zack couldn't stand it and stood. "How about another round or two, Jamie?" he asked. "They know we're using the dance floor, so they'll slow the delivery of our food."

"Your staff is well trained." She stood with an enticing twist of her body. Hell, who'd have guessed a seductress was hiding at the Little Blue Fruit Stand?

The band was playing a faster piece, giving him less of a chance to put his arms around her waist. On the other hand, her supple movements were a feast for the eyes, and he wasn't the only man who thought so. One of the single men staying at the resort stood at the side of the floor, watching with appreciation. As the music switched to a slower selection, Zack twirled Jamie to the opposite side to prevent her admirer from cutting in.

"That man looked nice," said Jamie with a saucy look. "You could have introduced us. You did with everyone else the other night."

"That particular introduction wouldn't enhance the image of us as a couple."

"Anything for the cause, I suppose." She snuggled closer.

A pained humor went through Zack; she knew exactly what she was doing…and was enjoying torturing him.

"Careful," he muttered. "Remember what happens to girls who play with fire."

"Been there, done that," she answered, her exuberance fading as she withdrew a few inches.

"Something wrong?"

"Hmm. Bad memory. It doesn't matter."

He tugged her close again to distract her, wanting to lure the seductress back. "Tell me something. You've heard stories of my spicy childhood. What about you?"

"I've already told you I spent every August in

Warrington with my grandfather. What else do you need to know?"

"Well, was there ever anything between you and Curt Saldano? You seem to have a history."

"We were buddies as kids and engaged in a little heavy kissing as teenagers. He didn't dare try more than that with Granddad standing guard."

"That must have been frustrating."

"We were never serious. It was an experiment to see if we were friends, or something else."

"Being friends won?"

"Don't knock it. I'm a big fan of friendship."

"So am I, but I'm also a big fan of…that *something else*."

"Really?" Her eyes glinted. "I would never have guessed. Of course, maybe it depends on how you define it."

"You want to get together and compare dictionaries?"

She closed her eyes as if in ecstasy. "Gosh, an evening discussing semantics. You really know how to wow a girl."

Laughter and desire stirred together in his gut. It was a potent combination.

The music finished and they started back to their table while he cast about for another topic as a continued distraction. "What about you and your brother…David, is it? Did the two of you get along?"

"Same as kids in a candy shop. David's a few years older than me and we squabbled because there wasn't anyone else to fight with. We're good friends now."

"If he had a chance to tell a 'taco' story on you, what would it be?"

Her smile peeped out again. "There was the time when he was a senior in high school. I sneaked out and tied a just-married sign to his bumper right before he went on a date. He didn't see it for a few days and his friends were congratulating him for weeks."

"Bet that took the spice out of his dating life for a while. What did he do to deserve it?"

"He read my diary."

"Ouch. I don't have a sister and even *I* know that's asking for trouble."

"I must admit, the just-married sign was only the first of several calculated moves I made for vengeance, especially when I found out that he'd told my boyfriend a couple things from my diary."

At the table, Kim and Brad were starting on a new platter of appetizers.

"We should get started," said Zack. "They've got traction on us."

The salads arrived as they finished nibbling their way through a plate of "tasty bits," as Gordon called them. After the main course, they all went to the dance floor and didn't return to the table for quite a while, at which point they were presented with a tempting array of desserts.

"No, thank you," Jamie said. "I'm full." Kim was shaking her head, as well.

"How about sharing some of mine?" Zack asked.

Jamie cocked her head. "Maybe a bite or two."

So of course, Brad suggested the same to Kim.

"Another dance?" Zack asked as they sipped on coffee.

Jamie made an expression of regret. "It's been wonderful, but it's getting late and this has been a long day."

Damn. For a while he'd forgotten—she'd started her workday with the discovery of more vandalism. She had to be exhausted.

"Of course," he said. "Let me get you home. Kim, Brad, will you excuse us?"

They started to rise and Jamie waved them down. "Don't cut your evening short on my account. It was lovely spending time with you both."

"Good night," they said, almost in unison.

Satisfaction settled deep in Zack, at least on his brother's behalf. Brad and Kim seemed to be getting a clue that they could be a couple.

THE NEXT MORNING Kim stretched and rolled onto her side. As with everything at Mar Vista, the beds and linens were top-of-the-line...even more comfortable than her mattress at home. She *had* to find out where to get one like it.

She turned over again and smiled when she saw her gown from the previous night lying across a chair. Dinner as a foursome had proved to be both fun and surprising.

So, Jamie and Zack were getting cozy.

Maybe it was inevitable for two lonely people to hook up after spending several nights together in a tiny trailer. But given what Kim knew of them, they were as mismatched as lovers could get and the long-term outlook was questionable.

Too bad. Zack was a great guy who'd probably spend the rest of his life having brief affairs and being buried in ledger sheets. She'd long since realized they were never truly in love, which was a good thing since his business goals were his one true passion, even back in college. Mar Vista was undeniably a marvel, but hardly a substitute for home and family.

Of course, Zack wasn't the only Denning with a single-minded passion—Brad was pretty passionate about being a marine. For his sake, she hoped his military career hadn't ended. But even as she thought it, her stomach dropped.

Kim glanced at her watch, trying to push the sensation away. It was early. In the afternoon she was going over to see Jamie, who'd promised to close the stand early and show her the jewelry she'd been working on. Lots of time until then.

Brad was likely on his morning trek…maybe she'd sleep awhile longer, and see if she could catch up with him later.

She closed her eyes again, yet she kept remembering how good Brad had looked while they were dancing—healthy, the lines of pain on his face nearly gone...and very, very handsome. In his own way he was even more attractive than Zack, and that was saying something. They were so different, sometimes it was hard to believe they were brothers.

Kim smiled sleepily. She'd really enjoyed dancing again...and Brad was awfully good company.

JAMIE FIXED BREAKFAST and ate on the porch where she could watch the sun rise over the hills in the east and admire the ocean in the west. Her great-grandparents couldn't have chosen a better location for their home.

It had been a quiet night, and in the early-morning sunshine, any anxieties hardly seemed worth the effort. Of course, she hadn't seen the fruit stand yet, but that could wait. The glow from the evening at the Sunfish Grotto still lingered. Who would have believed she could have such an enjoyable time in Zack Denning's company? And what fun to flex her feminine power; it had been disappointing when fatigue took over despite everything.

When they'd arrived at the house, Zack had tried to initiate a kiss, but she'd shied away, knowing where it could lead. But he still insisted on checking every single window and door for security, and waited on the porch while she bolted the front locks...as if she needed to be told that it was smart to secure her own home.

When the clock ticked to 7:00 a.m., Jamie knew

it was time to face whatever was waiting at the fruit stand.

And it was bad.

She surveyed the damage bleakly. Cleaning up would take a while and it was questionable how well she'd be able to function that day. The display stands were in pieces again, but this time they were broken beyond repair. The canopy was down and ripped, with Bitch scrawled beneath the Get Out message. Her eyes burned. She swallowed and clenched her jaw. No asshole would make her cry uncle. Bullies didn't deserve to win.

She took a deep breath. Nothing was going to get cleaned up and fixed by standing there and looking at it. She snapped numerous pictures to document the damage, and called to leave a message for Curt, telling him what had happened and that she hoped to have pictures to help the investigation. The dispatcher told her not to touch anything until an officer came by.

A sheriff's car pulled up ten minutes later and the young deputy she'd met weeks ago climbed out.

"Gosh, miss," he said, studying the mess. "That's just plain *wrong.*"

An ironic humor struck her, but she knew he wouldn't understand if she laughed. "No one could have said it better," she agreed.

He quickly took his own set of pictures, and dusted the door of the trailer for prints. Jamie removed the memory cards from the video cameras and the young deputy carefully put them in evidence bags and labeled them. "I'll get these to the sheriff," he promised. "But maybe I could help clean up first. That is…*gosh,* I hate to leave you with it."

"No," she assured him. "Your job is more important. Help Curt catch the guy who's doing this. That's what I need most."

As he pulled out of the long gravel driveway, two vehicles passed him coming in. The first was Zack's SUV, the second a Mar Vista maintenance truck with three men in the cab.

Zack climbed out, his face darkening with anger as he surveyed the message written on the canopy. The three men in Mar Vista uniforms nodded politely at Jamie.

"Okay," Zack said. "Let's get this cleaned up as fast as we can. Ms. Conroe will have deliveries coming soon and will need new displays. Jack, you're good at things like that. Can you build something with that lumber we brought over?"

"No," Jamie said. "Don't worry. I can do it."

Zack exchanged a very male glance with the other men and gave her a hug. "Of course you can, but you shouldn't have to."

"But—"

"Go ahead, fellows," Zack said, then leaned close to her ear. "Here comes Brad," he whispered. "This will *really* cement the belief we're a couple in his eyes."

She didn't dare say anything or she might have

let him have it, in more ways than one. He appeared genuinely upset on her behalf, but he was also using the situation for his own benefit.

Leaning down, he kissed her cheek, for all the world to see, as though he were comforting her.

"Anything I can do?" Brad asked when he arrived, looking grimly at the mess.

"I beat you to it today," Zack told him. "It's a shame all the work the two of you did yesterday has been undone."

Jamie jerked, seeing one of the maintenance men go inside the trailer. "No, *I* will clean up in there," she said, but Zack held her arm and wouldn't let go.

The man came out of the trailer after a minute. "Not much mess inside," he said. "Bet he was scared off. A curtain has been jerked down and the mattress is slashed on the bottom bunk."

"Ah, hell," Zack whispered in her ear. "I was rather fond of that mattress."

She almost smiled. "That's not funny," she murmered instead. "This is serious."

"Believe me, honey, I was completely serious."

"You're hopeless."

"Not in the least. I'm *full* of hope."

Of course he was. After a long dry drought of no sex, he'd had a drink and craved another. So did she, except that didn't make it a good idea. She needed her independence; he needed to be a superstar in the resort world. Getting together might work out if they were both into casual sex and didn't mind the glaring reasons they were incompatible. But then, casual sex didn't require anything beyond a mutual need to satisfy an itch, and she didn't need to scratch that badly.

Brad stood with the men who were working on the displays, showing them what to do and how large they should be.

"Can't *anyone* in the Denning family let me handle things on my own?" she muttered.

"That's not very gracious," Zack answered.

"No," she said. "I'm a bitch, and now I've got a sign to prove it."

Zack sighed as he watched Jamie stalk away to greet the farmers bringing deliveries. She wasn't about to surrender her determination to keep her fists raised to the world.

Her sophistication from the previous evening was gone, though not the sexy allure, peeking out from a tight T-shirt beneath worn overalls. They were loose enough to make a man want to slip his hand down inside to explore… Zack shut his eyes and counted to ten.

The night before, he'd emailed instructions to the maintenance supervisor to have three men on the early shift ready to go with him on a special job. When he'd met them at the maintenance yard, he explained that they were driving over to help their neighbor who'd been having trouble with vandalism. They hadn't asked questions, just cheerfully followed. They were fast, too. Some of the repairs were temporary, such as the duct tape over the tear in the canopy. But the stand was in functioning condition in less than an hour. Jamie, of course, tried to pay them, which they refused, though they left with baskets of fruit she'd pressed on them.

When everything was put back in order, Brad continued his walk. Jamie rounded on Zack once they were alone. "I did *not* need you to rescue me."

"Hey, it made a good show for everyone. And it got you up and ready for business, so why complain?"

"You just don't get it, do you?"

"No, I don't. But never mind that now. Do you think your security cameras caught anything?"

"I did a fast review and it looked like an identifiable face was recorded. Curt will follow up."

"Did you recognize him?"

Jamie gave a quick shake of her head. "No. I don't even know if he's local or not, and I can't imagine why he'd care about the stand. He wasn't a teenager. I'm lucky he didn't do more inside the trailer, or he might have spotted the cameras."

"How did you sleep last night?" he asked.

"Like a log," she claimed, though he wondered if she was telling the truth. She'd played an extremely alluring game the entire evening at the Grotto, stirring him up enough that it had taken a long cold shower to settle down. It was hard to believe she'd escaped unscathed.

Tempted as he was to test his theory, Zack decided it was wisest to leave her alone—she'd had a tough enough start to the day. Besides, a customer was driving down the road, the woman waving at Jamie, so he kissed her cheek again.

Her voice followed him to the SUV. "The show is for Brad and Kim, *not* the general public."

At 11:00 A.M., Jamie assessed the stock she had left. In three hours she was supposed to meet Kim Wheeler. She'd either have to leave and let people put money in a box until she came back, or she could close early and pack it all up. She hadn't promised to hold anything, so it could go either way.

Annoyed as she was with Zack, there was no denying that the help from his men had made things easier. But she would reduce the charges on her invoice to Mar Vista for the day, to pay for the work the employees had done.

At one she decided to load her leftovers. Word had spread about the vandalism and many curious or concerned folks had come by to check things out and then to shop, so she didn't have much left anyhow. She drove home to brew coffee and pull cookies from the freezer to serve when Kim got there.

With lawyerlike punctuality, Kim arrived right on time and Jamie welcomed her into the house. "I've got coffee on if you want a cup," she said.

"Sounds great."

They sat in the living room, drinking coffee and

discussing the vandalism at the stand. After a while, Kim examined the trays of jewelry Jamie had laid out on the dining-room table.

"These are really good," Kim enthused. She pointed at one tray. "Especially that group."

"Those are the ones I've made for the art gallery. The rest of the pieces are for regular tourist shops. I've decided to make the higher-end ones in limited groups and number them."

"Like an artist has numbered prints," Kim said. "That's a good idea. You know...maybe I shouldn't say this, but these would fit in with the merchandise in the shops at Mar Vista. I could show a few pieces to Zack and—"

"No," Jamie cut in swiftly, then winced. After all, she and Zack were trying to make Kim and Brad believe they were a couple. And considering the passionate night they'd spent together, it wasn't entirely a lie, even if it also wasn't the truth. "I wouldn't want to presume, you know, on the fact...that we... see each other," she said, tempering her tone.

"Don't worry. Zack won't let that influence him."

"Even so, I wouldn't be comfortable. Things are tricky at this...stage."

"Brad said you wouldn't like it, but I wanted to ask."

Jamie tried to think if she could say something about Brad that might help push the two of them together, and she laughed to herself. The matchmaking bug was hard to escape.

It truly wasn't her business. Besides, she couldn't claim any expertise in the romance department.

"Any plans for dinner?" she asked instead. "I could fix a salad or something."

"Oh, thanks," Kim answered, suddenly seeming flustered…a very *un*-lawyerlike condition. "But Brad and I are going into town. There's an Italian place we want to try."

"You must mean Martine's. They're great," Jamie said, deciding that Brad and Kim needed no one to push them together; from now on they could figure it out for themselves.

It was just as well that Kim hadn't stayed. Shortly after she left, Curt knocked on the door. He was delighted to get the leftover coffee and polish off the rest of the cookies.

"I went by the fruit stand first," he said. "It's amazing. How did you get things going again after the mess I saw in those pictures?"

"Zack Denning insisted on having a group of his men clean up and do repairs," she said, hating to admit it.

"Zack Denning?" Curt asked.

"Yeah."

"Zack Denning of Denning Enterprises and the Mar Vista Resort?"

"That's the one."

"Wow. I never saw that one coming. Do you think he could be sending a vandal out by night, and cleaning up by day?"

"When did you get so cynical, Curt?" Though Jamie had teased him about getting elected sheriff, it was something he'd talked of doing when he was a boy—with visions of being the Grand Marshal in the Founder's Day parade and riding a white... squad car.

"Working in law enforcement doesn't leave you innocent."

"Look, I'm pretty sure Mar Vista isn't involved, but I can't figure out who *could* be doing it."

"That I can answer. We've got the jerk under arrest. His name is Gus Hewitt. He's a local guy, never involved in anything major, but pretty seedy." Curt's voice got low and gruff. "He was hired and dunno why and can't finger his boss cuz he didn't meet the dude, just got the dough in the mail, see?"

Jamie grinned at the impersonation. "Sounds as if Gus has seen too many old crime shows."

"No question. I'm also sure he knows more than he's revealing and actually *has* met his boss. I suspect he's hoping to get more cash to stay quiet. Do you have any ideas? You say you don't think the Denning fellow could be involved, but are you certain? The man was plenty pissed off about the fruit stand."

Jamie shook her head. People could be incredibly two-faced, few people knew that better than she did, but her instincts said neither Zack nor his people were responsible.

"No. This isn't because of the resort. It's..." An

unsavory suspicion suddenly occurred to her. Could it be Tim? Hiring someone to do his dirty work sounded exactly like her ex-husband's style. He was basically a coward at heart, tearing other people down to make himself feel more powerful.

"Don't keep it to yourself if you've thought of something," Curt prompted. "All possibilities should be considered."

"It's just that my ex-husband… Well, he didn't exactly take the end of our marriage as the final word."

Curt pulled out a notebook and pen. "What has he done?"

"Nothing in person, at least nothing I know of. But he kept calling last winter, even after I changed my number. And he asked our mutual friends to talk about him. I thought he'd given up, only now he's started phoning my parents, putting on a concerned act about my welfare out here."

"Is he the kind of man who would do something like this?"

"*Yes.*"

He looked at her sympathetically. "I'm sorry, Jamie. Sounds as if it was a rough breakup."

Jamie hesitated, hating to admit how bad her judgment had been in picking a husband, and decided there wasn't any point in keeping her mouth shut. If Tim *was* behind the vandalism, everyone would wonder how she'd gotten together with him anyway.

"The most galling part is that I didn't realize

before we were married what he was really like," she said slowly. "It was only later, gradually, that his true character peeked out."

"Some people put on a good show. When I started out as a deputy, I once let a guy go because he said he had to get his wife to the hospital because she was having a baby. It turned out she had fifteen pounds of cocaine shoved beneath her shirt."

"How'd you find out that?"

Curt grinned. "Well, because I'm a lunkhead and believed him, I decided to escort them to the hospital. When the car turned the opposite direction, I got suspicious."

It was good to laugh and release some tension. Curt poured himself another cup of coffee, loading it with cream and sugar.

"What's your ex-husband's full name?" he asked.

"Timothy Wendell Gardiner."

Curt wrote it in his notebook and tapped the paper with his pen. "If your ex is responsible, he couldn't have simply picked Gus Hewitt's name out of the phone book. He would have to have known Gus was the lowlife type."

At the implication, Jamie wrapped her arms around her stomach. It was true. If Tim was the one behind all this, he must have come to Warrington, perhaps numerous times, watching and planning. Those times he'd called her, he could have been parked outside the house or down the driveway.

"You're right," she agreed. "He must have been

here long enough, or often enough, to figure out who to hire."

"That means I can show a picture around and see who might recognize him. It might even scare Gus into turning evidence against his boss. He'll be shopping for a deal since we can try him on several different counts—the D.A. wants to throw everything possible at him, including stalking charges. With his record, the judge won't be lenient. Do you have any pictures I can use? Or did you cut them all up into tiny pieces after the divorce, the way my sister did with photos of her ex?"

Jamie chuckled ruefully. "I considered it, but some of those pictures have people I care about in them."

She fetched her photo album and they went through it until Curt spotted a couple he thought would be good to use.

"We'll get right on it," he said, tucking the photos in his pocket.

As he went to his car, she noted that the late-afternoon sun was now hidden behind a deep fog bank. A cheerful fire would be nice. With Gus Hewitt in jail she shouldn't find any vandalism tomorrow, and she might have a chance to start sorting out the emotional garbage that had collected. But not tonight. This evening she planned to sit in front of the hearth and try to forget everything for a while.

CHAPTER FOURTEEN

IT WAS LATE that afternoon when Zack stopped by
the front desk to greet some arriving guests, and
stayed to chat with the clerk, Michael Brookings.

"You sound British," Zack noted after a while.
"How did you end up in Warrington?"

"I came as a tourist and met a girl. We've been
married five years last April."

"Did you come from a small town in Britain?"

"No, quite the opposite—London. But I enjoy living in Warrington, even if it is tiny by comparison."

"I'm glad you decided to make it your home."

"Thank you."

Zack continued toward the Sunfish Grotto, thinking the conversation had flowed better than most
he'd had in recent months with employees. He'd
been trying to get to know them, but it wasn't easy
with such a large number, and they often appeared
reserved when they were around him.

Strangely, things seemed to be running more
smoothly at Mar Vista. The vague uneasiness he'd
had over operations was starting to diminish; things
were getting better. Was it because he was handling

things differently? He'd have a chat with Trudy on Monday to get her impressions. She was still thinking about the promotion he'd offered...and he genuinely hoped she would take it. He was three kinds of an idiot not to have suggested it earlier. And somehow the way he felt about her pregnancy had also changed; in the beginning, he had worried about the impact on the resort—now he was truly glad for the Lopezes. He'd even suggested the possibility of an employee day-care program, which had put a pleased gleam in Trudy's eyes.

Zack suspected a day-care center was the sort of thing Jamie would applaud, probably with an it's-about-time comment. And he couldn't deny that some of the shifts in his thinking may have come from his contact with her.

At the Sunfish Grotto he checked to see if they had a table available for that night in case Jamie found something she felt comfortable wearing. They did, but it would be in the overflow area, a group of tables in the banquet room. It was still elegant, and had the bonus of being on the other side of the dance floor's aquarium wall. The tables were less private, but they still had terrific atmosphere.

"I'm sorry, Mr. Denning," the maître d' apologized. "By noon, our regular table reservations were filled from six to nine. We can't book too tightly because people enjoy lingering over their meals more than usual at the Grotto. I could bump someone if you insist." He ended diffidently, obviously concerned that as Mar Vista's owner, Zack would be upset if denied seating.

"Absolutely not. Having people stay longer because they appreciate our atmosphere is a nice problem."

The man beamed in return. "Very true. We're getting quite a few calls from local hotels for their guests. But we've been saving some of the private tables so Mar Vista guests have first choice."

"Excellent. Whose idea was that?"

"One of our dishwashers, Sue Griffin."

"Put her down for a bonus. Those are ideas we need and I'm glad you listen to everyone."

"Thank you, Mr. Denning."

Elation filled Zack. It wasn't his imagination; things *were* running more smoothly. What troubled him was that he didn't know all the reasons. It was a humbling lesson; owning his own resort wasn't quite the same as simply managing it for someone else.

As he was leaving the Grotto he saw Don and Nina Courtland on the way out and stopped to say hello. Don had inherited a fortune from his industrialist grandfather, and the time he didn't spend on the family's philanthropic foundation, he spent on golf. He'd fallen in love with Mar Vista's course and wanted to move his foundation's annual golf tournament to the resort. It was a major event that would bring in top golfers from around the country and raise Mar Vista's profile even higher.

"Don't you have a contract with the current home of the tournament?" Zack asked.

"It's coming up for renewal," Don said, waving his hand. "I haven't been happy with their management for the last couple of years anyway."

"Have your coordinator call and we'll talk."

"Will do."

The Courtlands' meal was delivered and Zack left them to eat. It was an incredible opportunity—he'd managed a facility on the PGA Tour and knew how much work a major tournament entailed, but it would be well worth the effort.

Better yet, the proceeds for the Courtland Foundation Tournament went to help families in crisis.

The thought reminded Zack of the conversation at dinner the night before...about how he'd become interested in building his own resort. Until Jamie had asked, it hadn't occurred to him that his mom and dad could never have afforded such a high-end resort as Mar Vista when he and Brad were kids. It was disconcerting to realize that he'd focused so much on luxury that he'd outpriced most ordinary families, even if they were splurging.

His original goal was still possible. Once things were more secure at Mar Vista, he could find land in the Warrington vicinity and build something special for people who weren't wealthy. Or maybe it wasn't necessary to wait; he didn't need investors for Mar Vista, but he could work on putting a group together for a new project.

Buoyed by the idea, he strolled back into the reception area and saw a sheriff's deputy talking with the desk clerk. He hurried to the man's side.

"Is there a problem?" he asked.

"Not exactly, sir," Michael said in a low voice. "The deputy showed me a picture and wanted to know if the man had been a guest. I explained he's stayed here periodically."

"Hello, Officer. I'm Zack Denning, owner of Mar Vista."

"Arthur Harris. Nice to meet you." The deputy handed him the photo and Zack also recognized the man; he'd stayed several times, always keeping to himself and showing no interest in the resort's amenities.

"What's his name?"

"Timothy Gardiner," said the officer, "though according to your registration desk, he registered as Thomas Smith."

"Our records show he had proper identification," the clerk asserted quickly. "He also paid cash in advance."

Some guests walking through the lounge on their way to dinner were staring curiously at them, so Zack gestured to a door next to the reception area. "Shall we go into an office? I'd like to know what this is about."

"Certainly."

Seated in the small, elegant room established for private consultations, the deputy seemed uncomfortable, so Zack offered him a cup of coffee. But before he could even ask for some to be brought in, the clerk knocked and handed him a tray.

"Thank you," Zack told him quietly and set it on the polished-wood table.

"One thing they told us at the police academy," the deputy said. "Don't turn down a cup of coffee honestly offered."

Zack laughed. "Good advice." He poured two cups and sat back with his own. "Is Gardiner wanted for something? Naturally, I have a concern for the safety of my guests."

"I understand, Mr. Denning. You see, today we caught a man who's been committing vandalism locally and—"

"The one who's been hitting Jamie Conroe's fruit stand?" Zack interrupted quickly.

"Yes, sir. I suppose you would have heard about that, but he wasn't doing it on his own initiative and we're hunting for whoever hired him."

"Why would this Gardiner fellow care about Jamie's stand?"

"I understand that he's Ms. Conroe's ex-husband."

Jamie's ex-husband?

A chill went through Zack. An ex-husband could make things personal. *Very* personal. It was bad enough to have someone angry about a fruit stand, but this must be a private vendetta. And, once again, Jamie hadn't called and told him a thing that was happening.

"Do you know if he's presently in the area?" Zack asked.

"There's no way of knowing for certain. Your clerk checked and he wasn't currently registered, but he could be staying elsewhere." The deputy drained his cup of coffee. "I should be going. I'm making the rounds of hotels on the west edge of Warrington and should get to the next one."

"Yes, of course, Officer," Zack said. "Thank you for explaining the situation. We'll inform you immediately if Mr. Gardiner shows up at Mar Vista."

"Thank you."

Zack tried to appear casual as he returned to the desk and told Michael that if Timothy Gardiner checked in, he should complete the registration without making the guest suspicious, then discreetly call Sheriff Saldano.

"He's not likely to be dangerous to anyone at the resort," Zack told him. "But we wouldn't want to take a risk in any case. I know I can rely on you and the rest of the staff to handle it appropriately."

The clerk flashed a pleased smile. "Yes, sir."

Zack took the back route to the employee parking area where the SUV was parked. He was heading to Jamie's house to spend the night, and he wasn't taking no for an answer.

KIM FUSSED AT her hair in the mirror. She couldn't get it right. It took only a few minutes to dress professionally, but she didn't want to look like a lawyer tonight. Finally, she did a French braid and secured it with combs. The clothing seemed right—a simple blue dress with a full, graceful skirt. Nothing too fancy. The restaurant they were going to was nice, but not as high-end as the Sunfish Grotto. That suited her fine. As pleasant as it was to go someplace extravagant, everyone at Mar Vista knew who they were and it would be nice to be an anonymous couple.

She gathered her handbag in time for Brad's knock. He wore a good pair of slacks and a corduroy sports jacket. On some guys, the military haircut might appear odd, but on Brad it was just right. He seemed to approve of her appearance, as well.

"Ready?" he asked, his voice a trace husky, and Kim felt the balance of her world shift. Was it her imagination, or was that serious heat in his eyes?

"Sure. I'm not a woman who keeps a man hanging around."

"You'd be worth waiting for."

Pleasure flashed through Kim's veins. "Thank you."

She took a silk shawl-type sweater from the wardrobe and handed it to him. He held it for her and she slipped her arms into the sleeve portion and wrapped the rest around herself. Brad's eyes darkened as he gazed at her.

"You're always so elegant," he said. "That was one of the first things I noticed about you."

"What was the second?" she asked.

"Can't say."

"Can't...or won't?"

"You were my brother's girlfriend. Sometimes there are things you can't afford to notice, except on an intellectual basis."

"And what did you notice on that basis?"

"That you had a sense of humor."

"Liar."

He laughed and offered her his arm.

JAMIE SAT CURLED in the large armchair near the fireplace, working on ideas for a new bracelet. There would be no brilliant sunset that night, just a gray evening, slowly turning into darkness. Ordinarily she enjoyed the fog; tonight it seemed oppressive. But inside, the fire crackled, pushing back the gloom, and a steaming cup of tea sat next to her, along with a bowl of popcorn. Marlin lay behind her neck, stretched along the top of the chair, his purr rumbling. Every once in a while, he roused to lick her ear and she reached up to scratch his neck.

The doorbell rang and she sighed. Tempting as it was not to answer, it could be Curt with an update. She went to the door and peeked through the security window. Zack...*oops.* She'd forgotten all about their arrangement to eat at the Clam Shell.

Jamie opened the door. "Zack, I'm so sorry. I forgot all about dinner. If you still want to do it and you don't mind waiting, I could get dressed and—"

"Why didn't you tell me the police suspect your ex-husband hired that creep to trash the fruit stand?"

"Oh." She blinked. "Good heavens, Zack, it only came up this afternoon. Curt asked if I had any ideas and it suddenly occurred to me that Tim might be responsible."

"Didn't you think I'd like to know?"

"I would have mentioned it the next time I saw you."

He ran fingers through his hair in frustration. "Okay, okay. Look, you can't stay here alone."

"Don't be ridiculous."

"Your ex-husband may have paid a man to vandalize your business. This is very personal, and very dangerous. You're either coming to the resort with me or I'm staying here. Don't bother arguing."

Resigned, Jamie waved him inside. "Didn't you bring dinner?" she asked with a feigned expression of shock. "You invited me, as I recall."

He gave her a grim look that wasn't the least bit amused. "I was in too much of a damned hurry to get over here before it got dark."

"Your sense of humor has certainly suffered," she muttered. "Go sit by the fire and have popcorn for an appetizer. I'll scrounge something in the kitchen."

She hadn't planned to fix a meal, but there was vegetable soup in the refrigerator and she could make sandwiches. It wouldn't measure up to Gordon

Chen's cooking, but that was Zack's fault for show-ing up in the first place.

"Ready," she called after setting the kitchen table. "Let's eat in here."

They ate in silence, then he helped load the dish-washer. "I didn't expect such an up-to-date kitchen," he said finally.

"Granddad had it remodeled several times. He said he would have kept it updated for Leah if she were alive, and tried to choose things she would have liked. The last time it was redone was a cou-ple of years before he died. I—I think he wanted it to be new when he left it to me."

Emotion caught at Jamie's throat as she explained. Though she'd been temporarily absent from Grand-dad's life, she knew he'd thought of her often. The kitchen was a reminder. He'd done it in the colors she favored, using natural stone and glass in the backsplash and putting in hardwood floors. When she'd first moved in, she found a card in the bowl of a fancy new stand mixer. She knew the message he'd written by heart.

Jamie,
You'll never know how much your visits each August meant to me. In a way it was as if my dearest Leah had returned, in your laugh, your insatiable love for the ocean and the un-derstanding you had, even as a child, for the beauty of this place.

I wasn't a good father to your mother—however much I loved her, she needed more than a sorrowful recluse as her only parent. But I pray that I was a good grandfather to you and David. Perhaps Leah can tell me when we meet in heaven. I know it will be soon. These days I hear her singing to me more clearly than ever before.

Don't grieve, darling child. I will be with Leah, and we will both look in on you now and then.

Jamie's eyes burned as she remembered the loving words, and she ducked her head so Zack wouldn't see.

"Let's go in and sit by the fire," she said.

Mist shrouded the house in a bank of fog so deep that the evening light was barely visible, though the sun wouldn't be down for a while yet. Zack threw another log on the fire while Jamie settled into her chair and picked up her sketch pad again. Marlin stared balefully at Zack on the couch before resettling on the space behind Jamie's head.

After an hour, she went in to make a pot of hot chocolate and brought Zack a mug along with her own. "You probably don't serve anything so homey over at Mar Vista," she said when he thanked her.

"Sure we do, several kinds, including a comfort-food version like this. You can have room service deliver a pot, then sit and drink it in front of your own personal fireplace—gas, though, instead of logs."

"Sounds like a nice thing to be able to do on vacation, especially when it gets cold and damp the way it is tonight."

Zack leaned his head on the back of the couch and closed his eyes. "That's what I thought." He was silent a few minutes before rousing again. "I wish they still had the old fog horns here. There's something about the sound that I love."

Jamie's hand jerked with surprise and she erased the mark she'd accidentally made with her pencil. She wouldn't have expected Zack to appreciate fog horns; they were too old-fashioned. Yet some of her dearest childhood memories were of lying snug in her bed and listening to the muffled, mournful call of a fog horn. That sound had meant that she was really home...because Granddad's house had felt like home more than anyplace else.

"You could put one in," she suggested.

"I've considered it. Unfortunately, it would be more for me than anyone else."

"I promise to enjoy it, too."

He chuckled. "I'll see if my bank loan will extend that far."

She glanced at him. "I accused you of being a wealthy jerk, but maybe you aren't. Not yet, anyway. Not until your loans are paid and Mar Vista's income belongs solely to you."

He cocked an eyebrow at her. "You never accused me of being a wealthy jerk."

"I'm sure I did."

"Maybe you just thought it."

"Possibly." Stretching, she went to make another batch of popcorn. The evening was as different as it could be from the previous night at the Sunfish Grotto. It was full of cozy warmth, and if she didn't look at Zack too often, she could ignore the other kind of warmth, the kind that was settling deep in her belly.

ZACK ATE THE last bit of popcorn from the bowl on the side table and gazed around the room. A few weeks before, the outside of Jamie's house had surprised him with its classic architecture. The inside was inviting, a real home.

"Is all the furniture and decor yours?" he asked as Jamie came back. "Or did it belong to your grandfather?"

"Most of it was his," she said. "I got rid of a few pieces of furniture and bought a couple that suited my style better. Leah did a number of the paintings and there are others that belonged to my great-grandparents. I arranged things a little differently than Granddad, but he changed it every year or so anyhow."

It sounded as if Jamie had left her marriage with few belongings, though she might have just wanted a clean break.

"Then George didn't make a shrine of the house, keeping it the way Leah had left it?"

A smile played on Jamie's lips. "No. It was the beachside land he wanted to preserve, the ocean always changing and always staying the same. Anyway, apparently Leah rearranged on a regular basis. He told me he found her shoving the bed across the room when she was eight months pregnant. It was the third time that year she'd rearranged the furniture."

"He must have had heart failure."

"Close to it." Jamie got up to pull a book from the built-in shelves and sat down again, flipping to a page in the middle. She seemed to be making a comparison to something in her sketchbook, her forehead creased in concentration.

"What are you drawing?" Zack asked when she put the book aside. It appeared to be a book on Russian art.

"Just some ideas."

He got up and glanced at the page. "What's that?"

"A bracelet. I had an idea about a Russian theme, but I don't know if I can make it work for silver casting."

"It looks nice. I didn't realize you did that kind of jewelry. Maybe I should look at your stuff and see if it's right for one of our shops."

"I'm sure it isn't." She flipped to a blank page. "You also choose the stock for your stores? Is there *anything* you don't control over there?" she asked.

"Control? You've got to be kidding." He sank onto the couch again and rolled his eyes. "Lately I've been much less attentive than usual. And it's odd, because things are going really well the last week or so. I don't know what made the difference."

Jamie started laughing. "Of course it's getting better. You haven't been micromanaging everything to death."

The comment shocked Zack and he sat for a moment in stunned silence. That was exactly what he'd been doing and it was utterly contrary to his normal management style.

"Damn, Jamie, how did you figure that out? You've only been to Mar Vista twice."

She put the sketch pad aside and focused on him. "It was obvious from stuff you let drop. And I also overhear employees talking while they're shopping at the stand. But don't expect me to be your personal spy. I won't tell who said what."

Zack held up his hands in mock surrender. "I don't want you to. If I'd had a better working relationship with them from the beginning, they might have told me on their own."

She cocked her head in curiosity. "Is it really that different being an owner? According to Brad, you were great at management."

He grimaced. "I have more on the line as an owner, and I've been determined to make it work, partly because of my...investors."

"I didn't know you had investors."

"Just two."

"Your parents, right?"

He should have known she'd guess. "It's really important to them to show their support for anything Brad and I do. Don't tell anyone."

"It's none of my business, and no one else's, either."

Zack sighed. He felt like an idiot, not realizing he was the source of the problems at Mar Vista. Trudy had implied the way he was looking over shoulders had been causing stress, but he hadn't listened.

"I hate to admit it, but you're right. I've got good people in management," he said. "I've known these men and women for years and I can trust their work."

"That's great for them, but what about the locals?" Jamie persisted. "Couldn't you provide opportunities for advancement? They think you're only willing to hire them for cleaning toilets and pulling weeds."

Zack nodded thoughtfully. In the beginning, it made sense to bring in management personnel that he'd worked with previously. They were experienced with how a resort functioned and could train the rest of the staff. But it was discouraging for employees if they never saw a chance to move upward. Hell, if he hadn't had those opportunities, he'd still be a bellboy.

All at once he winced, remembering the management positions that had opened *since* he had opened the resort. He'd continued to hire people he knew from outside the area without considering whether anyone local was qualified.

"Wow," Jamie said. "Aren't you ticked off that I said all that?"

"No, I welcome valuable ideas." Maybe he *would* have gotten furious before he'd gotten to know Jamie, but she had good insight into people, something he'd been struggling with lately.

Jamie checked the clock over the mantel and stretched. He gulped as the fabric of her T-shirt pulled tight against her breasts.

"How about a movie?" she asked. "I may not have cable television, but there's a selection of DVDs."

What Zack wanted was to pull Jamie onto the couch and explore her curves in the firelight. A movie was safest, but he wouldn't have any excuse to look at her.

"Do you have another Scrabble game here, or is the only one back at the trailer?" he asked, deciding he'd enjoy teasing Jamie with a little sexy wordplay. "I'd like a rematch."

Brad was far more comfortable at Martine's Italian Restaurant than the Sunfish Grotto. It was nice, but not over-the-top elegant. Besides, Kim added all the elegance that was needed. God, she was beautiful. It made a man feel ten feet tall to escort such a woman.

"I'm glad you suggested coming here," Kim told

him as they ate their salads. "This place has the kind of character they write about in travel magazines. Look at that stained-glass window. It's got to be an antique."

"Along with half the stuff in here," Brad agreed. "I heard it's been around since the original owner came back from World War II, in love with the pizza he'd discovered in Italy."

"We're so used to pizza that we forget it's relatively new to the United States. I think I read somewhere that the use of oregano jumped phenomenally after the war."

"Never underestimate a soldier's capacity for enjoying food."

The waiter took their salad plates and delivered the eggplant Parmesan they'd both ordered.

"We get our food more quickly here than at the Grotto," Kim said. "Though I really enjoyed dancing with you last night."

"It was great," Brad answered, not sure of the appropriate response. Had Kim's manner always been this warm and intimate? Obviously she and his brother *didn't* have a future together, or want one, so the whole thing had been in his imagination.

Their conversation wandered through food and music, movies and books, never touching on anything personal. Once he might have been glad— now he wasn't so certain.

"I can't get used to reading a book on an electronic screen," she complained at one point. "I prefer turning pages and feeling the paper beneath my fingers."

Brad shrugged. "So do I, but it's easier to pack a gadget loaded with a ton of books into a duffel bag."

Her eyes widened. "True. I hadn't thought of that. Are you, uh… How do you keep it charged?"

"I don't always. It depends on where I'm stationed." He suspected that Kim had almost asked about his future plans regarding duffel bags and active service, but had shied away from the subject at the last moment.

Their waiter was amiable about them staying long after dinner was concluded, refilling their coffee cups each time they were half-empty. After a couple of hours, they ordered dessert before heading back to Mar Vista.

When they arrived, Kim glanced at the thick mist. "I know it's foggy and late, but I'd love a walk."

"No reason not to," Brad said. "I've got an extra jacket if you need something warmer to wear."

"I'm fine. Are you sure you don't mind?"

"It would be a pleasure," he insisted. And it *would* be pleasurable in one way…though immensely uncomfortable in another. The pain in his leg seemed minor compared to the ache of desire every time he looked at her.

CHAPTER FIFTEEN

JAMIE STUDIED HER Scrabble letters. She'd won the first turn, but there wasn't much she could do with the tiles she'd drawn. Finally, she played the best word she saw out of the seven letters.

"RIDER," she said. "With the double-letter and double-word squares, that makes fourteen points." It wasn't very high, but unless you drew fabulous letters, the starting player often didn't get a great score.

Zack grinned. "Great. I can get rid of an awkward letter right at the start." He put an *S* and an *X* on either side of the *E* in *RIDER.*

She raised her eyebrows. "You could have made the word *SIX,* and gotten more points with the double-letter squares."

"What do you know about that?" he said with exaggerated surprise. "Guess I'm blind."

"I don't mind if you move your tiles."

"No. I'm sure there's an old rule saying you have to leave your letters where you first put them."

"Right," she agreed drily, wondering if he'd somehow managed to sneak the *X* out of the bag so he could yank her chain, or if that had been pure dumb luck. It was obvious what he was doing, and she was both flattered and wary. They were getting along all right for now, but that could change in a flash.

Feeling curiously melancholy, Jamie studied her letters. With either her *IST* or her *Y* she could build on Zack's word. She hesitated. It would open up the board to play more letters and send a message that she wasn't letting him get to her, but forming *SEXIST* would get her fewer points than playing the *Y* since it was worth more and she'd get a double-word score.

Slowly she put down the *Y*.

"Ah," Zack said with a gleam in his eye. "Trying to make things more challenging, I see. *SEXY* gives me fewer openings to build from."

His next word was innocuous. *AROUND*.

Jamie earned extra points, putting in an *O* to make *DO* and *OX*, and figured Zack had decided to compete more seriously when he put down *Y* and *O*, making *SOY* and *OR*. But he sneaked in a few suggestive words when he saw the opportunity. Of course, *NECK* should have been innocuous, except she recalled too well the way he'd nibbled his way from her ear to her shoulder…and from the gleam in his eyes, he was remembering it, as well.

Zack's tactics distracted her, but she still won since he wasted opportunities for better scores in order to spell spicier words…including a few that her mom would blush to see on a game board.

"Another round?" he challenged.

She was pretty sure he meant an entirely different sort of game, but pretended he referred only to Scrabble. She dumped the tiles back into the cloth bag that she'd made years ago to make it easier to play.

When she drew the *X* midway through the match, she realized she could get a lot of points making a two-word match of *AX* and *OX*. On the other hand, she also had an *E,* with an available *S*.

Jamie stared at the letters for a long time. Before she could make up her mind, a noise outside caught Zack's attention. He jumped to his feet, flicked off the light and hurried to the window. Jamie went to the one next to the front door and peered outside, too. Something had triggered the motion sensor, turning on the security lights. She stared into the foggy darkness for several minutes until the exterior light went off and didn't come on again.

Zack came to her side. "Anything?"

"Nothing. You know, those lights go on and off all night. Sometimes I sit on the porch and watch the show for hours. There are deer, coyotes, skunks, raccoons…all sorts of critters. That's why I don't let Marlin out at night. He might mess with a skunk, or a coyote could grab him for a tasty treat."

"Really?" Zack stood close, his breath fanning the side of her cheek.

"Yes," she answered, clearing her throat.

"Why would they want to pick so much fur out of their teeth?" His arm crept around her waist.

"They…they wouldn't know how thick it is until it was too late," she managed to say. "Don't you want to finish the game?"

"We've already spelled *SEXY* and *NECK*," he answered, his head dropping down to caress the spot where her vein pulsed wildly. "And I know how to spell *SHOULDER* and *LIPS* and…"

The rational part of Jamie's brain said that if she didn't want to play this new game, it was time to quit. Zack would respect her choice.

The problem was that she didn't want to quit; she wanted to touch and be touched. Her fingers traced Zack's lean rib cage and muscular shoulders. He was taking entirely too long to get to her mouth, so she started an assault on his neck while tugging his shirt free to touch bare skin.

He dipped a hand into the gap of her overalls and she barely breathed as he explored.

Zack groaned. "Should we adjourn to the couch?" he groaned, pulling her against him.

"We'd have more room in my bed," she murmured, taking a breath and backing up with him into the hallway and through her bedroom door. "Unless you prefer the couch."

"Lady's choice."

His lips closed over hers while he unbuttoned his shirt, before working on hers again, only to get stymied by her overalls.

"What the...?" He stared at the buckles. "How do you get these things undone?"

She giggled as she unbuckled them. Zack took over when she was done, slowly pulling the old denim down to her thighs. There was little to hold them up at that point, and the overalls settled in a heap at her feet. The lacy briefs she was wearing made him gasp and he ran his fingers under the edge of the silky fabric. He took his time, nibbling her legs as he eased her panties down. When Zack reached her ankles, he tumbled her onto the bed and pulled the fabric free.

She reached for the bottom of her T-shirt, only to have him stop her, removing it himself in the same slow, deliciously torturous way he'd taken off her briefs. When his tongue finally began teasing her breast, she thought she might jump out of her skin.

"You...you're overdressed," she managed to say, but he took considerably less time getting rid of his own clothing. She was more than ready for him, hardly able to stand it while he stopped to don protection.

"Should we turn off the light," she said, panting as his weight settled over her.

"Not now. Maybe next time...or the time after that," he murmured.

MUCH LATER JAMIE listened to the lonely hoot of an owl that lived in the woods just south of the house. The moon shone through the high, open windows, illuminating the bedroom she'd chosen when she moved in the previous year. She'd decorated it according to her taste, not frilly, but simple, with touches of blue and white to lighten the beautiful old wood furniture she had collected from the other bedrooms.

Zack lay on his side next to her, deeply asleep, his arm resting on her bare hip.

Their first encounter in the trailer had been explosive; tonight had proved that wasn't a fluke. If anything, this time was even more intense...more than once. Zack had amazing stamina.

How could she feel so good, yet so bothered? She did *not* want to care for Zack Denning. From the moment they'd met, she had recognized he was the opposite of what she would want in a man, if she'd wanted one in the first place. Declaring romance a dead issue was so much easier than dealing with it.

Jamie frowned. Whatever was happening between her and Zack, it wasn't romance...or was it?

The whole thing was so frustrating. She did *not* want to be involved with a high-powered entrepreneur who measured success through his account books. If she was going to get involved with a guy, it should be with someone similar to Zack's brother. In some ways Brad even reminded her of Granddad.

By sheer logic, Kim was the best match for Zack, and Brad was the best match for her. Yet she felt only friendship for Brad, and he was head over heels for Kim.

Jamie turned her head to look at Zack's handsome face in the moonlight. She'd already decided she didn't want a casual, sexual relationship with him, or any guy, yet here she was, in bed with the man again.

Boy, did she have a talent for getting involved with the wrong man.

KIM WOKE BEFORE DAWN, not sure she'd gotten any quality sleep. All she'd dreamed about, all she could *think* about, was Brad.

She considered herself a rational woman. Lawyers had to be. Even in college she'd evaluated her relationship with Zack, analyzing and measuring how she felt and the goals they both had. She hadn't doubted his affection, but she'd left him when she'd realized how far down she came on his list of priorities.

Now, Brad...he was a man who could get his priorities straight.

She groaned and rolled over. Who could have guessed she'd get off balance this way? All her reasons for taking minivacations were a crock and it was time to face the truth. She'd wanted to see Brad. And now, since their double date with Jamie and Zack, she was sensing heat in his gaze...the kind a woman hoped for. The night before, they'd talked for hours after dinner, and then walked along the shoreline, returning to sit in a romantic garden near the pool.

Why hadn't he kissed her?

She'd sent every possible signal she knew, and Brad hadn't picked up on any of them. Was she so out of practice?

Kim glanced at the lit face of the clock. She'd told the registration clerk that she might stay till Monday, but hadn't made arrangements with her office.

Grabbing her cell phone, she dialed Chloe's work number to leave a message. "Hi, it's Kim," she said. "Please shift my early appointment to one of the other partners and move everything else to later in the week. Please also apologize for me. Thanks."

She disconnected and settled back. Maybe she could get more sleep. Bags under the eyes weren't the most attractive thing to present to the world... especially to Brad.

THE VARIED CHIRPING of birds urged Zack awake. Jamie was still asleep; no doubt she was accustomed to the sounds of nature living on the edge of the salt marsh.

He gave a start as a feline head rose and stared at him. The cat had insinuated himself into the narrow space between their legs and Zack had a strange discomfort. It was an animal, for heaven's sake. What did it care if the humans in his household had sex or not, especially since he'd probably been fixed. Of course, maybe Marlin was jealous, no longer possessing the parts that could bring the pure enjoyment he and Jamie had shared the night before.

"Sorry, pal," he whispered. "I really hope you find pleasures to make up for it."

The cat blinked sleepily before snuggling closer to Zack and closing his eyes in contentment.

"Is something wrong?" Jamie asked quietly.

"No, it's just the cat."

She glanced down and yawned. "He's decided he likes you." Her eyes closed again and her breathing deepened.

Zack checked the clock. It was almost six-thirty and Jamie had to be at the stand by eight. Much as he wanted to stay and make love to her again, he knew her alarm would go off soon. The least he could do was brew a pot of coffee.

Marlin meowed a complaint as he eased from the bed, then thumped onto the floor himself and followed. Zack quietly found his clothing and dressed before heading to the kitchen.

Checking the cupboards, Zack discovered a whole shelf filled with different kinds of coffee. A handwritten note was taped to the inside of the door providing measurements. Intrigued, he carefully spooned various coffee beans into the grinder. For one dark-roast variety, the instructions said "3 beans only." With a grin, he counted them, ground the coffee and started the coffeemaker.

By the time Jamie wandered into the kitchen, he had breakfast ready.

JAMIE STARED AT the toast and scrambled eggs with diced vegetables. Who'd have guessed that Zack could cook? "That looks good."

"I figured we could both use a healthy start."

He handed her a cup of coffee and poured one for himself. "Hell," he exclaimed after tasting it. "This is good."

"You used Granddad's recipe," she said, recognizing the flavor.

"I thought you were joking before."

"Nope. He experimented for years until he found one he thought was the best."

Zack half closed his eyes and sipped appreciatively. Jamie knew how he felt. But she'd figured it tasted so good to her simply because she had a sentimental attachment to anything related to Granddad.

"Would you mind if I made a copy and showed it to Gordon?" Zack asked. "If he likes it, we could offer it on the menu as George Jenkins's Private Blend."

"Fine with me."

He jumped up immediately and scribbled down the information from the cupboard.

Jamie brightened as the coffee took effect, and tucked into breakfast with more energy. Zack sat again and ate with her, glancing at her now and then as though he had something else on his mind.

"I was wondering," he said as they were finishing. "Why would your ex-husband target the fruit stand? Revenge?"

Jamie put down her fork and sipped her coffee, her brow creased. "I don't think so. I think he's hoping I'll run to him for protection. He was quite confident in divorce court that I'd never make it on my own."

"Has he done this kind of thing before?" he asked.

"Not that I know of. Tim's an ass, though. In business he'll do whatever it takes to make a profit—cut a shady deal, lie his head off."

"He doesn't sound like a very nice guy, but it's a big leap from corrupt business practices to the violence of this vandalism."

"True." She didn't want to say anything more, but Zack was obviously suspicious.

"Jamie? Was he violent?" Zack pressed. "Was he, I mean…?"

She bit her lip and sighed. "He had his moments. I feel like an idiot for not realizing what a jerk he was. Our marriage was doomed from the start, though it took me a while to acknowledge the truth."

"He hit you?"

"Not…often. I should have walked the first time he did something out of line. He wants to win and will try anything before giving up. All this stuff with the fruit stand— If he's responsible, it isn't because he loves me. He just wants to prove he was right."

"I'm staying here until he's arrested," Zack declared. "You shouldn't have to deal with him alone. Bastards shouldn't get fair odds."

Warmth flooded Jamie. Zack believed the odds were even between her and Tim, at least on an intellectual level. Still, she couldn't relax her guard. Zack was temporary; she couldn't make the mistake of starting to rely on him.

"I have to get going," she said, checking her watch.

"Too bad we're not people of leisure. We could…"

He raised his eyebrow suggestively and she gave him a strained smile. Much as she wanted to head back to the bedroom with Zack, it was a bad idea.

"You're spending too much time with your wealthy guests," she answered lightly. "They forget you're a working man. But whether you do or not, *I* have responsibilities."

"Okay. If there are any problems, and I mean *any,* call 9-1-1 and then dial me immediately. Aside from that, I'll see you tonight."

"You really don't have to."

"Yeah, I really do."

THEY HEADED TO their respective vehicles and Zack watched Jamie climb into her old truck and drive out.

No wonder she was so determined to prove her independence. Her ex-husband must be desperate to think he could make Jamie question her ability to take care of herself. How dare he try to torment her with acts of violence and cruelty? But Tim wouldn't get the better of Jamie; she was smart, beautiful and feisty as hell.

Jamie turned onto the road toward the beach and Zack forced himself to head to his apartment. He *wasn't* a person of leisure, but it was time to back off and let his staff do their jobs. No more daily rounds. No checking purchase orders and invoices. No more reviewing every detail of how his department supervisors were handling things, inevitably giving the impression that he didn't trust them. He had a sudden urge to contact the prior maintenance supervisor and ask if that was why he'd left. No. Best to cut his losses and move forward. He'd return to the management style that served him best in the past... one that didn't scream "insecurity" and "paranoia." It might even be a good idea to take a day off.

When Zack walked into the living room of his apartment, he was struck by how cold it seemed in comparison to the pleasant home Jamie had made in her grandfather's house. Of course, he hadn't intended to live permanently at the resort. Someday, down the line, he'd figured on building his own house and using the apartment for his convenience or for an on-site manager.

"Good morning," Brad said from the kitchen. "Where were you all night, or do I need to ask?"

"I was at Jamie's house. Turns out her ex-husband might be the person who hired the jerk doing the vandalism, and I don't think she should be out there alone until it's all sorted out. Hope you don't mind me deserting you, but I'll be spending the nights there for the next little while."

Brad frowned. "Good idea. From what Kim says, I gather the house is isolated."

"Sure is. Nice for privacy, not so great for a woman alone with a jerk on her tail."

"Yeah. You know, I guess I'm not too civilized. I'd give a lot to find her ex and show him what it means to be scared."

"You and me, both," Zack agreed. "Might as well accept it, brother—we're only a step or two out of the cave ourselves. But there are worse things than wanting to protect the women in our lives."

"That's true."

Zack scratched his neck. "I've been thinking of taking the day off. You want to do something?" He didn't know what to do with free time after being so obsessed over Mar Vista.

"Kim and I were going sailing. Would you like to come?"

"No, thanks. The two of you go. I don't want to be too far out of touch, in case Jamie has a problem."

"Why don't you spend the day with her? She says Sundays are slow at the stand."

"Not a bad idea, big brother. Not bad at all."

Zack showered and changed, thinking about it. Why shouldn't he go down to the fruit stand? He could pick up lunch at the restaurant; she hadn't had time to pack anything before she left this morning. They could eat, play a game and maybe take a walk on the beach if she had a lull between customers. It was a far better option than sitting in his apartment, forcing himself to do nothing. Working seven-day weeks needed to become a thing of the past.

He called the kitchen to order a picnic lunch and dashed down to the reception desk.

"Hi, Betty," he said, glad he remembered the woman's name without checking her brass name tag. "I'll be off the grounds for part of the day. I can't imagine anyone will need me, but if they do, you've got my cell number, right?"

"Of course. But Mr. Cole stopped by the desk on his way to breakfast to ask if you were free this afternoon to join his party for golf."

"I'll talk with him," he promised.

Zack went into the Clam Shell and asked the server for Greg's table. Greg waved as Zack approached.

"Zack, old buddy. How about it—can you join us for a round today?"

He wavered. Greg Cole was an avid golfer who could spread the news of Mar Vista far and wide. But Zack wasn't an activities director any longer; he owned the resort and wanted to spend time somewhere else for once.

"Thanks, Greg," he said casually. "I'm afraid I've got plans. Maybe another time."

"Sure thing. This place of yours is tops. We've got to get a tournament going here."

"I'm open to it." Zack couldn't tell him that Don Courtland was already talking about moving his tournament to Mar Vista. For one thing, it might not happen. For another, Don needed to talk to his own people before it got around that he was considering a new site for the prestigious event. At any rate, having more than one tournament would be terrific.

"Great. We'll break into the circuit somehow, and I'd be willing to make it worthwhile for a pro. We can call it the Greg Cole Classic, or something equally grandiose."

It was a fantastic offer and Zack smiled. "Perhaps I'll hire an event organizer."

"Good idea. Get someone who knows what they're doing."

"Will do. Have a nice day, Greg."

"I'm sure that won't be a problem."

Zack went into the kitchen to collect the picnic basket. He'd finally said no to a guest and the world hadn't fallen apart.

"The message said No Strawberries," the chef in charge said hesitantly. "Was that right? I went ahead and put in a selection of chocolate-dipped berries. They're particularly good now and a popular picnic item, but we can take them out."

"That sounds terrific. Plain strawberries are plentiful where I'm going, but chocolate-dipped is another matter," Zack answered easily. "I'm sure what you put in is fine. You all know what you're doing."

"Thank you, sir."

Now, time to get out before he succumbed to the temptation to do or say something else.

CHAPTER SIXTEEN

ON WEDNESDAY JAMIE sat in her chair staring at an ocean so blue it didn't seem real. In fact, at the moment her entire life didn't seem real. Zack had shown up at the stand on Sunday, carrying a picnic basket, and spent the afternoon with her. He'd said it was her fault for alerting him to the mistakes he'd made overmanaging his resort, so now she was required to help him resist temptation. Somehow he'd made it sound erotic.

He had taken the table from the trailer and set it up outside so they could play chess in the open air, and later they ate lunch, the Pacific Ocean providing atmosphere that was every bit as appealing as the Sunfish Grotto. He'd even charmingly assisted with selling vegetables to some of his own employees, putting them at ease with a few humorous comments.

She'd been a little surprised—and disappointed—that he hadn't tried to lure her into the trailer, but he'd made up for it that night at the house.

The next morning he left, cheerily saying he'd see her that evening.

Temptation… Jamie dropped her head and groaned.

Zack wasn't the only one who needed to resist temptation.

She'd called Curt and asked him to tell Zack it wasn't necessary to stay at her house every night. Unfortunately, Curt thought it was an excellent idea that she had company. So then she'd looked into an alarm system, figuring Zack wouldn't have an excuse to come if she was otherwise protected, but the company couldn't give her an installation appointment for more than three weeks.

A seagull lit on the other chair and sidestepped a few times, looking at her hopefully. He was one of her regular avian visitors, identifiable from his unusual markings and the cockeyed feathers on one of his wings. It didn't seem to impair him, though; he could fly and appeared quite well fed.

"No handouts," Jamie informed the bird.

He squawked and hopped to the arm of the unoccupied chair, flexing his wings.

"I ate my sandwich early. You're out of luck."

A louder squawk came from the gull and it took off, swooping low and landing on a sand dune thirty feet away. He padded about, keeping a close eye on her, plainly suspecting she had food she wasn't sharing. It was true, but she didn't dare feed the seabirds strawberries or other fruit; they'd surround the place and bring friends.

Jamie's faint humor faded as her thoughts drifted

back to Zack. For all his cordiality, especially under the sheets, she knew he remained unhappy about the fruit stand. The carefully planted evergreens and other native shrubbery along the edge of the course kept it from being seen easily by golfers. But anyone going to the beach or horseback riding saw it, and they often appeared surprised by her presence.

"Hi, Jamie," Brad called, interrupting her thoughts. Now that Kim was gone, he was back to his normal morning exercise. The days of rest seemed to have been helpful for him.

"You're looking good," she commented. "Am I imagining it, or are you moving more easily?"

He hadn't shown up until late Monday afternoon, mentioning that he and Kim had spent most of the day together—the weekend, actually. Jamie hadn't fished for details, but it sounded as if he was still stubbornly resisting his feelings, which was Zack's opinion of the situation, as well.

"I think I've passed the hump," Brad said. "There's a point, after an injury, where it hits you that you're definitely getting better. I've been there before and know what it feels like."

She nodded, remembering that "hump." Emotional injuries could have a hump, too. She'd gotten past hers during the winter. The vandalism at the stand and realizing Tim was likely involved had dug everything up again. But she could deal with it, though she was looking forward to the final resolution—basically, Tim being found and arrested.

Once she might have said "castrated," but he didn't warrant that kind of hostility.

"Do you have any immediate plans for the future?" she asked.

"No. I'll have a medical evaluation at some point. That will determine if I'm fit for active duty."

It amazed her that he was still interested. "I've never really known anyone in the military. Now that I do, it's hard to think of you going back."

"Thanks, but it can't always be someone else's friend or relative who goes."

"No. Uh, Zack mentioned you'd had several surgeries. Are those finished now?"

"The doctors say so. The last was a couple of months ago." He ate some strawberries and sat in silence awhile. "Zack told me about your ex-husband."

"Guess I could have saved everyone a bunch of trouble if I'd thought of Tim earlier."

"There was no reason to suspect him until you knew the vandal had been hired."

"Maybe not."

It was more awkward being with Brad than usual. After all, his brother had been in her bed the past three nights. She hoped Brad didn't sense her uneasiness; she couldn't detect any sign that he did. He ate more berries and they discussed the baseball standings—she was a rabid Dodgers fan because of her grandfather, and he was equally devoted to the Cubs.

"I'd better get going," he said after they'd mutually agreed that there was always next year for each of their teams.

Once she was alone again, Jamie wanted to take a nap—extracurricular activities had cut into her sleep lately—but a busload of tourists showed up and cleaned out the stand. All that was left were the berries she was saving for several women who worked at Mar Vista.

She sank into her seat again when everyone was gone. Working every day was tiring, and the summer was less than a third over. It hadn't seemed fair to hire anyone until the vandalism issue was resolved, but maybe when they caught Tim, she could hire a manager. Part-time would be much better—she'd have more opportunity to work on her jewelry, and more solitude to get back the serenity she'd found before meeting Zack Denning.

"SO WHAT DO you think?" Zack asked Trudy on Thursday morning as they sat and drank the coffee he'd brewed.

"It's the best I've ever had," Trudy said blissfully. "Why didn't you introduce me to this ambrosia before I got pregnant and could have more than one cup a day?"

"Gordon likes it, too, though it won't suit everyone."

"No, of course not. But if Jamie doesn't mind, it could become Mar Vista's signature brew."

"That's what I had in mind. We're planning to call it George Jenkins's Special Blend."

"A nice tribute. I'll miss my coffee even more now. I hope you appreciate my sacrifice," Trudy told her still-flat tummy.

Zack grinned. "Hey, look at it this way—you don't want junior to stay up all night on a caffeine binge."

"Perish the thought. The doctor keeps reminding me that I'm not a teenager and need my extra rest."

"I'm glad you're paying attention to him. Now, what about my proposal on increasing opportunities for local employees?"

"I think it's a great idea. It'll be popular."

"No question of that. It's...been a challenge for me to let go of managing too much. Thanks for your patience over the past few months."

Trudy grinned. "You didn't make it easy. Rick kept saying, 'Give him time. He'll settle in.'"

Five days after making a concerted effort to stop micromanaging, Zack could see further improvement in the way Mar Vista was working. Employees were relaxing and conversed with him more easily. The supervisors were less tense and genuinely welcoming when they did see him. With the ones he knew best, he'd discussed the matter bluntly, also asking their opinions on how to provide promotion potential for local employees, something *they* were interested in, as well. Now Trudy could pass on the official policy. She'd also assured him she would come back after maternity leave as his general manager. He hadn't mentioned his idea of starting another resort, one that would be more family oriented, but he knew she'd approve of it, too.

Forcing himself to take time off had been hard, and rewarding. The past few days he'd spent more time with his brother than he had since they were kids. They'd discussed Brad's experiences in the marines and what it took to move past the trauma of the violence. Brad showed equal interest in how Zack had marshaled everything through the years to finally build Mar Vista, admiring the organization and discipline it took. They talked of their parents and world events, of sports and food and wine. They'd talked about nearly everything...except Kim and Jamie.

Obviously something was still holding Brad back from a relationship with Kim, but he'd have to work it out on his own, and Zack didn't want to pry. As for Jamie, maybe it was old-fashioned, but it didn't feel right to admit he was doing more than standing watch at her house.

Thinking about it was enough to shorten his breath and get him rigid with anticipation.

"Uh, Zack?" Trudy drew his attention.

"Gosh, sorry, Trudy. My head was a million miles away." He gulped some coffee, knowing he'd lied. His head was only a few miles away, in Jamie's bed.

"What about the fruit stand? Is it going to stay where it is? Rick wants to know if more plantings will be needed. He's got his eye on some stuff the Warrington nursery is carrying—they specialize in native vegetation. I'm voting for huckleberry bushes—that way I can pick them every year and make jam."

Zack had come up with a new idea to negotiate with Jamie, but hadn't discussed it with her yet. There were a couple of options he would offer. He'd have to swallow his pride, along with some of his plans, but he thought it might work.

"I'll have to let Rick know," he said. "Can he wait a few days?"

"Of course."

"Thanks."

His challenge now would be to sit and calmly discuss business with Jamie. Since he'd had dinner with Brad the past three nights, he'd arrived at her house an hour before dusk and the evenings had fallen into a pattern. He read while she sketched or worked on her silver casting. At some point one of them made a hot drink, and by the time their cups were empty, the bed wasn't.

That night, to keep his mind on business, he'd asked her to dinner at the Clam Shell. He didn't dare suggest going to the Grotto—if she wore that green number again, his brain would be too befuddled for a rational discussion.

JAMIE DROVE THE daily receipts into town to deposit and stopped by a small dress shop. It was silly to buy something just for tonight; she had a perfectly suitable skirt and blouse she could wear. Zack had mentioned discussing a proposal for the land, so it was a business dinner.

She went into the shop anyway.

It took a while, but she finally found something she liked—a midnight-blue dress that left one shoulder bare, gathered at the waist with a Grecian flair and swirled to below the knees. It could serve for either casual or formal functions, and seemed the kind of gown that would throw a man off balance. The mystery was why she was playing with fire. Zack was becoming far too important; he was a temporary lover and this was an unreal interlude.

Back at home, looking at herself in the mirror with the dress on, she smiled. If it had to be an interlude, she might as well make it a memorable one.

The doorbell rang at seven. She hadn't given Zack a key; it would make him seem too much a fixture in the house.

With the habit of caution, she peeked through the door to be sure it was him. Marlin curved around her ankles yowling. Zack had become one of his favorite people, and to her surprise, Zack reciprocated. After all, the man had never enjoyed the privilege of a pet and was now discovering its delights.

In the golden glow of the evening sun, Zack was too handsome for her own good. But she raised her head, smoothed her new dress and opened the door.

"Hi, I just need to get my purse." She strolled to the living room, savoring how his jaw had dropped when he'd seen her. "Ready," she announced.

He was still staring. "Are you, uh…? Don't you need a coat or something?"

"Hmm." She shrugged elaborately and he paled, watching the fabric shift over the single shoulder it draped. "I suppose I could bring a shawl. It might get cool, though we aren't staying late, are we?"

"No, I suppose not, no…not late at all."

Picking up a black silk shawl, she raised her eyebrow at him. "Are we going?"

"Yes, of course."

She climbed into his SUV, allowing her skirt to shift and show an expanse of bare leg. To keep the casual look, she'd chosen not to wear stockings.

At the Clam Shell they were escorted to one of the tables in the upper section, overlooking the cove. The view was magnificent.

She ordered the special of the evening, then leaned forward. "So, what is this proposal you have about the land?"

The muscles in his throat contracted. "You don't play fair, do you?" he murmured. "Wearing a dress like that sends a man's sense reeling."

"You want me to go home and change?"

"Hell, no."

"Then don't complain," she advised.

"Believe me, I'm not."

"So what's your…proposition?"

ZACK FASTENED HIS gaze on Jamie's face and tried to ignore everything else. Her gown didn't reveal much, not even the edge of her bustline, but it stimulated the imagination. For example…was she wearing a creative bra, or going without? Was the strip of fabric over her shoulder secure, or could it slip down?

"I had a couple of ideas," he said hastily. "First, let me say that I know how badly I acted when we first met, and later, as well. You have a right to be in business and that's that."

She nodded. "Thank you."

"If you agree, I could refurbish the trailer to make it a little less…startling. And I could have other signs painted that are visible, but not so colorful."

"You suggested that before."

"I thought I'd mention it again. The other option is new. I've bought a piece of land near the highway, a couple of miles from here. My architect has sent me several different plans and I could have an attractive building put up, one with running water and a restroom, maybe even a kitchenette."

"That isn't new, either."

"Yes, but the rest of the idea really *is* different. In return, I won't develop the rest of the land your grandfather sold me. You'll keep your section and it will all be left in its natural state. People can hike there, go horseback riding, have picnics and swim at the beach, but I won't build, or put anything else on my sections. I'll put it in writing so the land will be protected, no matter what."

Zack could tell he'd surprised her.

"You don't have to answer right away," he said. "Think about it."

Jamie nodded slowly.

"In the meantime, the Clam Shell has a dance floor, too. It would be a shame for your dress to miss its chance to shine."

"I thought this was a business dinner, not a date."

"Honey, you changed all the rules when you left that shoulder bare."

"Whatever you say." Jamie stood and they passed the server as he arrived with their salads.

"We'll be back," Zack told him. "Can you hold the main course?"

"Of course, sir."

The dance floor was similar to the one at the Grotto—the third wall of the triangular aquarium gave it atmosphere, though the lighting was brighter and more casual. Zack pulled her into his arms and they danced for several minutes.

"Zack, old buddy," a voice interrupted. "You can't keep the wealth to yourself." It was a bachelor guest from New England wealth who had frequented the resort Zack had managed prior to building Mar Vista. "How about it?" he prompted, holding his arms out for Jamie.

"Trent," Zack said, "no one is that generous."

His laugh followed them across the floor.

JAMIE TILTED HER head back and looked up at Zack. "You didn't ask if I wanted to dance with him."

"Did you?"

She waved her arm with the bare shoulder. "Not really."

"That's good. He's a wolf." Zack pulled her closer and she decided to drift with the moment. Part of her brain wanted to think about Zack's offer, but it could wait. Tonight was probably the last time she'd dance with him; she didn't want her memory of it to be about real estate.

The meal slipped by with small talk. They watched the daylight fade over the cove and ate the excellent food from Gordon's kitchen. They danced again and Zack persuaded her to share a slice of ti-ramisu.

"Mmm," she said as the delicate whipped cream swirled across her tongue. "This is good."

He reached out and brushed the corner of her mouth with his thumb. She lifted an eyebrow at him.

"I thought I detected a bit there."

"Really?" Jamie licked her lips and saw perspiration break out on his forehead. *One more night,* she thought. One more night together, then she'd resist.

"How about a walk on the beach?" Zack asked as they left the restaurant.

"That sounds nice."

Instead of the public beach, he drove down and parked behind the fruit stand. She kicked off her shoes and he held her hand as they climbed over the dune. It was a magically silver night, not that different from the evening when he'd kissed her and she'd repulsed him. Strange how things changed.

When they were on the firm sand, he tugged her close and began a slow dance to the rhythm of the waves. After a while, she stumbled.

"Your feet must be cold," he whispered. "Come on."

They climbed back over the dunes, and with a laugh, he picked her up and carried her toward the trailer.

"Are you nuts?" she said. "I haven't replaced the mattress yet."

"I told you I was fond of that mattress. You threw some sheets and blankets over it, didn't you?"

"Yes, but—"

He cut off her words with a long, slow kiss.

All right, so tonight would be really memorable.

ZACK HADN'T PLANNED to coax Jamie into the trailer. Romantically sharing George and Leah's beach had seemed right, but once there, the trailer was too good an opportunity to miss.

Inside, with only the safety light for illumination, he eased the zipper down on Jamie's dress and the silky fabric fell to her waist. As he'd suspected, no bra.... She'd felt too soft and natural against him. He kissed and nibbled his way down her neck to her shoulder and...

His cell phone rang.

"Hell," he growled, groping in his pocket to turn it off. The cell flipped out of his hands and Jamie deftly caught it.

"Trudy Lopez?" she murmured, reading the lit caller ID. "Isn't she the woman who answers at the Mar Vista business office?"

"Sorry," Zack muttered in frustration. If it was Trudy, it had to be important. "I should get that."

Jamie returned the phone and sat on the bunk, slowly pulling her dress back up. He groaned and hit the button.

"Hey, Trudy. What's wrong?"

"Zack, I'm sorry to call, but there's been a car accident—a couple of our employees on their way to work. I don't know how badly they were hurt."

In the small space, Jamie could hear the words as well, and she leaned forward, her brow creased with concern.

"Where are they?" he asked.

"At the local hospital. I don't have the address. The highway patrol reached me on my way home. I'll go, but I'm still an hour away."

That was right. She'd gone into the nearest city to shop for the baby. He put his finger over the cell for privacy and looked at Jamie.

"I can show you where the hospital is," she said softly.

"I don't know how long I'll have to be there."

"It doesn't matter."

He uncovered the speaker. "Don't worry, Trudy," he said. "I'm going there now. You need to get home and rest. Don't forget the doctor's orders."

"Yes, boss."

Jamie finished pulling her dress on, but he reached behind to help with the zipper, unable to resist bending to kiss the curve of her neck. They stepped out of the trailer and he looked at her feet.

"Where are your shoes?"

"They should be next to the truck."

He lifted her again and strode to the SUV.

"I can walk," she protested.

"This is faster."

He helped her into the seat and found her sandals, slipping them onto her feet. On the road, he pushed the speed limit toward town until Jamie told him to turn at a crossing beyond the resort.

"Isn't it in Warrington?"

"No, we share a hospital with another community. This is the fastest route. What was that about doctor's orders?"

"Trudy's pregnant. She's supposed to get extra rest."

"Is everything okay?"

"Sure, but she's thirty-seven and a first-time mother, so they're taking extra precautions. I… uh, knew she wouldn't have phoned unless it was urgent," he said awkwardly.

Jamie continued to give him directions, and he

marveled at her ability to recognize a number of badly marked turns in the dark. They arrived at the emergency room in less than ten minutes.

"Go on," she said. "I'll follow."

WATCHING ZACK SPRINT to the emergency-room entrance, Jamie pressed her arms to her stomach. He was obviously concerned and she didn't want to see that side of him.

Groping for her shawl, she draped it over her arm and swung her legs down from the SUV's cab. The emergency entrance hadn't changed much since she was a kid. When she was sixteen, Granddad had cut his hand and she'd driven him here for stitches. The responsibility had scared her spitless, but he'd encouraged her, and the experience had given her confidence.

The man at the security desk glanced at her, then gave her a much longer look. "Hello. May I help you?" he asked.

"I'm with Zack Denning, who just came in. He's checking on two of his employees from Mar Vista."

"Oh, he's over there." The man pointed to a corner of the waiting room.

Zack sat with a disheveled man. To her relief, they were both chuckling, albeit feebly, so the injuries from the accident couldn't be too severe. Zack saw Jamie and came over.

"Everything should be fine," he said softly. "I'd

like to stay awhile, though. Frank's wife is inside and he's alone."

"Stay as long as you need. I'll take a nap in the SUV."

"Are you sure? I can give you the keys so you can go home. I'll call Brad to give me a lift—"

"No, it's okay. You do what you need to do. Besides, the seats in your SUV are quite comfortable."

"Well, okay. Thanks." He gave her a quick kiss and walked back to the middle-aged man, whose face sagged in forlorn fatigue. She could imagine how he felt. It didn't matter if the doctor said your loved one would be all right; part of you didn't believe it until you saw them for yourself. Having someone wait with him would help.

Jamie smiled at the security guard and went back to the car. It was nice that Zack wanted to be with his employee. But Mar Vista was everything to him, and she reminded herself that taking care of the staff was also good business. It didn't mean he'd suddenly turned into a humanitarian.

She knew she wasn't being fair, but she also needed to keep her sanity. Falling in love with Zack Denning was a sure road to heartbreak.

CHAPTER SEVENTEEN

WHILE ZACK WAS sitting with Frank, a highway patrolman came in and explained the accident had been caused by a bus driver who'd lost control while texting someone on his cell phone.

"Unbelievable," Frank muttered. He glanced at the treatment room where the doctor was still working with his wife.

"Yes, sir. The district attorney will decide what charges should be filed against him."

"That won't help Edna."

"I know," the young officer said awkwardly. "I hope your wife will be all right."

"She'll be fine," the doctor announced, coming out. "Mrs. Irving has several cuts we stitched up, a broken rib and a mild concussion. We did a CAT scan to be sure and we'll hold her a couple days for observation, but everything looks good. We're taking her to a room and you can see her once she's settled."

Frank sagged into his chair. "Thank God."

Zack clasped the other man's shoulder, still feeling somewhat awkward. He was skilled at light conversation with guests at the resort, but this was different. He and Frank had talked for nearly two hours and he'd learned the couple's fortieth anniversary was approaching. They had four children and two grandchildren...and were devoted to each other. They'd even taken the jobs at Mar Vista because they could work the same shift and commute together. The Irvings reminded Zack of his parents—the romance in their marriage was still strong despite the years they'd been together.

"I was really afraid she'd never get that trip to Italy," Frank muttered. "Edna so wants to ride the gondolas in Venice and see the Pope. We've been saving up. It's supposed to be our greatest trip ever."

"You'll get there," Zack assured him. "How about a ride home, after you see your wife?"

"Thanks, Mr. Denning, but I need to stay with her."

Zack waited until Frank was sitting at Edna's bedside before hurrying downstairs. He checked his watch as he went through the double doors to the emergency area. 2:00 a.m. The parking-lot lights shone on Jamie through the windows of the SUV. She'd put the seat back and was asleep, her head pillowed on her shawl; he hated to wake her, but she roused as he unlocked the driver's-side door.

"Hi." She yawned and raised her seat. "How's Frank's wife?"

"She'll be fine. Sorry to make you wait so long."

Jamie didn't answer and he saw she'd dropped

off again. He reached over and gently fastened her seat belt before starting the car.

At the hospital exit, Zack tried to recall the twists and turns they'd made getting there. In the dark and with the poorly marked roads, he was probably safest using the GPS, so he punched in the resort's address and followed the directions until he came to the turn for Jamie's house. She woke up again as the car bumped over the rough driveway.

Jamie got out of the SUV and stumbled toward her front door, reminding him of a drowsy child. So he put an arm around her waist to guide her through the front door and into the bedroom. He left to lock up before returning to lie next to her.

Good God, she was beautiful. What would happen once the real-estate issue was resolved and her ex-husband's hash was settled? They'd traveled a long way in the past few weeks and it was hard to imagine becoming merely neighbors again.

JAMIE WOKE IN the gray predawn. As usual, Zack was on his side, his arm around her, with Marlin happily snuggled between them. The growing familiarity scared her. Familiar, that was, aside from the ache left by the previous night's unfinished business.

Almost as if he'd heard and responded to the thought, Zack stirred and pulled her closer, mumbling, "Good morning."

His hands began exploring. Marlin meowed and scooted off the bed, disturbed by their shifting bodies. Jamie considered saying no…for about three seconds, then let rationality drift away.

"A VERY GOOD MORNING," Zack said, a trifle smugly, as Jamie was coming back into herself. She was too relaxed to poke holes in his arrogance.

Marlin landed on the mattress a few seconds later.

"Do you suppose he watches us?" Zack asked curiously.

"No. I saw him in the mirror. He went for a snack."

"Hmm."

Zack dropped back asleep and Jamie tried to drowse as well, but she had too much to think about. Zack's second suggestion about the land had surprised her. It was a generous compromise. He had everything he owned at stake and was also trying to protect the investment his parents had made. Building rooms or cottages with a private beach would have been a profitable move, yet he was willing to forego it.

Granddad would have preferred keeping the entire section in its natural state, but he'd also wanted to leave a bequest to both her and her brother. If she accepted Zack's compromise, she'd never be able to sell fruits and vegetables there again, but preserving the land would have been Granddad's first wish.

After stewing on the subject for an hour, she slipped out of bed and went to make coffee and breakfast. Reluctant to talk with Zack just yet, she left a note by the coffeepot and drove to the fruit stand to do more thinking.

It would be best to accept the offer. She wouldn't enjoy running the stand if it wasn't by the beach, but she could hire a manager. It would still earn her a living, maybe almost as much, since she could keep it open year-round on a limited basis. And Zack was right that she'd get more business on the highway—by increasing her daily stock, she could partially make up for what she paid to an employee.

Beyond that, once the issue with Tim was resolved, Zack wouldn't have a reason to come around. That would be best for both of them. She couldn't start counting on him and forget how to take care of herself. Eventually, he'd move on and she'd be alone, picking up the pieces.

ZACK WAS DISAPPOINTED when he woke again and found Jamie gone; from the silence in the house, he guessed she'd already left for the fruit stand. Marlin lay next to him and he petted the cat, marveling at the untamed wildness in the animal's eyes. The line between domestic and primal nature seemed thin, but it was that way for humans, too. They simply disguised it better.

He snorted.

A fine moment to get philosophical.

Right now he should get to the office and see if Trudy needed him.

"Hey, boss," Trudy greeted him as he walked in. "Any news?"

"Frank Irving is okay, just bruised, and he insists on coming to work tonight," Zack explained. "Edna has a broken rib and will be out for a while, but nothing critical."

"That's a relief. I hope I didn't interrupt anything important last night."

"Don't worry about it," he said, thinking how painful the interruption had been, though he couldn't explain to Trudy. "You know what a real emergency is, so never hesitate to call."

The day zoomed by. He ordered flowers for Mrs. Irving and finally played golf with Greg Cole. They discussed Mar Vista hosting a tournament in greater detail. Greg was a noted sportsman and obscenely wealthy; he would love to have his name on a major event. And if it made the PGA Tour, he'd be ecstatic.

Zack met Brad for lunch at the Clam Shell and he seemed moody, but wouldn't say what was on his mind. Zack could make an educated guess—he'd checked the reservations and seen that Kim hadn't yet made one for the weekend. He was tempted to interfere, but figured there were times when a brother had to butt out.

In the early afternoon Zack left a message on Jamie's phone saying he'd bring dinner again that night—one of Gordon's new recipes. The chef had been using them as guinea pigs.

At seven he arrived and Jamie let him in.

"Something wrong?" he asked, noticing how pale she was.

"No, of course not."

"Jamie."

"Okay, there was a rosebush run down in the yard. Maybe it happened when we were at the hospital, or during the day when I was at the stand. I didn't see it until I got home tonight."

He reached out for her, but she ducked away. "I'm okay and I'm not falling apart," she insisted. "It's only a rose. I put in a support post and it might even survive."

They ate together in the kitchen and Zack jotted down their comments about the meal for Gordon's benefit. Afterward they sat in the living room and Marlin jumped up to lie next to Zack.

"I've decided to accept your offer," said Jamie abruptly. "The one to move the fruit stand and leave the land undeveloped. It comes closest to Granddad's wishes."

"That's terrific." Zack longed to touch her, but she was too reserved and distant. Unbelievably he found himself asking, "Are you sure?"

She focused on him. "Yes. I'll hire someone to run it and that will give me more freedom to work on my jewelry. I can use the solitude."

Zack sighed. He wasn't sure where the walls between them had come from, but they'd been erected since that morning. There'd be no snuggling tonight...or anything else.

Jamie picked up a calendar. "How long do you think it will take to build the stand?"

"A week or two. I can get a crew on it right away, if you're in a hurry."

"It'll be best to get things settled."

Having the Little Blue Fruit Stand gone was exactly what Zack had wanted, so it was strange that she was now the one pushing for speed. Or was she trying to get rid of him?

"We can probably have it done by the week after the Fourth of July holiday."

"Sounds good," she said, pausing before going on. "You know, I need an early night."

"Alone?" he couldn't resist asking.

"Yeah, I'm not in the mood for company. There's a clean bed in the room down from mine."

"I'll try the couch by the fire. That way I can hear anything from the front of the house better."

"Suit yourself."

She disappeared down the hall into her bedroom.

Perhaps it was for the best. It would give them both space to think. Yet a few minutes later, he groaned when he heard the shower running. One evening they'd showered together in the generous walk-in stall and made love in the splashing water. *Made love.* He didn't know what else to call it, though Jamie didn't seem to like the phrase. *That* was clear from their discussion the morning following their first night together. Yet *sex* seemed a cold description of what they'd shared.

Damnation. He didn't know what was happening to him. Ever since he was a kid, he'd had one goal. Yet while Mar Vista had been his focus for so long and he was proud of what he'd accomplished, it wasn't what he'd started out to do.

When did over-the-top luxury and five-star ratings become essential to his vision? Jamie had suggested more than once that he cared so much for his ambition that he'd lost sight of people. She could be right, though he was trying to correct that, even start planning something closer to his original idea.

He stuck a pillow under his head, pulled a quilt over him and tried to sleep.

JAMIE LAY IN her bed trying not to sniff for the scent of Zack's aftershave. Finding the rosebush flattened hadn't scared her; it had made her angry. Tim knew she loved roses and was trying to use the destruction to make her feel vulnerable. Fat chance. He'd taught her the pitfalls of feeling helpless and sooner or later he'd find out she was no longer a pushover.

But it *had* pushed her to settle the matter of the fruit stand with Zack. He'd grown far too important for a temporary lover; there was too much danger she'd fall in love with him, strange though that would have seemed a few weeks ago.

Stubbornly, Jamie rolled to the side of the mattress where Zack had slept the past few nights. She refused to pretend he was there or to imagine his arm lay around her. After a while, Marlin slunk in, meowing plaintively, as if complaining about having to choose between bed partners.

"Don't get used to him being around," she advised the cat. "He's only an interval."

It took a while, but she finally drifted off to sleep.

CRASH.

Jamie bolted upright as Marlin scrambled away. Even from her bedroom she heard the sound of splintering glass and crunching metal. Grabbing her robe, she dashed into the living room, where a large rock lay on the floor among shards of glass from the front window.

"Watch the bare feet," Zack growled and bolted outside to face the intruder.

"It's not worth it," Jamie called after him.

There was a screech of tires as a vehicle sped away.

She went to the door and in the security light saw Zack checking the crumpled fender on his Mercedes SUV. That was going to cost plenty. Why hadn't she told him to put it in the garage, where it would have been more protected?

Wearily, she went back to her bedroom, got changed and slipped shoes on her feet, renewed anger sweeping through her. It was like Tim to throw rocks in the night; at heart he was a coward and no different than a school-yard bully.

"I've called the sheriff's office," Zack said as she returned. "They should see the damage first."

They waited as the deputy snapped pictures and took information for his report. The officer was very happy to accept the recordings from the video cameras that Jamie had set up after finding the flattened rosebush. Hopefully, they would be as illuminating as the ones she'd gotten at the trailer.

"It's going to be all right," Zack said once they were alone again.

"I know. Tim is a bug. Someday he'll get smashed on somebody's windshield. I hope it's a garbage truck."

Grimly she began sweeping up the splinters of glass on the living-room floor. Outside, Zack nailed boards over the window while she filled the trash can with glass, then ran the vacuum to get the smaller splinters. When she switched it off to move a chair, Zack tried to pull her into a hug.

"I'm okay," Jamie said, shrugging away.

"For pity's sake," he exclaimed. "Letting someone close enough to give you support doesn't make you weak."

"It doesn't make you strong, either," she snapped.

"Maybe it does, if it's two people making each other stronger."

"Yeah, well, that sounds nice, but I live on the other side of the mirror."

Zack gestured around the house. "Do you want to be so fiercely independent that you're just like your grandfather, a strange old hermit who was eccentric as hell?"

"How *dare* you?" she snarled.

"*You* called him 'eccentric,' and if I hadn't said you were like him, you wouldn't have had a problem with it. But I will admit one thing—even if your grandfather was alone, at least he was memorializing a magnificent love. All you're doing is turning your back on the world because you don't trust yourself to be strong unless you're alone. Why would you let a jerk of an ex-husband have that much power over your life?"

"You don't have a clue what my life is about, so don't try any mumbo-jumbo, pop psychology on me," she declared. She shoved the vacuum toward him. "You want to help so much? Finish cleaning up."

She stalked to her bedroom and slammed the door. He didn't get it. Sure, she'd been hurt by her failed marriage, but Zack was the problem, not Tim. She wouldn't have even met Zack if he hadn't gone ballistic over Granddad's fruit stand for fear it might damage the image of his precious resort.

He might have cleaned up his act with his employees, but Mar Vista was still his obsession. He lived, drank, slept and literally *ate* everything connected with it. And who knew when he'd get irrational about some other dumb thing?

What did he expect her to do? Go nutty and throw herself into the arms of a guy who cared more about a piece of real estate than he did her? He might be a magnificent lover, but as soon as she needed him for something, he'd probably say he had to play golf with a guest or check registrations. She had more self-respect than to remain involved with a man of that sort…a man who could easily break her heart.

The sooner he was out of her hair, the better.

JAMIE TRUDGED THROUGH the next week. The broken window was repaired. She put up signs saying she was relocating, which piqued her customers' curiosity. The ones who knew about the dispute with Mar Vista tended to be annoyed at first, but cooled off once they heard the details. Others were disappointed, while acknowledging the new site would be convenient. But everyone agreed it was great to keep the shore and dunes undeveloped for people to enjoy.

Zack showed her several plans for the building, and offered to have them altered, even to incorporate the little blue trailer. She considered it, then decided to retire the trailer to the barn where her grandfather had kept it every winter. Maybe, someday, if she got ambitious, she'd take it on a road trip, visit Yellowstone and travel Route 66 like her grandparents had on their honeymoon. In the meantime, she needed to forget her *other* associations with it.

Zack was excruciatingly polite. He came each evening without fail, spending the night on the couch. Marlin split his attentions between the two of them; he was going to be miserable when Zack was no longer there.

Aside from the two incidents at the house, nothing more happened, and Tim seemed to have dropped off the face of the earth. Curt had checked with her ex-husband's office and they said he was out of touch on a business trip. On the next inquiry, they explained he was taking an extended vacation. Jamie knew Tim had plenty of vacation time saved, but she doubted he'd abandoned his plan to intimidate her so he could go sit on a beach in Hawaii.

At night, she slept poorly; it was hard knowing how much comfort and pleasure was available on her living-room couch. But hard as it was, she had to think of the long-term instead of what she immediately craved.

AFTER SO MANY days of being near Jamie without touching her or getting any closer, Zack was suffering extreme frustration. He had tried to get her interested in the plans for the new fruit stand, but she'd barely glanced at them and said they were fine and to pick the one he thought would work best. He couldn't tell if she was angry, or simply too tired to care. It was obvious she wasn't getting much rest and he missed those few days when their fatigue had come from giving each other pleasure.

He also hated seeing Brad's grim demeanor. What was going on between Kim and his brother? There was no evidence of an argument, and they weren't the type to hold grudges anyway. So what could it be?

"Has Brad said anything about Kim? Did something happen?" he asked Jamie one night as they sat in the living room in a semblance of cordiality.

Jamie's face warmed, becoming less remote. "He hasn't mentioned a problem, but he doesn't talk about Kim anymore. At first he did—that's how I knew he had feelings for her. Now he sticks to baseball, or telling stories about places he's been, kids he saw overseas, that kind of thing. When he talks at all, that is. He's quieter now than when he first began coming by the stand."

Zack tossed aside the book he'd been pretending to read. "I really thought we'd gotten them together."

She regarded him with more sympathy than usual. "They still might figure it out."

"I'd like to light a fire under his ass and get him to San Francisco somehow. I considered asking him to hand deliver something for me, then realized that might be too obvious."

"A little," Jamie agreed in a dry voice.

"Any suggestions?" he asked.

"No. I'm going into my workroom to cast some pendants. Maybe I'll think of something."

"Sure. I'll…finish my book."

Zack would rather have watched her work; he enjoyed seeing the deft way she handled the molten silver and how the pieces she'd designed emerged for the final finishing touches. After a couple of times, though, she had said it made her nervous to have someone observing her, so he'd left her alone.

He stood and looked out the windows into the dark woods that half circled the house. The night before, Jamie had irritably exclaimed she wished Tim would do what he was going to do so the waiting would be over. With everything in limbo, Zack almost felt the same. It was his private desire to personally catch the slimy bastard and plant a fist square on his nose.

KIM STARED INTO her fireplace at the flames dancing over the gas log. There hadn't been any need to light it for warmth; San Francisco was in the middle of an unusually warm June, but she'd craved the cheer and energy of a fire.

She'd accomplished little at the office for more than a week. And just as she'd begun to find her focus, she'd gotten a call from Zack asking her to draw up a very specialized contract. Jamie was to receive unlimited free use of a building on a new piece of Zack's property. In return, she would leave the beachside parcel unoccupied, and he agreed to do the same for all of the adjacent land.

The compromise surprised Kim, especially since it appeared to be Zack's idea. In fact, he'd become almost passionate about keeping the land natural for people to experience, saying Jamie had mentioned it was her grandfather's original plan and that was what had given *him* the idea. It didn't necessarily mean Jamie was happy about the arrangement, but at least she'd agreed.

Zack's enthusiasm surprised Kim even more than the compromise; if she hadn't known better, she'd think he was changing. Yet it was hard to imagine him no longer being utterly driven and intent on success.

So she had written up the contract and sent it to Mar Vista—her one real accomplishment that week. But it had stirred emotions about Brad that she had been trying to ignore. Even while performing the simplest of tasks over the past week, she'd found herself replaying the hours they had spent together. Finally, she had to ask one of the partners to review her recent briefs and contracts. It wasn't fair to clients otherwise. Thankfully, so far they'd found nothing amiss except for a few grammatical errors.

Picking up the phone, she called her mother in Southern California. They chatted about inconsequential subjects until her mother grew exasperated.

"Kim, this isn't like you. Why don't you get to the point?"

It made her smile. Her mother should have been a lawyer. Her dad always said it was Mom who'd passed on the analytical brain that powered his daughter's law career.

"No...there wasn't any particular reason.... Well...that's not true," Kim admitted. "Wasn't Dad in the navy when you two met?"

"Yes, you know he was."

"Did he worry about being with you because of that?"

Her mother was silent a long moment. "He was aware of it. The Vietnam War was over, but there was always a chance something could happen. He didn't want me to be one of those women you see on TV, trying to be stoic as she watches a flag-draped coffin come off an airplane."

"The two of you got together anyway."

Her mother's voice became soft. "Kim, honey, have you become involved with a military man?"

"Uh...yes. Sort of. He's holding back."

"And you think he might be worried that it's unfair to you."

"I honestly don't know. But he was badly injured, so he's especially aware of the dangers in today's world."

"Brad Denning?"

Kim closed her eyes; how had her mother guessed? "Yes."

"I've always had a feeling about the two of you. He's a fine man."

"He won't even kiss me. We do things together and he's pleasant...but that's all."

"Who says you can't make the first move? If I'd waited on your daddy, right now you'd still be a young law-school student."

Kim laughed.

"Just one thing, honey," her mother continued. "Be sure you're ready for what you're getting into. For the spouse of a soldier, a police officer, a fireman...any of those careers...it takes a toll. Be fair to yourself and to Brad, and don't get so carried away by romance that you forget the reality of what will come in the years afterward. Talk to your aunt. She came very close to losing Graham in that embassy incident."

The reminder was sobering, and Kim knew it deserved serious examination.

CHAPTER EIGHTEEN

JAMIE OPENED THE large envelope Zack had given her that morning; inside were legal papers regarding the land use. As far as she could tell, the agreement was simple and straightforward. In drawing it up, Kim Wheeler had avoided the legalese that could mean anything or nothing to a nonlawyer.

Deciding she should be smart, Jamie dropped it off at the office of her grandfather's attorney and met with him the next day. Zeb Barney had known Granddad for years, and was one of the few people who'd visited him during the isolated winters at the house.

"It's a fair contract," he told her. "Denning is giving up more than you are, and putting money in also, for the land and building."

"Then you think it's safe to sign?"

"Certainly, and I admit it makes me feel good to know that whole section will stay the way it was when I was a boy. It's also what George would have wanted."

"That means the most to me, too," Jamie agreed.

"He still would have put your welfare first."

Her throat grew tight with grief. "I know, but I think this is a good compromise."

Afterward she stopped at the bank to discuss handling deposits, now that she'd hired a woman to run the stand. Presently Susan was working at the trailer for a few hours in a trial run. Susan came with high recommendations, and since Jamie had said she could have her daughter with her, it was exactly the kind of job the young mother had been looking for to supplement the family income.

It felt strange to be an employer. Before making the decision to hire someone, she'd felt an urge to consult with Zack, only to immediately dismiss the idea. Maybe getting your life tangled up with other people wasn't such a horrible thing, but that didn't make it smart to rely on them.

Finishing at the bank, she ran by Curt's office to check in, but there'd been no developments in her vandalism case and Tim was still the invisible man.

"If he comes through here, we'll deal with him," Curt assured her. "I've also talked with the police in Miami, so they're aware of the situation."

"What about Gus Hewitt?" she asked, wondering if he'd be going after the fruit stand again. "Has he made bail?"

"Nope. We're mostly holding him on a parole violation. I figure he's staying in jail for a reason, probably to make Gardiner nervous enough to offer hush money." Curt chuckled. "Old Gus doesn't know it won't do any good. The lab lifted your ex-husband's fingerprints off the instructions he sent to Gus. I, uh, neglected to give that information to Gus, so don't tell anyone."

"Not a word."

Back at the stand, Susan was happily finishing up a sale. "I love this job," she exclaimed. "It would be even nicer if it stayed near the beach, but the other location is good, too. There are those trees and it has a pretty view across the valley. And when my daughter goes back to school this fall, she'll have a place to come in the afternoon and do her homework."

Susan's enthusiasm was one of the reasons Jamie had hired her. Once she'd left for the day, Jamie sank into a chair and watched the ocean for a while. Maybe she'd leave the chairs here. It would be a nice place for people to come and sit and watch the water. She'd ask Zack if he minded the idea; he probably wouldn't. They were attractive and would blend into the landscape.

She had a steady flow of customers for the rest of the afternoon, with the final flurry of off-duty Mar Vista employees between three and four. Lately they'd had a change of attitude concerning their employer. They were delighted with a new policy offering advancement potential, and the time he'd spent with one of their own at the local hospital had given a jump start to their approval.

It was another reason she was glad Susan would be taking over the stand soon. The last thing she needed for her peace of mind was to constantly hear about Zack Denning or Mar Vista.

As Brad completed his third full round of the property for the day, he thought it might be time to request a physical review and get on with his life. He'd begun running the route, recalling his basic training, and it was going well. It wasn't that he felt 100 percent, but he was making rapid progress, and he hated the uncertainty of wondering what he was going to do next.

Back at the resort, he dropped by the office to see if Zack wanted to kick back with a cup of coffee.

"Hi, Brad," Trudy greeted him. "A guest came by looking for you earlier."

"A guest?" His senses went on alert. Unless his parents had decided to make a surprise visit, Kim was the only guest who'd be looking for him.

"It's Kim Wheeler." Trudy confirmed his conclusion. "She was hoping you might be free for dinner. Apparently, she tried your cell phone, but it was off."

"Is she in the same room as before?"

"No, it was occupied, so they put her in 108, two doors down. She said to come by if you have a chance."

Brad went upstairs to shower and change, then walked slowly to Kim's room. It was an unusual time of the week for her to get away from the office, unless Zack had needed her for legal purposes.

At 108, he knocked. A second later Kim opened

the door and waved him inside. "Want a beer or something?" she asked. "I had room service deliver several options."

"Are you expecting someone?"

She smiled. "Yes. You." In a swift move, she wrapped her arms around him and landed a kiss that began hot and progressed to sizzling.

"Holy cow," he gasped when she finally loosened up on him. "What was that about?"

"If you don't know, you're even rustier with women than you say you are. Look, Brad. I accept that you're a soldier and I'll admit the idea of you returning to active duty scares the hell out of me. But if that's why you're keeping so much distance between us, quit shielding me. I've had some long talks with my mom and my aunt. If they can thrive as navy wives, I can handle it with a marine."

"You're not... I mean, it's not the same as when your dad and uncle were in the service."

"No, it's not, but so what? We are both consenting adults and you can't tell me that you're not attracted to me."

"You... I need to think." Brad grabbed a bottle of beer and drank down half, chewing on what to say. Kim had virtually proposed to him, and while it was tempting, it wasn't that easy.

"You think too much—that's your problem," she said.

"I'm trying to be realistic. You're a lawyer with a five-star reputation in a tough city. Zack told me that you have meetings with the mayor of San Francisco, for God's sake. The last thing you need is a banged-up soldier hanging around. I don't even know what I'm going to do with my life or what I'm good for...."

Sparks practically flew from Kim's eyes. "That's insulting. How could you imagine your physical condition has anything to do with me wanting to be with you? And as for what you're going to 'do' with your life, if you can't serve on active duty, how about teaching or another assignment? Surely the military can use a highly trained officer with battle experience in places that don't require you to bench-press a battleship."

Bench-press a battleship?

Brad's sense of humor asserted itself. He despised self-pity even more than he hated being pitied by other people. He'd admired Kim forever...wanted her without realizing it. She felt the same for him. Apparently, it was time for action.

He pulled her close and returned her kiss with enough heat to melt one of those battleships.

"Not bad, soldier," she murmured as his hands roamed around her waist and rib cage.

"So, what else did you talk about with your mother and aunt?"

She gasped as he neatly dispatched her blouse, but tried to talk in a normal voice. "They just gave me a few tips and some really valuable advice."

"What advice?" he said, sinking down upon the bed with her.

"Mostly that I didn't have to wait for you to make the first move."

"Mmm. I knew I liked those two women."

Zack studied the new structure for Jamie's fruit stand. It was half-completed and rested on land along the main drag out of town. It looked good—obviously more permanent than the trailer, but that wasn't a bad thing. They'd gotten permits to tap into the water main and bring electricity in, so there was a restroom and an indoor room where someone could relax or fix a snack, though the display space was a roofed area outside. He'd also bought a walk-in commercial cooler, where the stock could be stored, if necessary, for short periods.

A paved driveway provided a clean area for deliveries and the Mar Vista pickups. The project didn't have the resort's grand size or luxury, but it was attractive and functional.

"Hey, Zack." It was Jack Sawyer coming around the corner with his long lanky stride.

Instead of getting contractors, Zack had decided to use the Mar Vista maintenance staff to build the stand, making Jack the supervisor. In his off time, the man was a freelance contractor in Warrington, so it seemed a good way to demonstrate his intention to give the local employees advancement opportunities. Jack was a total professional, with a sense of humor that he'd let loose once he grew more comfortable around Zack; he had made more than one joke about Zack and Jack building a shack.

"You guys are doing a great job," Zack said.

"Thanks. We're all putting a token inside the walls. I'm putting in a stick."

"A stick?"

"Sure. Sure, the stick that hit the cow that kicked the dog that chased the cat that ate the rat that chewed a hole in the house that Jack built."

Zack grinned.

They discussed the flooring for the interior and decided on a quality laminate since it would be more durable and attractive than some of the alternatives. A low decking would provide the flooring for the outside sales and display area.

"We're knocking off now," Jack said at length. "But I'll have the crew back early tomorrow. A few days should do it."

"Terrific. I'll let Ms. Conroe know."

"She's a nice lady. A shame some louse had to make things hard on her."

Zack followed the truck back to Mar Vista. He stopped by the office to read a status report from Trudy and sign a few letters.

Jamie had insisted on providing dinner that night and was expecting him at nine. The later hour was her idea, not his; she'd probably decided it was a way to limit the time he spent at the house. It was so frustrating. He was certain Jamie still desired him, but she wouldn't acknowledge it and kept pushing him away.

The extra hours did provide an opportunity to take a run on the ocean bluff. Now that he wasn't spending every second trying to perform everyone else's job, he could do some personal things. Sixty minutes later, he arrived back at the apartment and decided he'd have to get out more often. The adrenaline burn felt good.

In the parking lot, Zack did a double take—Kim and Brad were headed toward his car, hand in hand. Somehow he'd missed seeing Kim's name on the reservations list. She looked as happy as he'd ever seen her and the pair kissed before Brad opened the passenger door. As Brad came around to the driver's side, he spotted his brother; Zack grinned and gave him a thumbs-up.

Feeling even better, Zack trotted up the stairs to his apartment. Somehow Kim and his brother had gone from nowhere to okay in nothing flat.

The phone rang and it was Gordon, asking if he *really* shouldn't provide food for that night. To placate the generous chef, Zack suggested appetizers and a dessert; after all, if they didn't eat them, Jamie could stick them in the refrigerator for another day. Gordon seemed pleased and Zack suspected he saw himself in the role of matchmaker, using food to smooth the road to romance.

Romance.

Brad and Kim finally had gotten it right and he

had a feeling it wouldn't be long before Kim was not only a friend, but a sister-in-law.

As for Jamie?

Zack's mood sobered sharply. Years ago, Kim had broken up with him, saying she refused to come second to his ambition. As a brash college student, he'd dismissed her reasoning out of wounded ego—after all, what was wrong with ambition? But brutal honesty made him admit that she *had* come second... and not even a close second.

Was that the problem with Jamie? She'd seen him as a determined entrepreneur, attempting to have a woman thrown off her land because he didn't like the appearance of her business. In the beginning, he'd used various business ploys on her to try to get control of the situation. Was it any wonder she hesitated to trust him?

He wanted her in a way that threatened to disable him whenever he thought of how she touched him in bed. More than that, he enjoyed simply being with her, and appreciated her humor, intelligence and insight.

Jamie deserved to come first and he had to decide whether he was ready for that kind of commitment...assuming she even wanted it from him.

In the meantime, he was determined to protect her while Tim Gardiner was on the loose. And tonight he had some other good news to share—Jamie would surely be pleased that Brad and Kim had finally gotten together.

JAMIE DECIDED HER pride had gotten the better of her. She'd insisted on preparing the evening meal as a move toward self-reliance or something—she was a little hazy as to the reason—so now she was stuck. Also, it was awfully domestic, cooking a meal for Zack Denning, a man she'd been trying to push away for more than a week.

Having him sleep on the couch every night was an exercise in torture. She'd never expected to like Zack, much less feel anything stronger for him. It would have been so much easier if he'd stayed a rude, arrogant jackass, demanding things he had no right to demand.

The doorbell rang and she glanced at the clock. Eight-thirty—he was early, as always, determined she wouldn't be at the house alone after dark.

"Fantastic news," he said as he came through the door.

"They caught Tim, so it's all done?" she asked.

"Uh…no. But from what I saw in the parking lot a while ago, Kim and Brad have finally gotten together."

"Really?" Pleased warmth flooded through her. Brad deserved to be happy, and Kim was a nice person, too. "You're sure?"

"They were holding hands and kissing. That's a good clue."

Not *that* good a clue, she thought. She and Zack had done more than kiss or hold hands, and it hardly made them a couple. Nonetheless, it was a positive sign because Brad *had* been holding back.

She saw a Mar Vista bag in his hand. "I told you I'd fix dinner."

He grimaced. "Gordon wanted to send something, so I suggested appetizers and dessert. You can put them in the fridge for your lunch tomorrow if they're not needed."

She shrugged. "We can have the appetizers now. The casserole has to be in the oven for another twenty minutes anyway."

Gordon had sent some of her favorite spicy appetizers with a sweet peanut sauce. They reminded Jamie of something she'd eaten once at a Vietnamese restaurant.

"I kept it simple," she said, when the buzzer went off. "A casserole and salad." She wished Zack would show displeasure or disdain at the prospect of something so simple.

"Sounds great. Even Gordon admits he likes plain old mac and cheese instead of gourmet all the time."

She'd fixed a rice-and-chicken casserole with a vegetable salad on the side. Zack stared at the salad in amazement. "How many vegetables did you put into that thing?"

"Fifteen. Three kinds of lettuce, cabbage, broccoli, jicama, avocado, carrot, onion, kohlrabi, spinach, peas, beets and radicchio."

"Is that fifteen? I lost count."

"So did I. Maybe it's fifteen, or maybe I miscounted. Oh, I forgot the radishes. And I should have asked if you liked beets. Some people despise them."

"Not me. I'm a fan of most veggies, though I've never heard of kohl...what?"

"Kohlrabi. It's just a fun crunchy vegetable. The farmers bring bits of stuff for me to try marketing, and once in a while I have leftovers. It's fun to see how many veggies I can get into a salad or soup."

"What's your record?"

"Twenty-four. But at that rate, you don't get much more than a few bites of each one."

He seemed to enjoy the meal. Since she'd just planned to serve cookies and ice cream for dessert, she pulled the chocolate truffle cheesecake from the bag Gordon had sent.

"He likes to feed his friends," Zack said.

It probably *had* been Gordon's decision to send the food, or at least quite a bit of it, but Zack had started the pattern. Even when he'd still been at odds with her, he'd brought food to the trailer. He didn't have to; he could have eaten and then shown up.

After dinner, Zack put on a movie from her DVD collection and she left him to watch while she went to work in her studio. She wasn't very effective, thinking more about Zack than anything else. He'd changed since she'd met him, or perhaps was showing another side of himself. The man who'd arrived at the fruit stand yelling that first day hadn't seemed to be someone who could acknowledge mistakes or make compromises. Yet in the past two weeks, Zack had done both. And while it might have also been good business to go to the hospital, his concern for his injured employees had been genuine.

She picked up a sketch pad and doodled. Beyond everything else, Zack had proved to be a considerate and passionate lover, but great sex didn't mean they had a future.

Tossing the sketch pad aside, she went to the window and stared out. The moon shone over the water beyond the salt marsh, turning the foam on the waves to silver. Granddad had lived alone in this house for many years, the surface of his life only gently ruffled by other people. The deep currents had been his memories of Leah and his art. It had seemed an uncomplicated life to Jamie, attractive after the messy end of her marriage. But was it realistic to think you could avoid complication? Was it truly desirable to be disconnected from people?

And why did it have to be Zack Denning who made her ask those questions? He'd been steadfast in wanting to protect her, but that could be a pride thing. It had certainly started that way, because of the suggestion that he or his resort employees were responsible for the vandalism, and it would have been hard for him to back out once it was clear someone else was to blame.

She went into the kitchen to make a pot of decaf coffee and took a cup into the living room. Zack had turned off the movie and was leafing through the newspaper, Marlin snoring beside him.

"Here," she said. "I'm taking mine onto the back porch to look at the view."

"Mind some company?"

"I'm perfectly safe out there on my own."

"That's not what I asked."

She sighed. "No, I don't mind company."

In the kitchen, she loaded her coffee with cream and sugar, while Zack looked on in surprise. "I thought you took it black."

"Once in a while I turn it into dessert."

She led the way to the wide porch. The motion detectors flicked on, brightly illuminating, switching off soon after they were seated on the comfortable outdoor sectional. The moon shone so brilliantly that the trees cast sharp shadows. Zack and Jamie fell silent as a herd of deer nibbled their way across the landscape. Zack stiffened uncomfortably as a skunk meandered along in front of the porch, but Jamie squeezed his arm and kept him still.

"Generally there's no danger," she whispered once it was gone. "As long as you don't panic. I've sat here dozens of times with no ill result."

"I can't help wondering what one of those would do to a guest room at the resort."

"Worse than a raccoon, that's for sure." Something thudded near them and Zack jerked. "I think that's Marlin," she said, twisting around to look at the window behind them. Sure enough, the big black cat was sitting on the interior windowsill, his eyes gleaming as he stared at the moonlit scene.

A fox delicately picked his way across the landscape and met another fox, sniffing and flirting... obviously it was female, and likely in heat.

"He's got the right idea," Zack murmured, his arm sliding around her shoulders.

"Careful," she warned with the last bit of rational reason she possessed for the evening. "You don't want to startle them. A fox can stink things up almost as bad as a skunk."

"Some things are worth the risk," he returned, pulling her close so his lips could start nibbling on hers.

Okay, so she'd known what could happen if they went outside together....

CHAPTER NINETEEN

ZACK PUT DOWN a length of the laminate flooring and used a mallet to tap it firmly into the tongue-and-groove fitting. He'd enjoyed planning and building the new fruit stand far more than he'd anticipated. A month or two ago, he probably would've thought it was too small to bother with, his head so preoccupied with size and luxury that not much else would fit. Fortunately, Jamie had knocked sense into him and life was more fun now.

"Is this right?" he asked Fred Harrington, who was directing installation of the flooring.

"Sure is, boss. You learn real fast."

"It helps to have a good teacher. Who taught *you* how to install flooring?"

"My wife—her dad is a contractor in Southern California. My father-in-law offered me a job when we got married, but I wanted to live in Warrington."

Zack paused and looked out the door, watching the afternoon fog drifting into shore. There was a tall cypress grove to the right, the small highway on the left and, across the valley, a few houses on the hills.

"I like it here, too," he agreed. It was true, and for the first time in years, he realized a place was beginning to feel like home. Jamie flashed across his mind, in her overalls and ready to take on the world. Was it Warrington that seemed like home, or Warrington with Jamie Conroe in it?

He held another piece of the laminate while Fred cut it to the correct length. At first he had driven out to see how the stand was progressing. After a while, he'd picked up a hammer. The men had good-naturedly corrected his goofs and showed him better ways to do things. It hadn't taken long before they stopped the formal "Mr. Denning" and began calling him "boss" or "Zack" the way Trudy did.

Zack enjoyed the physical activity, and learning new skills was always good; he'd often wished he knew more about construction while Mar Vista was going up so he could better evaluate the progress.

The Little Blue Fruit Stand would soon be gone. It hadn't impacted Mar Vista as much as he'd feared, but a number of guests had mentioned its questionable appearance. Greg Cole was concerned in particular, despite his enthusiasm for the resort; he should notify him that the fruit stand had moved. Still, the layers of native evergreen and bushes effectively hid the trailer, and they provided an interesting hazard for golfers. As a result, Rick Lopez wanted to keep the plantings, even when the stand was gone.

Zack's mind drifted to the night before last. The

hours on the porch had been incredible and he'd wondered if a form of moonlight madness had come over them. By morning Jamie had retreated again behind her barrier with the no-trespassing signs, and the next night he'd slept on the couch.... Comfortable though it was, that couch was too familiar.

"I thought we would have gotten this done today," Fred grunted as the two of them maneuvered the last piece into place. "But I didn't want to finish the flooring until the plumbing was finished, and we needed to find that lost diamond back at the resort. The guest really freaked when it popped off her wedding ring and went down the drain."

Zack had heard about the incident. "Did you find it?"

"Yep. There's a trap in the system. Sure was a mess to get, though. If she'd seen the gunk it was in, she might not have wanted it back."

"It was a pretty big diamond," Zack said. "Don't worry about the delay. We'll get this whipped the day after tomorrow."

"We could work on the Fourth of July if you need us to."

"No, I want everyone possible to get the holiday off. We'll still be able to meet the move date that Ms. Conroe has been giving her customers."

Satisfaction settled over Zack as he drove toward Mar Vista, and it occurred to him that the biggest reason he'd enjoyed his work on the new fruit stand was because he was doing it for Jamie. Not because it was getting rid of the trailer, or even because he genuinely enjoyed working with the crew on building it, but simply because he wanted it to suit Jamie's needs. The new stand was a reminder of how much she had come to mean to him.

KIM STUDIED THE ring on her left hand with extreme satisfaction. She was glad Brad hadn't apologized because it wasn't grandiose. He'd found it, he said, in a small antiques store in Warrington, and chose it for its old-fashioned charm. She couldn't imagine a better engagement ring.

They still had things to work out. Brad had inquired into teaching possibilities and found there was interest, both in San Francisco as well as at the Naval Postgraduate School in Monterey. But he might have to officially retire and be hired as a civilian, so he was considering it. She'd told him again that if he wanted active duty, then that was what she wanted for him. It was the truth, even if it terrified her.

Tonight they were having a celebration dinner at the Sunfish Grotto with Zack and Jamie.

Brad escorted her to the restaurant and she was proud walking in beside him. *My fiancé,* she thought giddily, more conscious than ever of the ring on her finger. It was like being sixteen again, with the excitement of a first romance; only this time it was going to last forever. The maître d' led them to the table where Zack and Jamie waited.

"Congratulations," Jamie said, standing to give Kim a hug. "I'm so glad for both of you."

"How about a dance before we order?" Zack asked.

Kim couldn't imagine turning down a chance to be in Brad's arms, and now she could punish him if he tried switching partners the way he'd done the last time they'd danced at the Grotto. A smile curved her mouth.... There were some delightful ways she could torment Brad, whether he did anything wrong or not.

"What are you grinning about?" he whispered in her ear. "You have a cat-who-ate-the-canary look."

"You'll find out."

From the corner of her eye she saw Zack; he seemed oblivious to everything except Jamie as they moved to the slow music.

There was something different about him, she thought idly. She'd teased him earlier about becoming Saint Zack to his employees, and he'd thrown it off with a joke. Actually, things *were* better, though the employees still appeared cautious, probably waiting to see if his policy changes were as good as they sounded on paper. He'd discussed the resort for a while with her, but didn't seem as zealous as usual. He was still enthusiastic, just not so intense.

Was it possible he'd found something—*some-one*—more important to him than Mar Vista? As they returned to the table, Kim felt a faint chagrin stemming from feminine pride. *If* Zack was reordering his priorities, it was Jamie Conroe who'd gotten him to change, not Kim Wheeler.

She looked at Brad and her chagrin vanished. Life had turned out pretty damn good.

JAMIE HADN'T WANTED to eat dinner at Mar Vista with Zack, but couldn't refuse since it was a celebration for Kim and Brad. She'd decided to wear the off-the-shoulder blue gown again. This time she dressed it up with silk stockings and long, elegant earrings that drew attention to her bare shoulder. She'd also fastened it differently, which showed more skin.

The other accessories completed the look and she was satisfied; Zack had swallowed hard when he saw her, and seemed to have trouble concentrating on anything except her bare shoulder. He'd left a trail of kisses down from her neck while they danced and her skin still tingled.

Firmly she reminded herself that it was a night for romance; after all, they were celebrating an engagement long overdue in the making. Kim had bubbled on the phone when she'd called and told Jamie about it. Since Kim was in her mid-thirties, they were planning to start a family right away. Jamie had pushed away her own angst. When she and Tim had gotten married, she'd wanted to get pregnant the first year, but Tim insisted on waiting; he'd wanted to be established in his career. Gradually she'd realized that he didn't *want* children, and by that time, she hadn't wanted to have any *with* him.

She just wished he'd make his move and get caught. Knowing he was out there planning something made it hard to put him completely out of her mind. Regardless, she was ready to face him down.

When their entrées arrived, so did a bottle of champagne. Zack poured their glasses and raised his. "To Kim and Brad," he said simply. "I'm thrilled my friend will soon become my sister."

Kim's face lit up and Brad reached over to kiss her before they all drank the toast.

"What kind of wedding will you have?" Jamie asked when she'd finished her meal.

"We haven't discussed it," Kim answered. "But I'd like something simple, with just a few guests."

"Hear, hear," Brad said.

As they left the restaurant, Kim turned to Zack. "It's the Fourth of July. Are there fireworks anywhere?"

"Sure," Jamie answered for him. "Down at the dunes near the fairgrounds. It's free. Everybody just comes and watches, but we should get blankets to sit on. I've got some at my place."

It took only a few minutes to pick up the blankets, then they drove down and found a good place to watch the displays as they burst overhead. Zack pulled Jamie against him, his arms around her. A yearning voice inside her said it was the perfect way to watch fireworks every year, and another voice crossly told her to shut up. But was a future together so terribly impossible?

"That was amazing," Kim enthused as they hiked through the sand toward the car. "It's so much better because the sky isn't lit up from the city, especially with those orangey streetlights they use so many places."

"It's the first time I've ever seen the fireworks here myself," Jamie confessed. "My brother saw them each year since he visited in July, but I always came in August."

A face slid past in the crowd and Jamie frowned. Tim? She stopped and studied the people around her but saw nothing.

"Something wrong?" Zack asked.

"Nope," she answered. With Tim on her brain, it would have been hard not to imagine glimpsing his face in a large group of people, particularly in the limited light.

They'd ridden down in Zack's convertible sports car, and as they came near her drive, Jamie suggested dropping her off.

"Not a chance," Zack said. "You're not going into that house in the dark alone, and I can't imagine you wanting to if Tim might have been there tonight."

"How did you…? Never mind." Jamie shook her head. Did guys have radar for that kind of stuff?

When they came back to the house after dropping Kim and Brad at the resort, Jamie suggested putting Zack's car in the garage. In past nights he hadn't wanted to, insisting that having the SUV in front was a deterrent.

"Your Beamer is a sports car," Jamie pointed out. "Something that would just dent an SUV could seriously mess up the BMW."

"It doesn't matter," Zack answered with a shrug.

"Fine. It's your car. I'll see you in the morning." She escaped as fast as she could to her bedroom.

ZACK SURVEYED THE finished building for the fruit stand with satisfaction. It was perfect. Other fruit-stand operators might end up making it look junky, but he knew Jamie would keep its appearance sharp.

The structure was simple, in a pseudo Arts and Crafts style. After an internal struggle, he'd offered to paint it blue, but she'd chosen muted shades of brown. Over the front, a carved, wooden sign proclaimed it was the George Jenkins Memorial Fruit Stand. Those letters were in blue, the same shade as the trailer.

Zack snapped several pictures before climbing into his SUV. If Jamie was busy, he could show her the photos; if she wasn't, he'd take her for a tour.

At the end of the public road, his foot hit the brake and the vehicle ground to a screeching halt. There was a sawhorse across the road, adorned with a sign saying the fruit stand was closed.

Jamie would have mentioned if she was closing early, and would have simply put the chain across the road. Besides, it didn't look like her other signs—she used sandwich boards, not sawhorses.

Zack's foot hit the accelerator and the sawhorse

went flying. He grabbed the radio microphone and told Trudy to call the sheriff, *fast*. Nearing the trailer, he fishtailed to a stop and leaped out, only to skid in the dust as he stared in astonishment.

"Aaaaaaaaaaa!" Tim Gardiner screamed, barely recognizable from the pictures Zack had seen of him. Gardiner's eyes were scrunched shut, tears streaming down his cheeks, and he clutched his crotch in obvious agony. Jamie, breathless and glaring, held her cell phone in her left hand and a can of pepper spray in her right.

Zack grinned as Jamie spritzed more pepper spray in Tim's direction and the man groaned.

Fists clenched, Zack stayed ready to knock the creep down again if needed, but for the moment Tim was occupied with pepper spray and the pain in his groin…likely the result of a well-placed knee.

A few minutes later, sirens sounded. Tim looked around wildly and tried to get up, but crouched again when Jamie gestured at him with her can.

Curt Saldano's car pulled up beside Zack's and he jumped out, gun drawn. He stared, mouth open at Tim Gardiner, Jamie standing guard. His eyes met Zack's and they both started laughing.

Shaking his head, Curt efficiently put handcuffs on Tim and hauled him to his feet.

"You're under arrest, Mr. Gardiner." He reeled off Tim's legal rights, which in Zack's opinion were far too generous.

"You can't arrest me," Tim managed to shout.

"As a matter of fact, I can," Curt said with a great deal of satisfaction. "Now, do you understand your rights as I've explained them?"

"You can't stop a man from talking to his wife."

"Ex-wife," Zack and Curt said together.

"She…she didn't mean it. She needs me."

"Like a hole in the head," Zack said. "Curt, take a look at the bruises on Jamie's wrist."

"Yeah," Jamie agreed. "He grabbed me and wouldn't let go. So I put a knee in his groin and used my pepper spray."

"Hmm. Mr. Gardiner, it looks like assault and battery, along with the other charges."

"You have no proof of anything. You—you—" Tim's protest ended in a string of curses that lacked creativity, to say the least. Zack could have done better when he was ten years old.

"Tim." Jamie interrupted her ex-husband with a smile. "I turned on my video camera the minute I saw you coming down my road. There's more than enough proof to send you to jail."

Gardiner still looked defiant, though the muscles in his throat began to spasm.

"Very nice, Jamie," Curt complimented her. "And I suspect the paint from Zack Denning's SUV will match the dent on that rental car over there."

"And is the video from the night he broke my front window usable?"

The sheriff's smile widened. "Definitely. Mr. Gardiner, there is a mountain of evidence against you. I've seen some dumbass jerks in my time, but you beat them all. By the way, Gus Hewitt is a parole violator and he's going to need a deal, so I have a feeling he'll flip on you in a heartbeat."

Gardiner deflated with the speed of a balloon losing air and Curt put him into the back of his cruiser.

Curt shut the door and turned to Zack. "Could you bring Jamie in to make a statement? It's best to get it on record right away. And I should probably have you do a witness statement, as well."

"I can drive myself," Jamie protested.

Zack rounded on her. "Hell, you could probably drive to Tucson right now, but since you nailed Gardiner without our help, let us preserve a shred of masculine ego by driving you into town."

"Well…" Her mouth quivered at the corners. "I suppose I could stretch a point."

JAMIE CLIMBED INTO Zack's SUV and buckled her seat belt. Adrenaline was running high and she felt extraordinarily good.

The radio signaled and Zack answered.

"Everything all right, boss?" Trudy's voice asked.

Zack chuckled. "Jamie had the guy down for the count by the time any of us got there. We're going in to make a statement." No matter what he'd said about wounded ego, he sounded proud of her.

With Zack running obvious interference at the house, she'd thought Tim might try something at

the stand when she was alone there. So she'd prepared ahead, tucking her camera into a discreet spot
among the leafy vegetables. It hadn't taken a genius
to know the score when a guy in a hooded sweat-
shirt put a sawhorse across the road; a moment later
she'd pressed the record button.

At first Tim had tried to sweet-talk her, saying
how much they loved each other and that he knew
what a hard time she'd had since the divorce and
how he was ready to help.

He hadn't taken it well when she laughed in
his face, telling him she knew that he'd hired Gus
Hewitt for his dirty work. Then she'd calmly explained that she would never turn to him and hadn't
loved him for a really long time.

That was when he'd grabbed her wrist and asked
how she'd like it if her grandfather's precious trailer
ended up as scrap metal. "I told Gus to go easy,
since you cared about that crazy old man," he'd
said. "But next time all you'll find is tiny pieces
of blue."

The whole sheriff's office was in stitches as she
told the story of kneeing Tim in the most vulnerable part of his anatomy, followed by a stream of hot
pepper spray in the face. She'd never realized such
a big wimp was hiding beneath the bully.

"My God," Curt choked out between gasps of
laughter. "You got him to confess on camera that
he was guilty? Any time you want a job with the
sheriff's department, just say the word."

"So, how many charges is Gardiner looking at?" Zack asked once their statements were signed and filed.

"That'll depend. It's hard to believe, but apparently, he never put two and two together that he was doing something illegal—guys like that can be pretty batty. Now he's panicking because of how his employers will react to this news. That's our trump card in keeping him away from Jamie."

Jamie didn't doubt it for a minute. Tim had risen to an executive position, but his high-profile company wouldn't appreciate this story at all. If she decided not to press charges, Tim would stay away from her, if only to keep them from finding out.

On the way back to the fruit stand, Jamie's elation slowly ebbed. Triumphing over Tim felt terrific, and she'd proved she could handle herself. Now Zack could spend nights in his own bed and leave her to the peace and quiet she craved.... Or at least she *thought* she craved it. With everything that had happened, she wasn't so sure anymore.

"You didn't have a chance to tell me why you came to the fruit stand this afternoon," she said. "Is anything wrong?"

"No," he exclaimed. "It's the new building—it's all finished and looks terrific." Excited, he stopped at the side of the road and showed her several pictures he'd taken.

He was right; it looked terrific. It was the kind of building she'd have chosen herself, except she wouldn't have put so much money into it. Of course, not having a restroom *was* awkward at times, and would have become a problem once she'd hired an employee in either location.

"There's a walk-in cooler inside," said Zack as he restarted the car and pulled back onto the road. "And a small kitchenette." He cast a look at her. "No bunk beds, though, so it has a definite disadvantage on the trailer."

She tried to appear demure. "I could always have some put in."

"Or just a good patio couch. They're not bad for… sleeping."

"Aren't beds more comfortable?" Jamie asked, at the same moment wondering why she was going along with his verbal game.

"It's always nice to have plenty of room, in case you get restless. After all, some nights can be just tossing and turning, turning and tossing."

He parked and fell silent. Jamie looked at the trailer, her stomach twisting with the realization that this was the last day for Granddad's trailer and the Little Blue Fruit Stand.

"You know what? We should get some pictures of you and the stand."

Zack had her pose and snapped several photos with both of their cameras. Several customers arrived and he asked their permission to shoot pictures of them buying strawberries.

"Have you decided when you'll open in the new location?" Zack asked after the last family left.

"I told everyone it would be tomorrow, unless they heard differently. But people will pass it on the way here, so they won't have to make two trips if they don't know about the move. It was mostly the suppliers who needed to have an exact date, and you thought it would be ready by then."

"It would've been done yesterday, but the crew had an emergency job at the resort."

"That's okay. Susan has been here two mornings with me already, so she knows the drill, but I'll be with her tomorrow to get things started."

Jamie glanced at the canopy that Granddad had rigged. With the damage done to it, she'd probably have to haul it to the dump.

Zack's voice was suddenly serious. "Jamie, if this really *isn't* what you want...well, don't worry about the contract. We can tear it up. I mostly had it drawn up so you'd know I would keep my word."

It was the last thing she'd expected him to say and she blinked several times. Why did he have to be so nice just before they reverted to being just neighbors? Friendly neighbors this time, with no bone of contention between them and no urge on his part to protect her. They'd barely see each other.... Her stomach went hollow at the thought of it.

But it was senseless to get weepy.

"Jamie?" he prompted.

"No," she answered firmly. "This is best. Except

if you don't mind, I'm going to leave the chairs here. That way anyone can sit in them and look at the ocean. They're nice quality."

"I don't mind at all. We can put a few extras out here, too, maybe in various places so people can sit quietly and enjoy."

She didn't know if the "we" he used meant Zack and Jamie, or Zack and the Mar Vista staff.

"That would be nice."

More customers were coming, so Zack smiled and waved as he walked to his car, turning back once to snap additional pictures.

Jamie decided she'd leave dismantling for tomorrow. Today she'd enjoy the stand as it was and celebrate her victory over Tim.

CHAPTER TWENTY

ZACK PHONED THE wine steward at the restaurant and asked him to have a bottle of champagne in an ice bucket ready at dinner, so he could carry it with him in the car.

"Are you going to Jamie's?" Brad asked.

Zack grimaced. "Yeah, hope you don't mind." Kim had flown back to San Francisco to meet with a client, so Brad would be alone that night.

His brother stretched and grinned. "Go. Just don't take as long as I did to straighten things out in your head. It took a kick in the ass from Kim to do it for me."

A laugh rumbled in Zack's belly. So *Kim* had made the first move.

"Don't worry, brother," he assured him. "My head's in the right place."

Brad raised a skeptical eyebrow, but Zack paid no attention. He'd told him about that afternoon, making Brad howl with laughter at how Jamie had dropped Tim Gardiner in his tracks. What Zack hadn't told his brother was the certainty that had hit him in the middle of everything—the terrifying realization that if something had happened to Jamie, he'd have had even less time than old George Jenkins had shared with his Leah.

A bleak picture of himself in fifty years had flashed across his mind...a lonely old man, tooling around a golf course before going to sit on Jamie's beach and remember what might have been.

Then he'd seen Jamie, her cheeks flushed pink with victory—alive and well in all her strength and beauty. And he'd known what he wanted—a partner for the years ahead.

With Jamie he could make a worthwhile life. He still had ambitions, even for Mar Vista, and he *would* build a resort the average family could more easily enjoy. But he wanted Jamie at the center, to smack him on the head if he ever forgot his priorities again. He wanted to love her and make children with her, to watch sunsets and enjoy the taste of strawberries with her. For him, she was first, now and always.

But what did she want? Even if she returned his feelings, was she still determined to make it alone? She'd already been burned by a guy with screwed-up priorities—would she give a lonely resort owner a chance to show he'd learned his lesson?

It was ironic. A few weeks ago he'd wanted to get her and her fruit stand as far from Mar Vista as possible. Now he wanted a lifetime, and even that wouldn't be enough.

JAMIE SET THE CD player volume on high and danced around the house. Tomorrow she'd say farewell to Granddad's stand and the empty space inside when she thought of Zack; tonight was the time for a victory celebration.

She ordered a pizza to be delivered at eight. The works—everything except anchovies. In the hallway, she ran in her stocking-covered feet and slid down the polished wood right to the end. Back and forth, like she'd done as a kid, while Granddad stood in a doorway and laughed, giving her scores for the lengths of her slides. Then she danced back through the living room and into the kitchen and kicked the laundry basket across the floor of the laundry room.

The doorbell rang and she danced her way back to the front door, flinging it open. It was Zack.

What the hell…she might as well make it a thorough celebration. She threw her arms around his neck and kissed him, no holds barred.

He groaned and returned the kiss for all he was worth. She giggled, and had begun tugging his shirt up when he grabbed her hands.

"Jamie," he said. "Much as I like the direction this is headed, we need to talk first."

She dropped her hands, leaned against the wall and studied his face. "So?"

"I love you," he said simply and her jaw dropped slightly. That definitely wasn't what she'd expected

him to say. Not that it wasn't a nice thing to hear…
depending on how genuine he might be.

Some of Jamie's elation ebbed. Love could mean
so many different things to people.

"Let's go into the living room," Zack suggested.
He gently pushed her down on the couch and sat
next to her. "Do you love me, too?"

Jamie bit her lip, unsure how to answer. Sure, she
loved him; she'd probably loved him from the minute he'd stubbornly stood outside the trailer door and
threatened to play Ella Fitzgerald all night. But loving someone didn't make it a good idea to *be* with
that person. And what did he want? Did he want to
be with her decades from now, or did he want to
spend Thursday and Sunday nights in her bed until
he tired of her?

"Okay," Zack said. "I rushed that. What I meant
to ask is, will you marry me?"

Chewing her lip, Jamie stared at him. Hope
started pushing its way upward, but she shoved it
down.

"Jamie?"

Ever since her marriage had begun falling apart,
she'd believed she had poor judgment when it came
to men. It had seemed so much easier to plan a future without romance or the possibility of loving
someone. Maybe it was just a cop-out, another form
of fear. She had made some good decisions and she
could take care of herself, but did she really only
want to take care of herself and no one else?

"Zack," she said. "I've already been married to someone who cares more about a business deal than he does about me. I'm not saying you're like Tim, but when we met, it seemed as if the only thing you cared about was your resort. Now I know you care about people, too, but it hasn't been that long since you charged the fruit stand to tell me I was trespassing."

He winced. "You're right, Jamie. I've worked hard all my life for one thing. I wanted the resort and got it. Mar Vista is everything I ever dreamed it would be, and I might have messed even that up if not for you. But now I also know that none of it means much without you. I finally get it, Jamie. Mar Vista is just a business. A life should be built around people and I want to build my life around you and a family."

She swallowed. He meant it.

The doorbell rang.

"Don't answer it," Zack said as she stood. "They'll go away."

"That wouldn't be fair. It's probably the pizza."

"I'll get it." He hurried out of the living room and she heard the murmur of male voices.

Loving Zack meant taking a chance and relying on someone again.

Zack *did* recognize the important things in life. And she suddenly understood why he'd questioned if she really wanted to let the fruit stand go...why he'd offered to tear up the contract. He was putting her first.

They would disagree now and then. Strong-willed people frequently did...but it was all right as long as they respected and believed in each other.

Zack came back in, holding the pizza box. "Now we've got two dinners," he said. "Gordon sent something over also."

She grinned. "That's okay. It'll give us something for dinner tomorrow."

Relief flooded Zack's face as he stared at Jamie.

"By the way," she added, "I love you, too."

Joy bubbled up as he tossed the box onto a chair and grabbed her in his arms.

What a future they could make for each other.

* * * * *